THE BITTER END

AN EM RIDGE MYSTERY
BOOK TWO

LINDA HALL

WILD SEAS PRESS

THE BITTER END

Formatting by Rik Hall – Wild Seas Formatting
Cover design by Elaine York, Allusion Graphics, LLC/Publishing & Book Formatting
Editing by Rogena Mitchell-Jones Manuscript Service

eBook ISBN: 978-0-9949550-0-5
Print ISBN: 978-0-9877613-9-2

08122015

DEDICATION

To my best friend, sailing companion and lover

*****

I admit it. I'm fascinated by conspiracy theories. The Bermuda Triangle? Even though all of the stories have one by one been debunked, I still like reading about it. Conspiracy theories are just plain fun. I knew that for Book #2 in the Em Ridge series, I wanted to explore this very busy area of water. And so, I present to you, *The Bitter End.*

I have been more than pleased at the lovely reception that *Night Watch* has received. I thank all of you who took the time to read the book, email me and put up online reviews.

My husband and I are still enjoying our summers aboard *Mystery*, our 34' sailboat. This past summer we added two new boats to our fleet - two Old Town kayaks. We spent a lot of the summer exploring little bodies of water and streams and inlets which we barely knew existed in our wonderful province.

And now for the disclaimer - The Portland, Maine in *The Bitter End*, only sort of resembles the real Portland, Maine. The tidal island of Chalk Spit does not exist on any map. I needed a place for Em to live and nothing in and around Portland, Maine quite suited. If Chalk Spit resembles anything, it would be Minister's Island, St. Andrews, New Brunswick which is only accessible by road during low tide.

Book Three in the series, *The Devil to Pay* should be out next year.

I'd love to hear from you and have you be a part of my newsletter community. "Pickers and Choosers" the first story in my book of short stories, *Strange Faces*, will be sent to you as a gift when you subscribe. Here's the link: writerhall.com/newsletter

Linda

The end of a cable abaft the bitts is the "bitter end." The common expression, "reached the bitter end," refers to a situation of extremity and has nothing at all to do with lees and dregs and other unpalatable things. It means literarily that someone has 'got to the end of his rope.' The Ashley Book of Knots by Clifford Ashley, 1944

CHAPTER 1

The speck out on the horizon was still. Too still. And it definitely contained alien life. At least that was the loud conclusion of Dr. Papa Hoho as he gasped and panted his way up the ladder to the flybridge. His binoculars bounced around his neck, and all that wild red hair of his was caught up around his face like dandelion fluff. So far, the search for the Entrance to the Gates of Hell had not gone well. We had been out on the body of water known as the Bermuda Triangle for twelve days. For twelve days, we had seen nothing but ordinary boats doing ordinary things on this very ordinary body of water.

I could have told him it was ordinary. I've sailed these waters more times than I can count, and I've never encountered anything but ordinary. Nevertheless, he'd hired me to ferry him all around the Bermuda Triangle for two weeks in July, and I needed the job. I would have chosen another time, though. I would have picked a month that wasn't so hot. I would have gone for a month in which hurricanes didn't threaten every other week, but you take what you can get when you have a job like mine.

Papa — as he'd asked us to call him — plopped down in the plush, white leather chair beside me and pointed. "You see that boat or whatever that thing is over there? I been watching it. Hasn't moved a bit. We been out here searching for almost — what is it — two weeks? This could be it."

"The Gates of Hell?" I tried to keep the sarcasm out of my voice. For twelve long days, I had tried with varying degrees of success to keep the sarcasm out of my voice.

I'd been watching it, too. I'd even tried hailing it on the radio. Nothing yet. Either we were too far away or their radio was turned off.

"Head over in that direction, will ya? I got a good feeling about this one."

"Already on it," I said. Unlike Papa, I didn't have a good feeling about this one. As we moved ever closer, inside of me began to grow a fearful queasiness. I was watching the speck grow to be a boat, a sailboat to be precise — a sailboat with a torn mainsail hanging limply in the becalmed air. I tried the radio again. No reply.

Behind me, Liam, my young crew member, was leaning against a stanchion and watching it, too. Down on the bow, Jason, the photographer, was trying to set up his tripod. Papa grunted. The Hawaiian shirt he wore today featured a snarl of pink and orange flowers. He always wore these huge shirts unbuttoned, so we got to enjoy all his reddish chest hairs, the folds of fat on his belly, and the scabbing and peeling sunburn on his formerly white neck.

"Can't you get this thing to go any faster?" he said to me. "I want to get over there. See what that thing is."

"It's a boat."

"Yeah, I know it's a boat, but this could be it."

"Aliens?"

He pointed at me. "Don't make fun."

"You want to go faster? Maybe Jason should move all his equipment from the bow. Wouldn't want him losing that camera overboard."

Jason was a gangly twenty-something who wore jeans and

t-shirts with the names of movie sets he'd worked on scrawled across the backs of them. Today's shirt was black. Most of them were black. Black. Let that sink in. Mid-July off the Miami coastline and he's wearing black tees and jeans. Made of jean material. Papa went back down and the two of them hefted the equipment to the stern. When they were safely off the bow, I pushed the throttles forward and could feel the power underneath me as we surged up on plane. The sudden wind felt good against my hot neck. I hailed the boat again on the radio. Again, no answer.

Liam came and sat beside me on the chair that Papa had vacated and said dryly, "I don't think there are aliens over there."

I looked over at him.

"But it could be the reptile people."

I laughed. We both did. We'd heard all these stories and more the past couple of weeks.

Liam is the fifteen-year-old son of Jeff and Valerie, my neighbors from two-doors-down. When Liam had overheard me tell his parents about my newest boat captaining job, his ears had perked up and he'd asked all sorts of questions. In the evening, he'd accosted me down on the dock in front of our houses. I'd been scrubbing out the propane compartment of my sailboat, *Wanderer*.

"Hey, Em, you need any crew for that thing you're doing?"

Before I had a chance to reply, he said, "It'll be in summer. I wouldn't have school then. I could go if you needed me. If I would be allowed. I could help out."

"Won't your mom and dad need you for the lobstering?"

"It wouldn't be that long, would it?"

"Two weeks. I'll talk to your parents, and then I'll have to talk to the TV people. How about I promise you that?"

"Cool."

I'm a boat captain. What I do is deliver boats. Mostly, I deliver luxury yachts owned by the rich and famous, from point A to point B. These wealthy people like the status of owning big boats, but usually, they have no clue about boat ownership or operation, or actually being out on the water, so they hire people like me. Many of my captain friends have permanent jobs on high-end yachts and get to go all over the world. So far, in my budding career, all I've gotten are short hauls. Which is okay with me. Even though I love the ocean, love being out here, I would miss my big, old dog Rusty and my little cottage house at the very end of Chalk Spit Island near Portland, Maine.

Sometimes, I get hired to take people places by boat. That was the nature of this work. I'd gotten the call from Papa three months ago, shortly after Rusty and I had returned home from Florida. I'd found work in a marina down there for five months during the winter. It being Florida, I use the term "winter" loosely. I'd also managed to get a couple of jobs taking yachts across the Gulf Stream to the Bahamas. Always fun.

While in Florida, I'd put out a lot of feelers for work. I'd nailed up my sailing résumé at every marina I visited. I hadn't been home a week before the crazy, ginger-bearded man, who was now leaning over the port railing, called me.

"Do you know who I am?" had been the second thing he'd said to me, the first being, "I would like to hire you."

"Sorry, sir, I don't." I Googled frantically. Had I ever worked for someone by that name?

"I host a highly acclaimed network television program."

"Oh." There it was, coming up on my computer screen now.

"Lots of viewers."

"I can see that." *Conspiracy Theories FINALLY PROVED!* was the name of the show. And yes, it did look to be quite popular.

"Do you know what the government is hiding from us?"

"No, sir, I don't." It was a weekly show. Eleven at night. Not prime time, but who cares in this streaming, TVOing world?

"Many things. Many, many things. You would be surprised."

"I'm sure I would be." Did he know what I did for a living? Hire me for what?

He was going on. "That's what I set out to prove. That and other things. I examine known conspiracy theories for their accuracy."

"Okay."

"I need to hire a boat captain."

"Really?"

"To take me all around the Bermuda Triangle. I've checked with the stars and rotation of the planets, and this summer, second week in July to be precise, is the perfect time out there."

Oh? "Oh." I could do that. It might be a hoot. "I know those waters well."

"Did you know that there's a theory that the Bermuda Triangle is the entrance to the Gates of Hell?"

I kept myself from snorting out loud. "No, sir, I did not know that."

When he told me what he intended to pay, I accepted on the spot. And that's how we happened to be out here on this July day, which was as still and as hot as a sauna on overdrive. I was beginning to believe his theory about the hot fires of the afterlife rising like steam from these waters.

Dr. Papa Hoho turned out to be as crazy as his name. For the past week and a half I'd learned we were governed by collusion of reptiles—you can tell by their eyes, he showed me pictures—and that an entire race of humanoids lived inside of our planet and that crop circles were alien prophecies of doom to come.

I'd never bothered with watching his show until I signed this contract. Then I binge watched nine episodes in a row, which left me feeling slightly queasy. Are there people out there who actually believe this stuff?

"We won't make it to 2050," he had told me a few days ago while we'd sat up here on the flybridge eating lunch. "They have something planned."

"Who?" I turned. "The government?"

"No, the aliens. Our days on this planet are numbered."

"Well, if I'm still here in 2050, I'll remember your words."

"The world will be gone by then. You mark my words. We can't last much longer."

"I suppose not."

All we'd done in twelve days was burn gas, lots of gas, thousands and thousands of dollars' worth of gas as we sped all over the calm waters in the heat. Each night, we'd head back to the marina in Miami where Papa put us all up in a five-star hotel. So far, we hadn't stayed out overnight on the boat, although he'd said that might be a possibility. I was getting the idea that he liked mingling with the tourists at the bars and luxuriating in his celebrity status. He would find being out on the boat at night far too lonely and strange.

Every morning at seven thirty, we'd be down eating our fifty-dollar breakfasts and then we'd head down to the boat. Thermos carafes of coffee, lunch, snacks, and drinks were delivered by the hotel staff and stowed in the appropriate fridges and coolers onboard *Townie,* the fifty-one-foot Sea Ray he'd chartered.

At first, it was fun, but after twelve days, I was becoming tired of this pompous man. I was getting anxious for this assignment to be over. I hated the way he brought his face too close to mine when he spoke, the way I felt I had to continually back up to be away from the line of spittle fire. I hated the way he continually made references to all the money he was making. I was bored with hearing about how many online followers he had, and how next year his TV show was going to be even bigger and better and be distributed to more networks than ever. Oh, yes, and that's not even to mention the constant talk about his seven-figure book advance. He dropped names of celebrities ad nauseam. I tried not to let him see how unimpressed I was. I needed — really needed — the money. Maybe I'd even be able to afford that new sail for *Wanderer* I'd been eyeing. Just two more days, I kept saying to myself. Just two more days.

And now, Papa was scrambling back up the ladder toward

me and barking out commands. "Jason, get that camera up here, will ya? We'll get some shots from up here. Hurry it up. Slow down the boat a little as we're coming in, will ya?"

We were closer to the disabled sailboat now, and through the binoculars, I focused in on the stern. The name across the back had been removed. Papa continued to snap out orders. "Get this shot! Get this coming in. Get my face on that shot. Come on. Hurry. We can't let this one go. This could be the mother-load. Film me now. I need a shot of me with that boat in the distance. Right now, Jason. Wait. My face is too sweaty."

He dumped a bottle of water on his hands and rubbed it over his head. "Get me a towel, dammit," he yelled to no one in particular.

Liam found a small cloth on the instrument panel and handed it to him.

"Greasy, sweaty face," he mumbled. "I can't be on TV with this greasy, sweaty face."

I said, "People will understand it's hot."

I was glad I was a bit upwind from Papa. His odiferousness got to be overwhelming in this heat, but at least he'd buttoned up his shirt now.

"Hey," Papa said to me, "when we get a bit closer, slow down. I want to get pictures as we come up on it."

"Someone could be in trouble," I said. "I've been trying to reach them."

He shook his head. "I don't care. This is perfect. This is so perfect." And then, more to himself, he said, "I knew this would happen. I just had a feeling that today was going to be my lucky day." He grinned as he pranced around the flybridge, looking, for all the world, like an overgrown garden gnome. "Twelve has always been my lucky number. Did I ever tell you? And this is the twelfth day." He stopped. "I should check that numerology. Maybe I can figure that in somehow. Did you happen to watch the episode on numerology?"

When I showed no signs of answering his question or

slowing down, Papa repeated, "I told you I want to come in dead slow. Now."

I ignored him. I held my hands tightly to the wheel. I stared straight ahead, my mouth dry.

"Captain Ridge, I said explicitly that you were to slow down as we came to the boat. Jason," he barked, "keep the camera going. I want to get some shots of us coming in on this boat."

I mustered up the courage to say, "No. I can't do that. There could be people hurt on that boat. This may be your TV show, but as captain, my first obligation is to whoever's aboard that vessel."

I was surprised he actually listened to me, but then I noticed the camera was up and running and aimed in my direction. He'd recorded what I'd said. Great. And then the camera was turned to Papa, and he was talking, talking and pointing. I had no idea what he was saying, and at this point, I didn't care.

"Jason," I said interrupting Papa's soliloquy. "You and Liam go on down. Get the fenders ready. Get him to show you what to do. We'll be alongside soon."

Papa answered for him. "Jason's busy with me up here."

I stood my ground. "He's needed down there. We have a boat possibly in danger, people possibly in peril, and we need everyone to help."

Papa turned quietly to Jason. "*Peril*. I like that word. You get all that recorded? Her tone? It'll make for good TV. Go on then." He pointed at me. "You better obey the mighty captain." He winked, and I turned my face away.

As we approached the boat, my hands shook. It was hot, tremendously so, but I felt a chill go through me as I looked down into the open cockpit of the silent boat. We were close enough that I could see two half-filled wine glasses set neatly on the snack table in the sunshine. Between them was what looked like a plate of crackers and cheese. And napkins folded into triangles. I kept my breathing steady as I idled in. I tried the radio again. No answer.

Down on the starboard side, Liam was telling Jason how high to tie the fenders while Papa tried to operate the camera by himself. When I maneuvered close enough to the sailboat, Liam expertly lassoed a line to one of the forward cleats. I pushed on the bow thrusters, and we sidled easily up to the boat. Liam hopped aboard the sailboat and tied her tautly, bow and stern.

"Hello? Hello?" I kept calling down to the boat. "Hello?"

By this time, Papa, himself, was holding the camera and yelling for Jason to get everything recorded. They needed the whole thing on camera, every bit of it, right from the start. That is if Jason wanted to keep this job after this, and it wasn't looking too promising if he continually disobeyed direct orders from his boss.

I ignored all of this and descended the rear steps to the stern of *Townie* and instructed Liam to go up and stay at the helm of the powerboat.

As I boarded the sailboat, a skinny, black cat emerged from down below in the cabin, stared at me with her bright green eyes and meowed loudly.

I grabbed hold of the rails and swallowed over and over to keep from throwing up.

CHAPTER 2

My mother's brother, Uncle Ferd, is the stuff of family legend. As far back as I can remember he's never lived anywhere else but on his boat. He has sailed from the southern tip of Patagonia to Norway, down and to the Mediterranean and then out and on to Thailand, India and beyond — Hawaii, Fiji, Australia, New Zealand. I don't think there is a stretch of open water anywhere that he hadn't sailed through, always on *Wandering Soul,* his thirty-three-foot Cape Dory.

How he came to own *Wandering Soul* is shrouded in family myth. One of the stories has him winning it in a card game down in Mexico. Another has him being bequeathed it by some woman he was with for a while. Still another has him finding the boat washed up one winter onto the shores of North Carolina's Outer Banks after a hurricane. And then there was the one about buying it after he crewed for the owner. Whatever the tale, I never remember my uncle owning any other boat.

"No," I whispered as I climbed aboard the sailboat and stepped into the cockpit. For several minutes, I tried to keep from noticeably shaking while the little cat mewled around my bare legs. A chill began in the top of my head and ran right down to my toes. "No. No, no." I was swaying and had to grab hold of the top of the compass on the binnacle to keep from falling.

I stared down at the wine glasses, the precisely folded napkins, the plates — everything perfectly aligned. An opened bottle of red wine sat in the center of the table. Tentatively, I touched the food on the plate. The cheese was hard, the edges crusted, the crackers soft.

I stood there, breathing heavily while the little cat looked up at me. I heard and felt movement behind me. I turned. Jason had come on board, his heavy camera balanced on his shoulder. Papa was offering a continual monologue for the recording as he attempted to move his bulk from one boat to the other. I didn't listen. I didn't offer to help. Wouldn't. Couldn't.

When I was around six and my twin sisters were babies, we began the yearly summer drive from Ohio to Maine to visit my mother's parents. Sometimes my Uncle Ferd was there. Sometimes he wasn't. When he was, he would take us out sailing on *Wandering Soul*. Even at that young age, I think my uncle saw in me a kindred spirit of sorts. Or maybe I saw that in him. I loved him. I loved the sea. Even on rainy, stormy days, I begged to go out. "It's raining at home anyway," I would protest. "So why not just go out on the boat?"

During one of our Maine summers, I acquired an old sailing dinghy. Uncle Ferd and I worked on it until it was not only sailable but also gleaming. We gouged out large sections of rot, and filled the holes in with fiberglass. Then we carefully sanded it, first with a rough grade of sandpaper and ending with the finest he could find. When it was all finished, we painted it a bright red. My choice.

At first, I wasn't very good, but with practice, I became better. When we weren't out in the wind on *Wandering Soul* with my Uncle Ferd, I was hiked out on my sailing dinghy weaving in and through and between all the boats in the mooring field, much to the encouragement of Uncle Ferd, the doubtful looks of my mother, and the shrieking fear of Mariana and Katie, my little sisters.

If I do say so myself, I was quite good at it.

"She's got the bug," said my grandpa. "Just like her uncle." My mother always frowned when he said such things.

I don't know where that old dinghy is now. Probably, it was gotten rid of when my grandparents died and the place along the water was sold. There were pictures, too. Lots of summer pictures of me on the dinghy. Of Uncle Ferd and me. Somewhere there is a photo of me—nine years old and dwarfed behind the wheel of my Uncle Ferd's boat, grinning in my big, bright orange life jacket, my hair blown into a mess around my face.

I haven't seen that picture in a long time.

Maybe my parents got rid of it and the dinghy after all the trouble happened. Even when I was a child, I could sense that a strange and awkward thread ran between my uncle and the rest of his family. A strange and awkward thread that blew up the summer I was ten.

But there was no time to think about that now.

A few weeks ago now, I'd emailed Ferd telling him all about my crazy new assignment.

Can you imagine? The Bermuda Triangle! Isn't that a hoot? If you're around, give me a holler.

When he didn't get back to me, of course I didn't worry. My uncle's emails and communiques were few and far between at the best of times and totally dependent on where he could get to shore and pick up WiFi. Answering email was often the last thing on his agenda.

I walked back to the stern, leaned over, and examined the transom. The name of the boat had been scraped off, but if you caught it in the right light, you could see the shadows of the letters there. The inflatable dinghy was also gone. It usually hung off the back, and while the lines for the davits were there, the dinghy itself was gone. Liam leaned over the flybridge on *Townie* and called to me. I raised one finger and gave him an imperceptible shake of my head. I knew he understood.

A sound like a whoosh caught my attention, and I glanced up at the sails. A slight breeze was drifting through the ripped mainsail like something ghostly.

A moment later, it was dead calm again. I bent down to pick up the cat and held him closely to me.

"Bear," I whispered. "Bear."

I knew this cat.
I knew this boat.
This was *Wandering Soul*.

CHAPTER 3

I stood there, clutching Bear to me, my whole body quivering while Jason and Papa attempted to brush past me and get down inside the cabin.

"Wait!" I said. "Wait, you guys." I had to be the first one down there. I needed to do this. Whatever we would find down there, I needed to be there first. I was captain, after all.

"I have to go down first." I put bear down and attempted to shove past them. When they didn't stop, I said as loudly as I could, "It's the law!"

They stood to the side and let me pass. It's amazing how many bald-faced lies you can get away with if you just speak loudly and put on an air of authority. I descended the teak steps into the main cabin.

"Hello? Hello?"

I halfway expected Uncle Ferd to come strolling out, a pipe wrench in one hand and a roll of plumbing tape in the other. *"Oh. You found me. Just trying to make some progress on this leaky head in there."*

But he didn't.

It was quiet, eerily so. I stood at the bottom of the steps and looked around me. I held up my hand to keep Papa and Jason from roughshodding over me with their loud talking and filming and cameras.

I called up, "I'll let you know when it's safe for you to come down."

This boat is an old wooden sloop of the skinny ocean-going design. It is a beautiful boat, gorgeous, with plenty of teak and ash down below. But in the classic design, there's not a great deal of room. Modern boats are beamy and made for comfort with hot and cold water, showers and microwaves and coffee makers and lots of molded plastic down below. This boat had none of that, but it could sail around the world with the best of them. This boat was brand new in 1980. A year later, my uncle had acquired it.

The table in the cabin was up and covered with a cloth of the same design as the dishes outside. It was a pattern I didn't recognize. When had my uncle gotten these? Two of the same themed plates were set with knives and forks precisely at the sides. Pots were on the stove in the galley, potatoes in one and peas in the other. I felt the sides of them. Cold. The potatoes were mushy and turning green around the edges, the peas congealed into their juices. A salad was composting in a glass bowl on the counter. A fry pan with what possibly were fish filets at one time sat on one of the burners. By the looks of it, Bear had made short work of them.

Bear! I looked under the cabin table. In place of her normal food bowl was an oversized cooking pot, empty now. The sink, I noticed, was three-quarters full of fresh water. Someone had, at least, thought about Bear.

I wasn't able to keep Papa at bay. The two of them were clambering down behind me.

"No one's here?" Papa asked.

"Doesn't look like it."

"Wow!" Papa said loudly. "Just wow! Get all this on camera, Jason. This is gold. This is platinum. We're going to need all of this on film. Keep that camera rolling. NOW! Get that black cat! What a great touch! A black cat! Wow! I did a whole show on black cats once. You happen to catch it?"

I didn't realize for several seconds that the question was addressed to me. Finally, I shook my head. "Must've missed that one," I muttered.

"They have a history of witchcraft, but there's a real reason for that," he said eyeing Bear. "It's been proved they do have mystical powers…"

On the counter was a kettle, two teacups, each with a teabag, the string laid over at the same place on both. There was a loaf of bread there, too, with a bread knife next to it. I touched the top of the loaf. Hard as a conch shell.

Bear continued to meow as I rummaged through my uncle's cupboards. I found a bag of kibble and brought it out.

"Feeding the cat," I said to no one in particular. "The people are missing, but someone needs to take care of the cat."

I poured a handful of pellets into the empty pot under the table. I also found a bowl and filled it with water, although it looked like she was doing just fine with the sink.

Jason carefully filmed the entire process. Bear went wild with eating, and Jason got the whole thing on camera.

My uncle has never sailed without a cat. When one cat dies, he simply finds another one at the next port. He names them all Bear, regardless of gender.

I took out my own phone and, head beginning to pound, I took lots of pictures of my own. Lots. I walked past Papa and Jason and went forward into the vee berth. This was the place I'd claimed as my own when I was a young girl and sailing with my uncle. I would come up here when I wanted a place to hide away from the storms while he was out there in the rain and wind getting us home. Part of the vee berth was neatly made up with sheets and two woolen Hudson Bay blankets. It looked too precise somehow, too neat. I opened the door to the small head. Everything stowed and in order. This place was painfully clean. Heads are notoriously difficult to keep clean. I took several more pictures.

There were minimal jackets and coats in the hanging locker and not many clothes in any of his drawers. Those that were there were folded in precise stacks with mathematically straight edges. Yes, my uncle has always been sort of a neat freak for an old single guy, but this? It was like the boat was made up for a movie set. I thought about that for a minute, and understood. Papa had set this up. My uncle was always looking for a way to make money. Of course. This had to be it. Next time I saw Uncle Ferd, I would scream at him for being so stupid. *"Anybody could have found that boat! What were you thinking? Are you that moronic?"*

I approached Papa. "Okay. The joke's over. I get it. Funny. Funny. But you're not using this for your show."

He stared at me for a moment, a tiny speck of wetness at the corner of his mouth. "What are you talking about?"

"This whole thing. You engineered it." I almost added, "with my uncle," but didn't.

He stared at me. "Is that what you think? Em, if you never believed me before, you have to believe me now. I have no idea how this boat got here."

Something in his tone made me believe him. Almost. Maybe there would be a way to find out. I decided to wait until I spoke with my uncle.

"Okay. Okay fine." I put my hands up in an attitude of surrender and went back to photographing the boat.

I paused for a moment as I stood in the main cabin and studied my uncle's vast collection of gardening magazines and plant books on the starboard bookshelf. Yes, my uncle has an odd hobby for someone whose back yard is the sea. He collects gardening books. He has a collection of pristine gardening magazines going back to the early 1990s. Some he keeps in plastic so as not to deteriorate in the salt air.

Jason and Papa largely ignored me as I took pictures of them. I went through every drawer and cubbyhole and took more pictures. I pulled up the top of his nav table. His gleaming old sextant was still there, along with the charts, rulers, and dividers. The boat logs were gone, however. I looked and looked for them, along with his passport and personal journals, but found nothing.

I knew where my uncle kept a secret stash of money. I reached my hand into the crevice behind the bookshelf, but the money compartment was empty. It was beginning to look as if all identifying information with his name or the boat name on it was gone. I went back to his clothes cupboards looking for something, anything.

While I did this, Papa and Jason were talking, filming, and exclaiming over things. I barely heard them as I tried to keep my hands from shaking. Was this a joke or was this happening? On my phone, I wrote a quick email to my uncle. It would send just as soon as there was service.

Found the boat. Got the joke. You can come out now.

I moved toward the stern, past Papa and Jason. The engine was under the cockpit and behind the companionway stairs. I pulled the stairs away and had a look at the engine. What I was looking for, I didn't know. Nothing was especially leaking or wet. Stuffing box looked fine. I checked the bilge. Just the normal amount of water you would expect. I wiped the gathering sweat off my face with the bottom end of my t-shirt and went back outside into the sun.

Maybe this wasn't my uncle's boat anymore. Obviously, whoever bought it had scraped the name off the back and bought new dishes. Maybe it had somehow become loosed from its moorings and had floated way out here. Yet, there were no lines dragging in the water. Plus, some of my uncle's clothes and personal things were still on the boat. But the dishes weren't his. I couldn't get any of this to make any sort of sense. I checked my phone. Barely one bar of service this far out. I took more pictures.

I had another thought. Maybe out at anchor, my uncle had set up the boat for visitors, he'd gotten in the dinghy to fetch them, and the anchor hadn't been secure. Maybe the bitter end of it was even now attached to the anchor and lying at the bottom of some bay.

I went up on the bow and saw the problem with that theory. Both anchors were attached to the fairlead rollers as usual. That also didn't explain the torn mainsail. Or the lack of any ID.

I was coming up with all these scenarios in order to avoid the logical one that was staring me in the face. If this wasn't a joke, my uncle had been boarded, robbed. Or maybe he had taken off in his dinghy, and was even now injured or drifting. All the froufrou with the plates and dishes and food? Set up by his captors because this is, after all, the Bermuda Triangle. Piracy happens. Even here. My uncle doesn't carry a gun. Never has. Told me he'd never needed one. Except for now, maybe. Or not.

I shaded my eyes and looked toward the shore. We were about twenty miles out, and I could see the hazy blur of Florida in the far distance. The problem with Florida is that the entire state is so low to the ground it's hard to find landmarks. The entire state is basically a beautiful marsh.

I stood next to the mast and fingered the ripped sail. I looked straight up to see that the halyard seemed to be jammed at the top. Maybe he had tried to pull it down and ended up just leaving it. Why hadn't he climbed up the mast steps and fixed it? Right now, the sail hung limp, but any breeze and this boat would be carried this way and that. Was that what had happened? How had the wine not spilled?

I put a hand to my head to try to stem an oncoming headache while I went back to the stern. I checked the lazarette. All of his fenders and outside equipment were organized with the same preciseness, his lines neatly coiled. The key was even in the ignition.

"Hey," I called down to the two in the boat. "I'm going to start the engine."

With that, I pulled out the choke and turned the key, and the old Universal started first crank. So that hadn't been the problem. I killed the engine. For now. It was enough to know that it worked, and we could maybe get this thing to shore. I checked the fuel. There seemed to be plenty.

Liam, up on the flybridge of *Townie,* was leaning over the rail. I knew he was itching to come down and see what was going on. I knew he recognized the sailboat. Two and a half years ago, when my husband Jesse died, Ferd sailed up and anchored in our bay and stayed with me for a month.

"What's going on?" Liam called down.

"I'll come up in a bit. We'll talk. I have to call the Coast Guard anyway. And I've got, like, only one bar down here."

I climbed across to the other boat, mounted the ladder to the flybridge, and sat down on the big chair, grateful for the shade. When I told Liam what was on the boat, his eyes went wide. "Wow, that's weird."

"Yep. Weird." I paused before saying, "Liam, please don't say anything to either Jason or Papa. The last thing I want is for them to know I might know this boat. I sort of thought this might be some sort of prank, but I'm not so sure. It's sort of out of character for my uncle."

He nodded. I could have used the open and very public VHF radio, but I didn't want to. Not with this. This was my uncle, after all. I got out my cell phone. It was higher up here on the flybridge where there is more reception for cellphones. I have a friend in the Coast Guard down here, and I called Russell on his private number and told him everything.

My words came out in a tumble. "I'm so worried about my uncle. He could be on his dinghy somewhere. He could be in trouble."

"Ferd? His boat? Wow!" He told me he would see what he could find out.

"It still could be a setup, but I just can't be sure. His dinghy is gone. The sail is ripped. The halyard's jammed. The name's even been scraped off the back. Yet, down inside the boat, you could eat off the floor it's so clean, and the table's all set up for a meal Bermuda Triangle style. I'm totally getting weirded out..."

"I'll check it out and get back to you, Em. Are you okay out there? You want anyone to come out?"

"No, it's like a millpond out here and hot as hell. We're fine. Did he by any chance call in a Mayday? Could you find out?"

"I'll check."

"It's so freaky. Everything's just a bit too neat, too made up."

"If I do remember correctly, your uncle *is* a bit of an old lady..."

"Not this much of an old lady." My voice went quiet. "Thanks, Russell. I owe you."

"No, you don't, Em. Friends don't owe friends anything."

Back almost a dozen years ago, the two of us worked at a marina in Fort Lauderdale. When Russell was falsely accused of slamming an owner's boat into some pilings, and, therefore, gouging a big hole in the side, I came forward and showed pictures I had taken with my then new digital camera. Russell and I had been together that weekend down on the Keys, and my pictures had the digital stamps to prove it, along with the smiling faces of twenty others at that beach party. We were a couple then. It didn't last. We were better simply as friends. Russell's married now with a couple of kids. He even has a real job with the Coast Guard, plus I like his wife.

Ever so slowly, I put the boat into gear and turned *Townie* toward the coast. Rafted up, we could start heading in slow. A few moments later, true to his word, Russell called me back.

"Nothing," he said. "No Mayday calls. No reports from Ferd, nothing. Why don't you bring the boat in?"

"You want me to take it to the Coast Guard wharf? Will they want to see it?"

"Any signs of foul play?"

"Aside from the ripped sail, I can't see anything."

"I would say just bring it in. Maybe the city dock would be good enough."

After I thanked him and hung up, I turned to my young charge. "If we un-raft this thing, you want to take *Wandering Soul* back to Miami?"

"What?" His eyes brightened. "By myself?" I knew he could handle her. He was a Maine coast kid, and like all Maine coast kids, he grew up on boats and was running his little runabout dinghy all over the bay before he'd even learned how to ride a two-wheeler.

The four hours or so it would take him to get there, we would be in constant visual and radio contact. It would be easier on both boats to sail them in separately.

I made another call. Because I do what I do, I have a bevy of friends up and down the coast. Somehow, I knew Skip and Sue would come through for me. They always did.

There are three kinds of people who live in Florida — originals, tourists, and transplants. The originals are the born and bred Floridians whose families extend back for generations. Their families have long histories in the state and lived there before air conditioning, Disney World, condos, hotels, and everyone from the north descending during the winter.

Second, are the tourists who spend the winter months in Florida and the summer months at their northern locales — Minnesota, New York, Michigan, Canada.

Third are the transplants. These are usually retirees who end up moving permanently into one of the thousands of 55+ communities.

My friends, Skip and his longtime partner, Sue, are originals. He grew up on the shores of a lake in central Florida where his dad fixed small engines. She lived in northern Florida with parents who worked the orchards. Up until eight years ago, they never had much. They lived in a run-down three-room shack right next to the lake and both did odd jobs around town when they could find work. When times were tough, they ate fish from the lake and grapefruit from their tree. When times were extremely tough, they'd roast alligator on the fire pit.

Six years ago, all of that changed when he inherited some prime land on the waterfront in Miami from a distant great aunt. He and Sue left the shack by the lake and moved east. Now Skip collects the rental money from his properties, but mostly, he still does what he always did — fish. Even now, he rarely even turns on the AC — says it makes it so you can't hear anything outside. He still prefers to sit out under the shade of a palm tree with a cold beer and a fishing rod.

I met the two of them when I rented dock space from him on a delivery that went badly right about here. Engine overheating for no apparent reason. He and Sue were more than kind. He'd ended up finding a blockage in the exhaust elbow, something I hadn't even considered.

When I told Sue about my predicament, she said, "Yes. You come. We got room on the dock. You need a place to stay? We're heading out later today, but you can have the house.

Like for showers and things."

"That's great."

"Oh, and Em? If you need crew to take the boat anywhere, my neighbor's daughter, Janice, is here and between crewing jobs. I can vouch for her."

"Thanks. I have no idea what I'm doing yet with the boat, if anything."

I went back onto *Wandering Soul* and told Papa what had been decided. When he balked, which I knew he would, I said, "It's what the Coast Guard has ordered. You have twenty minutes to finish up your movie-making," I said. I could have named any time frame, but I wanted to keep him happy but didn't want to be out here all day. "Then the Coast Guard will be checking back with us." I felt like a mother admonishing a child. "Just something else you should know," I said to Dr. Papa, "I will be claiming salvage rights on this boat." I figured if I said that, and it was a joke or a setup, now would be the time when he would come clean.

"What?" He leaned his short hobbit-like bulk against the table. His face was glossy with sweat. "What does that mean?"

"It means when you find something on the high seas, you get to claim salvage."

"So that would be me." He pointed his thumb at his chest. "I saw it first."

I opened my hands in a surrender gesture. "You forget one thing." I had to remain strong. "I'm the captain. This is my call as captain. It's what the Coast Guard has decided." I love making things up as I go along. "Believe me," I went on, "this is not a responsibility you want. It means I have to find a place for it and take care of all the cleanup. I'll also have to," I paused, "figure out who the boat belongs to and where they are."

He put a finger up. I stopped him before he started.

"I know. I know. You're going to say the aliens are responsible for all of this, but I live in the real world, and I have to find out where the owner of this boat is. Liam will be taking the boat in, and we'll go back on *Townie*. When we get to shore, you can take a few more pictures of it, and then we have to turn the whole thing over to the Coast Guard."

He rubbed his red beard and smoothed back his frazzled hair. "Okay, if that's the way it has to be." He pulled a white handkerchief from his pocket and mopped his slick brow.

Something in my uncle's ubiquitous collection of gardening books caught my attention while Papa said, "I want more pictures though."

"Look," I said holding out a small olive branch. "Finish those shots here and then we can head back up onto *Townie*. You can get some shots of the boat as we sail along beside her."

I was becoming more and more puzzled. Something on my uncle's bookshelf seemed very out of place.

CHAPTER 4

Russell was right. My uncle could be excessively neat—*old-ladyish* neat. When I sailed with him, he would admonish me like a maiden aunt—"A place for everything and everything in its place." When, as a teenager, I would roll my eyes, he would say, "It's the only way you can survive in a small place." If I dared to put the scissors, for example, back into the knife drawer rather than the scissor drawer, I soon heard about it.

Since I loved both sailing and my uncle, I soon learned to put the pencils away precisely where they belonged, with their sharpened edges facing forward, or make sure the toilet paper was rolled the right way around. I always suspected this is why he never married, never settled down—he couldn't find a woman who wouldn't "mess up" his stuff.

He also had what he called a "system" for his shelves, which allowed, he explained, for maximum strength when heeling. Books shelved his way had less tendency to dislodge during heavy seas. His books were arranged by height, and height alone. They were highest on the outside of the shelves and gradually became shorter toward the middle. A fiddle of teak across the front kept them in place. My fastidious uncle would never allow a book, a tall book, to stick out so obviously in the middle of a shelf. Like this one.

I glanced over at Jason and Papa. Backs to me, they were concentrating on getting more close-ups of the plates on the table. Quickly, so quickly they did not see me do it, I grabbed the tall, slim volume out of the bookshelf, placed it against my chest, turned, went forward, and laid it on the vee berth where I hovered over it, out of their view.

The book cover was a vase of colorful flowers. Prissy for my old uncle, but the fact that he collected these books at all was surprising. I opened to the first page. It wasn't a garden book after all, but a volume of poetry. I quickly flipped through it. The entire small book seemed to have one theme — love. My crusty old uncle had a book of love poems? With flowers on every page? And hearts, even?

I was about to close the book and put it back when I noticed a square greeting card sized envelope tucked in the back. I opened it and pulled out a card with blue embossed flowers on the front of it. Zinnias, if I wasn't mistaken. I ran my hand over them. The flowers had been cut from somewhere else and pasted on, almost like old-fashioned découpage, but not quite. Inside the card was a small square of folded paper. I pulled it out. The paper was soft and yellowed and permanently creased like it had been here for a very long time. I read the short message:

Please don't try to find me. I had to leave, E

I read it several times before I folded it and put it back. Inside the card was another handwritten message:

I know this is a lot to ask, but please take good care of her, E

I fingered the card. It seemed new, the paper crisp and white while the note inside seemed old. Or maybe it was just old paper. I'm sure my uncle has a lot of that around.

Bear came and purred around my ankles. Absently, still holding the card, I bent down to rub her neck. I read the message again and came to a certain understanding. "E?" My name is Emmeline. Was this card meant for me? "Her" could refer to Bear.

Ferd knew I would be here. He knew I would find this one odd book sticking out. Through this cryptic message, he was telling me to take care of things for him. I bent down, picked up the feline and snuggled her against my face. His cat.

Maybe when the pirates or thieves came, he just had time to pen this note and put it in a place he knew I would find before he was taken by gunpoint on his dinghy.

He also was warning me not to come and find him. *He had to leave.* What did that mean? Was he warning me of danger? *Please don't try to find me.* What did that mean?

I said in a whisper, "I'll take good care of Bear. I know she means a lot to you. I'll take good care of her until we find you. Wherever you are..."

I put Bear down and turned the card over. There was no manufacturer's name on the back of it. This card was handmade. Cruisers sometimes make crafts and sell or trade them for things like boat repairs or boat items no longer needed. I smiled when I thought of my uncle accepting handmade artistic greeting cards for maybe some fish he'd caught. That would be just like him.

I put the card and note in the pocket of my shorts, put the book back on the shelf, and said to Papa, "Time to get back aboard *Townie.* Liam's taking this boat to shore. We're going to a private dock I've contracted. We'll tie *Townie* up there briefly, and then we'll head back to Miami. By my records, we still have two more days together."

I went back outside and into the sun.

CHAPTER 5

Liam was having the time of his life. From the flybridge of *Townie*, I could see him there, tall and straight behind the wheel, proud and thrilled. The day was calm, sunny, and hot, and the only way he could have been happier, was if he'd been sailing instead of motoring. Sailing would have presented a problem with that ripped mainsail, however. Before we separated the boats and left, I'd climbed up the mast, freed the jammed halyard, took the mainsail down and folded it as best I could and crammed it up into the vee berth. I examined the rip, and it still puzzled me. It looked to me as if the sail had been cut cleanly with a knife, rather than frayed by the wind.

The whole scenario was worrying. Russell told me there had been no reports of pirates in the area or crimes of any sort like this. Still, I worried. Plus, Papa was beginning to second-guess everything I was doing.

"You sure you talked with the Coast Guard?" he asked me.

"I'm sure."

"And they said to take the boat in like this?"

"Yep." I was only half lying.

He mumbled and fumed and muttered things like, "The network, they're going to think I set this up." And then to me, "You'll vouch for me, right? You'll vouch for the fact that we found the boat like this? They'll have to believe me. They'll have to—" And then his voice would trail off and he would frown into the sun.

Five hours later, we tied both boats to Skip and Sue's private wharf. They were there to greet us and catch lines. After I made sure Bear had plenty of food, water, and a clean litter box, I locked her into *Wandering Soul*. But Sue would have none of that. It was hot aboard *Wandering Soul,* dead hot, and Bear would be far more comfortable in their house. She'd even get Skip to turn on the air conditioning for the cat. They also said they would happily watch the cat until I figured out what I was going to do with Ferd's boat.

As soon as we were snug in our hotel rooms for the night, I called my good friend and Portland police officer, Ben Dunlinson. The call went to his voicemail. "Call me," I told him.

Next, I forced myself to call my mother.

"Have you heard from Uncle Ferd?"

The pause was so long I thought maybe the phone had been disconnected.

"Mom?"

"It's sort of odd, you asking about Ferd."

"Why's that?"

Very quietly, she said, "I had an interesting phone call a few weeks ago."

"Yeah?"

"Someone called here, a man. He asked to speak with Ferd. When I told him that my brother doesn't live here and has never lived here, he insisted I tell him where he was. He seemed not to believe that I had no idea where Ferd was. Why are you asking?"

"Did you get a caller ID?"

"It was blocked."

"Mom?"

"Yes?"

"I might have some bad news..." I told her what had happened. "I think something may have happened to him," I said. "I think he's in trouble." I told her my pirate theory. It sounded ludicrous in the telling, but what other explanation could there be?

"That man who called," my mother said. "He said it had to do with some money Ferd owed him."

"What?"

"I hung up before this person could really explain himself. This has happened before, Em. I don't want to be a party to Ferd's penchant for gambling."

"Mom! He could be in trouble!"

There was an audible sigh on the other end, and then she said, "He's in South America, Em."

This stopped me.

She said, "I got an email from him. Just recently. That's where he said he was. It's obvious, Em, he's got a different boat now. You said the name was scraped off the back? I think you're making a mountain out of a molehill. My brother probably lost the boat the same way he got it, in a gambling game."

"But, Mom," my head was spinning, "a lot of his stuff is still there."

"You said all his papers were gone, right—wait a minute," she said. "I'm sitting here at my computer. I've got that email from him in front of me."

She read the short email to me. All it said was that he was down in Patagonia and would be for some time. It was dated three weeks ago.

I said, "I thought you said you and Ferd didn't keep in touch very much."

"We don't. Not at all. This came out of the blue. He didn't email you with the same information?"

"No."

I could hear her sigh, and then, "You know how your uncle is."

I said nothing.

"Okay," she said, "here's what I'll do. I'll call Aunt Alice in California. See if she's heard anything."

"Thanks."

Alice was my mother's younger sister. Ferd was the oldest. Five years later my mother came along, and ten years after that, Alice. If my mother and Ferd weren't close, Ferd and Alice barely knew each other. Alice was still a child by the time Ferd had set out for life aboard his boat.

After the phone call, I got out the flowered card my uncle had left for me, read it again, and had another idea. Down through the centuries, ships have been referred to with feminine pronouns. Maybe Ferd wanted me to take care of *Wandering Soul* for him. Maybe it was more than Bear. Maybe it was *Wandering Soul and* Bear.

I was beginning to come up with a plan. As soon as I finished my contract with Papa — we still had two more days — I'd make sure Liam got on the plane home and then I'd sail *Wandering Soul* up to Maine by myself. Maybe I'd call my friend Joan and see if she wanted to come and help crew. Or I could get ahold of Sue's friend Janice. Maybe she'd like to help take the boat to Maine.

There was a knock on my hotel door. Through the peephole, I expected to see Papa. Instead, there stood Liam.

"Liam." Quickly I opened the door.

"Papa just called my room. He wants us all to go down for our last meal together."

"Now? Does he know what time it is?"

The boy shrugged.

"Well, I don't know about that. It's a bit late, wouldn't you say?"

"Come on, Em. It'll be fun, won't it?"

The only reason I'd felt okay in taking Liam on this trip at all was because Papa had originally told us that we would be spending almost all of our nights out on the boat. That was okay with Liam's parents. When it got to be every night on land, I made sure that Liam's room was right next to mine, and then once he was in, he was in for the night. I told him I would be checking on him periodically throughout the night to make sure this was true. If he "dared" to leave, even to get ice from the machine, I would know immediately and he would be on the next Greyhound home.

"He says," Liam said, "that he tried to reach you. That this is his last night with us."

"Really? By my records, we have a few more days."

"I'm just saying what he said."

"Okay," I said grabbing my key. "We'll go down, but we won't stay long. And stay right with me."

He sighed. "Okay."

Down in the restaurant, the waitress led Liam and me to the back of the dining hall where a bunch of tables had been shoved together. There was noise and people, and at the head of the table, Papa was holding court. On the tables were pitchers with copious amounts of beer, and huge baskets of chicken wings. Surrounding him was a bevy of fans, mostly females.

"Liam," I said, "we're leaving."

"Why?"

"Well, for starters, you're underage. Your mom would kill me if we don't leave now."

Too late. Papa saw me. "Captain Ridge!" he hollered. "Get your pretty self on over here. You and Liam both. Liam, my best little crew member ever!" He motioned. "Get on over here, you two. Someone get a glass of root beer for my first mate, Liam. Captain Ridge, these people are doubting what we all saw. I want you and Liam to tell all these good people what we witnessed out there in the Bermuda Triangle today."

I stood there in the doorway, my arm on Liam's shoulder.

He came out from behind the table, sauntered over to us, and stood much too close for comfort. Prior to tonight, Papa, although he came too close many times, closer than I would have liked, never before touched me. And now he touched my shoulder with his right hand while he said, "Tell all these good people what we saw out there since this is our last night together."

I looked at him and said quietly, "Our last night together? By my records, we have two more days."

He shook his head. He was smiling. "Nope. This is it." He lowered his voice and said, "The network called. They decided that since we hit the motherlode, we have enough for the show. They love the pictures, by the way. I have a meeting with the network execs tomorrow morning. The big guys. They want to see me."

"Good for you," I said.

"Good things are happening," he said. "I can feel it."

A moment later, he was back with the ladies at the table. For the next interminable minutes, I drank half a beer. Liam had his root beer and ate a huge number of chicken wings, one right after the other, while I answered questions as best I could. I literally was saved by the bell. My cell phone rang. Ben. I wouldn't take the call here. I'd wait and call him back.

"Liam," I said. "We gotta go."

He seemed disappointed but hastily grabbed a bunch of wings and wrapped them up in a napkin to take with him. On our way out, he gave a few long looks at the scantily clad females as I took the back of his jacket and led him out of the room.

Everyone secured in their rooms for the night, I called Ben.

CHAPTER 6

Portland City Police Detective Ben Dunlinson and I are friends. We became so a little more than a year ago when I helped him out on a case. He's relatively new to Maine, and occasionally he calls on me for my "expert opinion" on all things boats and Maine and nautical. I'm sort of an attaché to the police. It's been fun and interesting being in on the ground floor, so to speak, on a number of police matters and cases.

We are, as they say, "just friends" and that's the way it is. Oh, there was a time about a year ago when I thought it might turn into more. This was after he rescued me from a rapidly sinking inflatable dinghy on its way to the middle of the ocean. While I recuperated from a painful broken ankle, he came over every day and we sat outside on my front porch, looked out over my end of the bay and talked. Later, I realized it was me who did most of the talking while he listened. After I was better, we went out for a couple of dress-up, adult dinner dates, but nothing happened. Even though I found myself attracted to him — and I still do, much to my chagrin — I was the one who backed away. The reason? The guy is married. Yep. He's married. I even know her name — Cindy. I've seen her picture. He also has a son somewhere. Why I had even agreed to go out with him at all when he has a family out west somewhere is still a mystery to me. I know better. Or at least I think I do.

His last policing job was in Montana, and according to an article in the hometown paper, and available online for everyone to look up, he shot and killed an innocent bystander during a drug bust that went horribly bad. Even though he was found not to blame — he was given faulty information —

he took stress leave. After that, he transferred here. Alone.

In the year I've known him, he's never mentioned his family, and I've never asked. When he's ready, he'll talk. Or maybe not. Maybe we'll never have that kind of relationship.

Out on our two fancy adult dinner-dates, his only topic of conversation was the beauty of Montana, his canoe, his stream, the mountains and fishing — mostly the fishing, fly fishing to be precise. Never about his wife. Never about his son. Never about his family. Never about what happened. At the end of our second date, after he had spent twenty minutes describing a specific fishing expedition, I feigned a headache and said I needed to get home.

"I get them," I'd said. "Headaches. And I'm no good to anyone when I'm in the middle of one of my migraines."

And that was that. We said not a word all the way home. I didn't invite him in. When he drove away, I sat on my couch and was sad.

A month later, he called me with a question about lobstering boats. We went to the coffee shop across the street from the police station — the very neutral place we always went — and had our discussion. I talked. He took notes. I advised. He took more notes. He told me a joke. I laughed. We were back the way we always were. Friends. Good friends. But, despite our failed attempt at being a couple, Ben is that someone I could call in the middle of the night if something really bad happens. Like now.

"It's my uncle." I choked back my tears. "You've heard me mention my Uncle Ferd? He's gone. I found his boat."

"Hold on. The last I heard you were on some job for a conspiracy theorist for a television program."

Trying to regain some control, I told him what had happened out there.

"What does the Coast Guard say?" he asked.

"As far as they're concerned, it's just an abandoned boat. Do you think you could check on my uncle? A friend in the Coast Guard did but couldn't find anything. My uncle didn't call a Mayday. He didn't file a sail plan..."

"I'll check. Are you okay?"

"I think so." I gave him all my uncle's particulars. I added, "I'm thinking of taking *Wandering Soul* up to Maine. I can't leave her here, and as of tomorrow, I'm free from my employ. I think Papa has taken enough pictures to last a lifetime."

"I've seen his show. It's nuts."

"Agreed. And Ben? Thanks."

"Anything for you, Em."

Really? I swallowed.

The following morning my mother called.

"I checked with Aunt Alice out in California. It seems she got the same email I did about Ferd being down at the bottom of South America. It was word for word. Em, are you sure the boat you have belongs to your uncle?" There was something in her voice that frightened me.

"I'm sure. I'm one hundred percent sure. Are you okay, Mom? You sound – different."

"That same man phoned again."

"What?"

"Last night. He demanded to know where Ferd was. He said he was sure I was holding out on him. I told him the last I heard, my brother was in South America. He talked again about money."

"Did you call the police?"

There was a protracted sigh. "Em, I'm used to his shenanigans, especially when it comes to gambling and money. So, no, I didn't call the police."

"I have a police friend checking on him."

"Where are you now?"

"Miami. In a few days, I'm going to start sailing Ferd's boat up to Maine."

"Really? You're going to do that?"

"Yes." I didn't want to tell her about the note. "I can't leave it here."

"What if he comes off his drinking binge and goes back to Florida looking for his boat?"

"Mom!" *Drinking binge!* "His boat was left abandoned. If I

hadn't found it, it would have been taken by the next person who did."

"Your uncle..." A long pause. "Em, you have always idolized your uncle."

"He could be in trouble. Mom, he could..."

"Oh, for goodness sake, he's not in trouble. I know my brother better than anyone does. He's probably bought himself a new boat with whatever money he stole from the guy who phoned me."

"Mom? If that man calls you again, could you see if you could get his name? Find out what this is all about?"

She promised she would, reluctantly.

Later that morning, I said goodbye to Dr. Papa and Jason. He gave me a nice big check, which I slipped into the front zipper pocket of my bag. He seemed in good spirits. "Hope you don't mind cutting your trip short a bit." He winked at me. "The network wants to see me. Today. And I'm going to do you a favor. Just so you know, I'm going to recommend you to them if anyone there ever needs a boat driver."

"Thanks. It was fun."

"And," he eyed me playfully, "you be careful out there on the Bermuda Triangle. You never know what still might happen out there."

"Right."

I ended up driving Liam to the airport in Skip's car. Even though he begged to come along on *Wandering Soul*, and even though I could have used the crew, Liam is, after all, only fifteen. I was sure of the safety of the boat, but not the safety of the mission, or when you got right down to it, my sanity.

On the way back to Skip and Sue's, I took the ripped sail to a sail loft I knew. They promised they'd put a rush on it and have it repaired by tomorrow. It's great having friends in high places. I deposited the check Papa gave me and bought a crap load of food. Back on the boat, I drained and refilled the water tanks, checked the batteries, the fluids, the ground tackle, the sheets, halyards and all the rigging. It was nice that Skip and Sue had power and water on their dock. I checked the electronics and the solar panel. Everything was in working order, which is so like my fastidious uncle.

A few key navigational items were missing from *Wandering Soul*, I noticed. Namely, the GPS and radio microphones, the one from the main set and the one from the helm. Odd? Maybe. But if someone had come aboard *Wandering Soul* and left her out there, taking these would have made it hard to call for help. Fortunately, I'd brought along my own GPS and handheld radio for the Papa Hoho trip. I always believe in having a backup, plus I have learned never to trust other people's equipment, so I always bring a spare. I would use it. I debated about buying a second GPS but decided against it. I did, however, replace the microphones. The paper charts were all there, plus my uncle's set of plotting tools, but I know these waters and this route like the back of my hand anyway. It would be like driving home.

I called Joan and she said she was tied up for the next week or so, but would be happy to meet me in the Chesapeake if I wanted crew for the second half of the trip. I said sure, fine, thanks. Joan is a good friend and a great sailor. She's been on many deliveries with me and is unflappable even in the worst conditions. She is smart and savvy and while she's not quite old enough to be my mother, she's old enough to be my aunt, if that makes any sense. Her husband, Art, has sailed with Ferd. Maybe they had heard something.

When I told her about finding *Wandering Soul* abandoned, she told me that she and Art received the same email my mother and aunt had. He was at the bottom end of South America. He was about as far as a person could get from here.

"I don't think he's there," I told her. "Unless he's got a new boat."

"With Ferd, you never know."

"No, right. You never know." I thought about what my mother said. "He left me a note." I said, "He told me to take care of his boat and his cat. He'd never go anywhere without his cat."

"The police know?"

"Of course. They're looking into it. I'm worried. His dinghy is gone, too."

"That's maybe a good sign."

"Yeah. I don't know. I don't know anything."

I contacted Sue's friend, Janice, who was young and keen for blue water experience. She was free now and would be happy to come with me until the Chesapeake. This would work out great. She'd get the delivery experience she wanted, and I'd get needed help on those long nights.

That evening, I stowed everything and made supper aboard *Wandering Soul*. Skip and Sue knew of a good used inflatable that was selling for a good price. I called and could pick it up tomorrow. Later that day, Janice joined me. She was small, spunky, twenty-one, and she reminded me of Liam in her eagerness. Attached to the front of her shirt was a ceramic pin with her name, Janice, in a kind of stylized script. During our time together, she would wear that pin everywhere. During our entire time together, I never asked her why.

But when she showed up that day on the dock, all she did was smile. She wanted to crew, wanted to please, wanted to sail, wanted to learn. Skip and Sue had told her so much about me, she said. I told her very little about this trip—just that I was taking this boat home to Maine, we were going to sail 24/7, and that I was glad to have her along.

We looked at the charts and studied the weather. If we went far outside the intracoastal waterway and sailed night and day, we could be in Baltimore in two weeks.

The night before we were to leave, I wanted to sleep aboard *Wandering Soul*, but with the night so still and so hot that the little cat was actually panting, the three of us decided on Skip and Sue's air-conditioned guest room.

The first morning out was gorgeous with the winds blowing a hair over ten knots. We put up Ferd's repaired mainsail, and it caught the wind beautifully. Eventually, we got both sails up and glided along at a steady fifteen-degree heel at six knots. These are the kinds of days sailors write about. These are the kinds of days you sit back and enjoy the sun, the breeze, the utter aloneness of space, the peace, and the calm.

My uncle is a true introvert and loves his own space and his own company. When life gets too much and there are too many people around, he simply sails off. I'm a lot like that. I would have preferred to be out here alone, instead of with talkative and gung-ho Janice who wanted everyone to know her name, otherwise why would she wear that pin? She would soon learn that, by and large, sailors are a quiet lot who prefer aloneness, and feel it's perfectly okay to go for hours without speaking.

I thought about my uncle a lot. As I adjusted the main sail, I wondered about all the places he might be. This boat has always been his home. Without it, he's basically homeless. A new boat? He would have emailed me. He would've sent pictures. Maybe. Unless. Unless what?

We'd been out there for around five hours when I saw a sleek silver boat behind me in the distance. Actually, I heard it first, that incredibly loud, thunderous engine sound of a super-fast cigarette boat. That name in popular culture comes from the fact that they are fast — very, very fast — so fast if they are smuggling something — i.e. cigarettes — they can outrun the good guys. Hence the name cigarette boat. They have also been called rumrunners, for obvious reasons.

I aimed my binoculars in the direction of the noise. The boat was silver with a zigzagged lightning motif along the side I could see, and it was gaining on me. Was this the sort of boat that had boarded my uncle's boat? Did whoever it was recognize *Wandering Soul*? In my haste, in my fear, I got out my radio to call the Coast Guard. All the while Janice was pointing and jabbering. "You see that boat over there? You know how much they spend on gas? You know how much those things cost? Ya gotta be crazy owning one of them. I had this boyfriend once…"

She went on and on. I put down my radio, deciding I was letting my paranoia get the better of me. When the boat in question abruptly turned and headed for land, I realized it was probably some rich kids out for a joy ride. It had nothing to do with me or *Wandering Soul* or my uncle or the Bermuda Triangle or some guy phoning my mother wanting to know where his money was.

I continued on, but the gloriousness of the day was slowly being replaced by a kind of wariness. Something real and awful had happened here. My uncle had been forcibly taken from his boat, and whoever it was who'd done this, would they come after me? Had I put this young woman, Janice, in danger? Despite the day, despite the sun and gentle breeze, I hugged my arms around me.

The first night, far offshore, even too far for cell reception, I told Janice to go down and get some rest. I'd sail for as long as I could through the night. Then we'd switch. I engaged the autopilot and leaned back in the cockpit. Out on the water at night is when you realize what a tiny speck you are in the massive universe and how little you matter. Sometimes I wonder if this is how it feels to be in outer space. Only one thing worried me a bit. I usually never go this far off shore without a satellite phone. I didn't have one now. Should I have sprung for one before we left? I furrowed my brow and stared at the water, at the glinting silver tops of the waves. The moon was high and almost full. No, I just wanted to get this thing home.

A few hours later, Janice came up, more than ready to take over.

I lay down in my berth but couldn't fall asleep. At one point, I thought I heard the sound of the cigarette boat again. It was part of a dream. It had to be a part of a dream. Not way out here. Not this far out. Not at night. A dream.

Days passed. We managed to sail, to eat, to talk a little. The only one who didn't feel the strangeness was Janice. She was so enthusiastic about pleasing me and doing everything right that it was slightly embarrassing. I finally had to confront her. "You're doing great, Janice. Don't worry so much. This is such a big help. I don't know what I'd do without you."

"But it's you." Her eyes were bright. "Skip and Sue have

told me so much about you, how great you are with boats and all..."

She told me she wanted to do what I did — get her captain's license, and I tried to be as nice as I could, but I was tired and headachy and too keyed up from worry to have long conversations about crewing, captaining and what was required. A weird fear began to settle down upon me like a heavy cloak that I couldn't push off me, no matter how I tried to lift the corners. I didn't want Janice noticing, so I tried to keep cheerful. As far as Janice was concerned, this was an ordinary delivery for an ordinary client. Yet, the further we got away from Miami, the colder I felt, the more my hands shook over simple tasks.

"You're tired," Janice told me on the fourth day.

"Yeah," I said. "I'm sorry I'm not the best of company. Family problems." I sighed.

She sighed theatrically. "I know all about *that*. That's why I'm staying with Skip and Sue and not my own mom and dad."

The sun was low on the horizon of the sixth day when again I heard the sound of a cigarette boat in the distance. I was awake. This wasn't a dream. This was real. What the hell? It couldn't be the same boat. Not way out here. Was it following us? I focused my binoculars on the glint on the horizon. It certainly looked like the same boat. I couldn't see it clear enough to see the lightning strikes along the side so I couldn't be sure.

"Does that look like the same boat to you?" I pointed at it.

Janice looked at me. "You kidding me? That was like four days ago."

"I guess you're right."

"Those boats, they all look alike."

"Yeah."

"Same crazy people. Spending a ton of money."

"Yep."

On the seventh day, I was lying in my berth at almost five in the morning when Janice called down,

"Hey, can you come up? Something's weird up here."

I pulled on my sweatshirt and climbed above. By the time I got up there, she was already down in her bunk and asleep. Odd, I thought, but at the helm, I kept blinking. The night was too dark, the water too inky black and solid looking. As I stood behind the ship's wheel, something felt out of place and wrong, but I couldn't think what. The dawn of that early morning was coming on too bright, the colors all wrong. I blinked several times.

The sky came out so blue it was as if a child had chosen an impossibly colored crayon to fill it in. The sun came up too yellow, and it even had those tendrils of lines of sunlight coming off it that children draw. What was the matter with me? Papa's words came to me then. *"You be careful in the Bermuda Triangle."* We weren't in the Bermuda Triangle anymore, though.

The sails were up, but it was like the wind couldn't make up its mind. It would settle down to nothing and then whip up around me like a wind nymph. It had a color, too. The wind had a color, and it was a very pale pink. Or was that my fanciful imagination? I went from putting up the sails to taking them down and motoring. I settled on using the mainsail only and kept the motor on while I noted an exceedingly strange cloud formation to starboard. Fog? But the weather had indicated no fog. No precip of any kind was forecast for the next three days. I know. I keep an eagle eye on the weather when I sail.

The boat swayed. The distance looked blue and calm, but directly beneath me, the ocean began to ruffle as if a hand the size of my boat was stirring a circle around me and I was in the middle.

I felt a cold wind like breath on the back of my neck. Shakily, I wiped the sweat from my upper lip and tried to get a grip. Maybe we should head ourselves inland, spend a night or two on shore. Get a decent shower. Feel the earth under our feet. I tightened in on the main sheet, my only sail up now, and took it off autopilot, attempting to hand steer while I continued to rock and sway. I checked the GPS. Way off course. I couldn't be more off course if I'd lifted the boat up and plunked her down in the opposite direction.

The sail flapped loudly and suddenly, I was looking at the side of the inside of the boat from my berth. I climbed out of it quickly. I'd been asleep. Dreaming.

I rubbed my eyes to clear them, groaned, got up, grabbed for my glasses, and climbed up into the cockpit where Janice was expertly sailing the boat. It was early morning. Everything was fine. Everything was right. The sky was normal. The sun was a yellow ball.

"You missed the most beautiful night," she told me. "And the dawn was spectacular. I've never seen anything like it. Look at that blue sky. It's still really blue. It was really, really blue about half an hour ago."

I swallowed and told her I'd take over and maybe she should get some sleep.

"I'll make breakfast first," the eager beaver said. "Do you want eggs?"

"Sure. Thanks."

For twelve days out on *Townie,* I had heard Dr. Papa recite every single tale about the Bermuda Triangle in popular culture. Strange fogs and winds. Lost radio signals. Planes going down and never being heard from again. Compasses going nuts. Boats going nuts. People going nuts. Sentinel to the Gates of Hell.

Right.

It was only a dream. Get a grip. It was only a dream.

I grabbed a bottle of water from the cooler and drank deeply. I needed to drink more water. Maybe less coffee. I'm too addicted to coffee. Most sailors agree that when you go nuts out here, nine times out of ten it's dehydration. I drank the whole bottle down in one go.

Eight days later, after sailing day and night, we entered the bottom end of the Chesapeake. That was when I heard the unmistakable sound of a cigarette boat engine again. No problem this time. There were lots of boats like that on the

Chesapeake. This was not the same one. The sound was over to my starboard. I picked up my binoculars. It was a silver boat with a lightning motif. How was that even possible? You'd never take that sort of a powerboat so far away from home. It would cost thousands of dollars in fuel alone.

I looked for a flag of registry and saw none. Neither did I see a name across the back or license numbers on the side. I tried hailing it on my radio. No answer. But somehow, I didn't expect there would be.

It was evening when I heard several sharp rings. My cell phone. We had crossed the threshold into cellular reception again.

One message from Joan and three from Ben. I called Joan first. She was going to be delayed, but she would meet me in four days in Baltimore if that was okay. Her calendar was pretty free after that. She was looking forward to it. She's always liked being on *Wandering Soul*.

I got Ben on the first ring.

"Hey, Ben."

"Em? Are you sitting down?"

"Yeah?"

"There's an APB out on your Uncle Ferd. He's wanted for questioning in connection with a murder."

CHAPTER 7

"**W**hat!" I sat down in the cockpit seat with a thud. "What?"

A breeze was gusting across the cockpit whipping my hair across my face. I fingered it back. "Ben, what? What are you talking about?"

Bear, who'd been curled up beside me, put her head in my lap.

"He's a person of interest, in any case."

"Why?"

"He was seen arguing with the victim the night before. Quite a heated argument, apparently. The police want to talk with him, and no one knows where he is."

"He's in South America."

"The authorities can't find him there. Have you heard from him at all, Em?"

"No. He emailed my mother, my aunt, and Joan's husband, Art. Where was this murder? South America?"

"Pennsylvania."

"What?" I stood up suddenly. "Pennsylvania? Where in Pennsylvania?"

"A town called Mount Joy, near Harrisburg."

I put a hand to my forehead and swept my hair behind my ears. How could my uncle be wanted for murder in Pennsylvania? My uncle never goes to Pennsylvania. Harrisburg is nowhere near the ocean. "He wouldn't go there," is all I said.

"All I'm telling you is what I've been able to find out."

"Where is this town exactly?"

"Around halfway between Lancaster and Harrisburg. Lots of Amish."

"Someone Amish was murdered? What happened, Ben? What do you know?"

"Ferdinand Hanson, apparently, was somehow involved in a murder which occurred outside a café there a month ago."

"I'm sure there's some sort of mix up. I'll have to clear this up, Ben. Who was murdered?"

"Someone by the name of Stan Hollander. Ring a bell?"

I said the name out loud. I had never heard of that person and told him so. "It has to be someone with the same name."

"Ferdinand Hanson was traced through his passport."

"What?"

"Apparently, the only ID he had on him was his passport," Ben said. "The police were given a photocopy of his passport by a clerk at the motel where he stayed."

I clamped my mouth shut. My uncle doesn't have credit cards, library cards, medical cards, nothing. The only ID he ever carries with him is his passport. But my uncle also doesn't get into fights. And, my Uncle Ferd doesn't venture more than half a mile away from the ocean. Ever. I explained all of this to Ben. "Someone has obviously stolen his passport. The same people who took him off his boat and left it out there floating."

"They want to talk to you as well. Officer by the name of Wayne Holden from Mount Joy has been trying to reach you."

"Me? I didn't get any calls."

"Your address in Maine was on his passport."

"Oh." I felt a small tinge of relief. The government requires that you have an address on the planet somewhere, and it has be a real address on land, so my Uncle uses my address. The phone number on his passport was probably from the days when Jesse was alive and we had a landline. I continued, "Give me his number and I'll clear this up."

He did.

"Where are you, Em?"

"I've just entered the Chesapeake. I can be in Baltimore in a few days. I have a crew member getting off, and Joan is

47

getting on to help me sail this boat the rest of the way up to Maine. I'll be up in Portland in a few weeks, maybe three. And Ben, it's not my uncle. It couldn't possibly be." But even as I said it, I wondered, how well did I know him? Hadn't my mother asked me that?

Ben continued, "There's a bit more. Or there could be a bit more. The police aren't sure how this is related, but shortly before he was murdered, a gas station attendant was killed, or at least left for dead, outside of a Sheetz gas station in Mount Joy. Does the name Simon Towers mean anything to you?"

I told him no.

He went on. "One of the Sheetz employees found him lying out back, covered in blood. He checked Towers, determined he wasn't breathing and then went inside to call 911 — this was at something like two in the morning. When he went back out, the body had been moved. By the look of the blood track marks, it was presumed the body had been dragged a distance. The police questioned Stan, but before they could formally arrest him, he was murdered."

"I don't understand what that has to do with my uncle."

"I'm getting to that. Stan Hollander, Simon Towers, and Stan's brother, by the name of — I have it here somewhere — Ronny Joe Hollander had jointly won a fairly large sum of money at a racetrack. I guess it was Simon who collected it, kept it, and when Stan went to get his and his brother's share, a fight ensued."

"Money?" I remembered what my mother had told me about her mysterious phone calls. "Where's the money now?"

"That's the thing. No one knows where it is."

"The police don't have it?"

"No."

"What about the brother? What did you say his name was?"

"Ronny Joe Hollander. Like your uncle, he's missing, too. No one has seen him since his brother died."

"Well, there you have it. He killed his brother for the

money and took off with it. Oh, and Ben? Someone phoned my mother out of the blue saying that Ferd owes him some money."

"What? When?"

I told him about the phone calls.

"Really? Holden will want to know about that. And, just so you know, they might want to search the boat. They have the bullet, the one that killed Hollander, but they still can't locate the gun. It was a clean shot, right into the neck. Small caliber bullet. Which is another curious thing."

"Why?"

"These three were into big guns. Assault rifles, from what the reports say. The small bullet doesn't fit any of their weapons."

"Well, it's not my uncle's. My uncle has never owned any guns. None at all. You should hear him talk about guns. He's opinionated, and this is one thing he has strong opinions about."

After we hung up, I sat there wondering. Why was my uncle in a place like Mount Joy, Pennsylvania mixed up with people like this? Ferd seldom set foot in any place further away than a hundred feet from the ocean. I don't think my Uncle Ferd has ever even seen a cornfield.

I grabbed another bottle of water before I called this Wayne Holden in Mount Joy. When he came on the line, I went through the whole story, adding that several people had heard from Ferd confirming he was in South America. No, I told Wayne, he hadn't told me that. I hadn't heard from my uncle in months. Yes, I'd look up my last email from Ferd and forward it to him. I told Wayne I was heading into Baltimore now by boat to pick up a friend who was going to help me sail Ferd's boat the rest of the way home to Portland, Maine.

"We'll meet you in Baltimore," Wayne said.

"You're driving in from Pennsylvania?" I said.

"Yes, and we'll need to search the boat."

"Okay, I guess."

I was told to dock the sailboat at the Coast Guard yard on

Curtis Creek. They would make sure there was space and meet me there. Fine, fine, okay, fine. I told him I was maybe a couple of days out and would call him when I cleared Knot Island. From there I would be only four or five hours away.

I realized I had to tell Janice something. She was under the impression this was just an ordinary delivery.

"We've run into a snag," I said.

"Yeah?"

"In Baltimore we're going to the Coast Guard. The police have to search this boat."

"Wow! Why?"

"The owner's run into some trouble."

"Oh. Okay. Wow! Does this happen often?"

"Not really."

That was all I said. It seemed to satisfy her. Down below, instead of catching a bit of shut-eye, I turned my phone into a hotspot and opened up my laptop—not caring how much bandwidth I was using up on my pitiful data plan—and googled the murder. I scrolled through and read every news story, every word I could find. I learned that the body of Stan Hollander was found outside and near the back door of Jacobson's Café early in the morning of three weeks ago. I studied the details. No mention of my uncle. None at all, other than the police were looking into various suspects. The article also noted that Stan had been questioned about the brutal attack of Sheetz gas station employee Simon Towers whose body had not been located.

I read to the end. It seems Stan Hollander had a police record—theft, a few DUIs, and one drunk and disorderly. Both Stan and Simon had spent time in jail. Ronny Joe had not. Or at least I couldn't find any information on him.

I searched for and found Stan's obituary at a funeral home site. His picture looked more like a mug shot. Jowly faced, no neck, short prison cropped hair, crooked nose—probably from being broken—and I couldn't be sure, but it looked like there was a tattoo. I thought I could see it snaking its way around his neck.

I read that Hollander had left behind a wife, Ocean Anne, a daughter, Corrie Tabitha, and a brother Ronny Joe Hollander. No mention of parents. No mention of anyone else.

In another article, I discovered that Stan Hollander, Ronny Joe Hollander, and Simon Towers were part of a survivalist group that had a clubhouse a few hours north of Harrisburg. To my way of thinking, there are two kinds of survivalists. There are those who plant their own organic gardens, and keep chickens and eggs, and put up solar panels, and then there are those who firmly believe the government is trying to poison us through vaccines and contrails — Dr. Papa Hoho would be proud — and they stash arms and foodstuffs in bunkers hidden throughout the countryside. Reading about the brothers led me to believe they were probably firmly in the second camp.

I also learned that Stan's wife had recently put out a restraining order against him. Well, there you go, I said. There's your murderer. Look no further. Not my uncle who has nothing to do with all you weird people. It was a small gun, right? Ben had told me the bullet was for a small gun — the kind a woman might carry, not a paranoid assault rifle-toting survivalist.

We would be in Baltimore soon, and I would certainly learn more then. I decided on a quick nap before it was my turn at the helm again, but I didn't sleep well. I kept waking up to noises, like people walking on top of the boat with heavy boots. Dreams. All simply bad dreams.

****

I was motoring up Curtis Creek while Janice sat in the cockpit, her stuff packed and ready to leave. Four officers were down on the wharf waiting for us. Up on the bow, Janice threw a line to a waiting officer, a chunky guy who looked overly warm and stuffed into in his uniform. I managed the stern and handed my line to a good-looking Coast Guard guy.

"Captain Em Ridge," I said.

"Captain," the good-looking one said.

"That's Janice, my crew member."

"Hello."

When the boat was secure, Janice carried her duffle bag out, I thanked her, and she hugged me and said, "I hope everything goes okay. I was just happy to help during this time." She hugged me again. "And I hope you think of me if you ever need a crew member again." She hugged me a third time and then she was gone.

The officer named Wayne was standing on the dock. I recognized his booming voice from the phone. Oddly, he turned out to look very much like the photos I'd seen of Stan. Stocky, thick-bellied, with an acne-marked face and a fleshy nose.

"Bear! Oh, Bear. Sorry," I called to the officer. "My cat!" Bear had jumped ship and was off and down the dock already wanting to explore other boats. When I cornered her, I secured the makeshift leash I'd made for her out of thin line. "Sorry," I said again as I picked her up.

"Your cat?" said the only woman officer, a pretty girl with hair the color of newly pulled carrots.

While I held a very squirming Bear who did not want to be held, I went through my story again. By now, I was getting practiced. Holden surprised me by asking if I thought my uncle was suicidal.

I simply stared at him. "Of course not. Why would you ask that?"

"It's one of the theories we're working on."

"I can assure you that is not the case."

"We may need to see some of his emails."

"I can forward them to you. As many as you like."

I had this horrible feeling that they were going to ask for my computer. This had happened to me before, and even though I really didn't want to lose it for even a few hours, I was ready. All of my important stuff was on two thumb drives in my pocket.

I asked, "Can you tell me what you know about

Pennsylvania?"

Wayne said, "This is what we know so far. Your uncle goes there. He checks into a motel and visits Jacobsen's Café a number of times. A whole bunch of times, actually. Makes friends. He keeps going back to the same café."

I asked, "Where did he stay?"

He told me the name of the motel, and I filed it away in my brain.

"He gets to know this young waitress there named Ocean Hollander."

I nodded. "She had a restraining order out on her husband."

He raised his eyebrows.

"I read it in the news," I said. "Go on."

"This Ferdinand Hanson becomes really chummy with the whole staff. One evening, Stan Hollander comes in, which is in direct violation of said RO anyway. I guess Ferdinand Hanson confronted him. According to witnesses, it was a very heated argument. Next morning, the café manager finds Stan's body out back by the dumpster. He was cleanly shot and killed. And then Hanson disappears. Doesn't even check out of the motel. So, you see why we're interested in talking with your uncle."

"Why did you ask if he was suicidal then?"

"Because he's been gone for almost a month. He left his boat abandoned out there."

"The dinghy is gone," I countered. "So he could be somewhere."

Wayne nodded.

"And the brother, I understand he's missing, too?"

Holden nodded. "We're also looking for him. But he'd been missing prior to the murder."

"This whole thing is extremely out of character for my uncle."

Bear managed to squirm out of my arms and onto the dock. She did not like me restraining her with the leash I had made out of a line, and voiced her protest with a loud meow.

"We have a search warrant for this boat."

"Okay. May I sit here in the cockpit while you search? I might be able to help. I know my uncle pretty well."

The carroty hair officer said, "Might be a long wait."

"How long?"

"Few hours. Maybe longer. There's a park just over there where you and the cat can go."

"I have to sleep on that boat tonight. Will it be ready by then?"

"Oh, it shouldn't take us that long. But after we're finished, you'll have to move it from the Coast Guard dock."

"Understood."

"There might be room in the Inner Harbor. You'll have to check with the harbormaster."

"Thanks. I'll do that."

Sometimes, I feel I don't have a lot going for me in my strange life, but I do have one thing. I know a lot of people all up and down this coast, and Baltimore, like Florida, is no exception. Maybe my friends, Barbara and Simone, were home and we could meet for supper or coffee. They don't live too far from town.

Barbara answered on the first ring. When she heard my sad sob story, she said, "Em, you will not sleep on your boat. You'll come up and spend a couple of days with us. And when the Coast Guard is finished with the boat, use the dock where Simone's boat usually is. She's away sailing on a course. You're welcome to the house. I have to head out to work in a couple of minutes. But come in, make yourself at home, and we'll talk later. Or in the morning. I'm heading to work. I have to work late. You know where the key is?"

"Under the kayak in the backyard."

"Yep. Come on in and don't worry about waiting up for me." Barbara works as a waitress in a high-end restaurant along the waterfront, and Simone teaches timid women how to sail on three and five-day cruises. I added, "I have a cat with me. My uncle's cat."

"Bear? No problem. I remember your uncle and his cat."

"Joan's coming in a few days."

"Well, the guest loft is made up. It's all yours."

"Thanks. Have you..." I paused. "Have you heard from Ferd?"

"No. Sorry. I'll ask Simone."

"Thanks so much. You are such a kind person."

"Oh, bah."

Bear and I walked up to the park, where we walked around for awhile. Then I went and got a coffee. I got some strange looks, walking up to the drive-through coffee shop, restless cat in arms. We went and sat in the park until I drank all my coffee. When we went back down to the boat, they still weren't finished, so Bear and I sat on the dock in the gathering darkness until they were.

An hour later, I was motoring the boat around to Simone's dock space. The police hadn't found anything, they said, although precisely what they were looking for, I didn't know. I presumed the mysterious money. I could have told them they'd find nothing. On the trip up here, I'd been through all of my uncle's things. Everything personal was gone. As I tied up on Simone's dock, I realized it was a good thing I was going to be spending a few days here. Down below, the police search had left the boat in a complete shambles. It would take me a few days to get it ready to go.

There was a marina cart at the end of the dock. I borrowed it and put all my stuff in it, including the box of cat litter, plus the cat sitting on top contained by his rope leash. Up at Barbara and Simone's, I easily found the key under the kayak. Inside, I fell onto their couch and began weeping from exhaustion. I settled the two of us into the guest loft and then found clean towels and took a long and well-deserved shower.

A little while later, I lay down on the bed in the guest loft. I could sleep here without worrying about silver cigarette boats and pirates and guns and murder and strange weather phenomenon out at sea. No one knew I was here. I slept. And slept.

I awoke to the sound of my phone. I didn't know where I was, and I shot up — my turn to take over from Janice! But, no, the sun was shining through big, square windows. I was in a house. On land. Barbara and Simone's. I had slept clear through to the next morning.

It was my mother. "The police called me, Em. What's going on?"

I shook the sleep out of my head and said, "There was some murder or robbery or something and they want to talk to Ferd about it. Apparently, he was there or something." I rubbed my eyes, reached for my glasses. She didn't say anything. "Mom?"

Finally, "I always wondered if something like this would happen to my brother."

"What do you mean?"

"Em, I have often worried about you. You don't know how he was. Why he left the way he did."

"Mom?" I sat up on the edge of the bed. Bear peered at me from the window seat where she had made herself comfortable. I didn't hear anything from down below and wondered if Barbara was still in bed. If she'd worked late, it was quite likely. I hadn't heard anything all night. I don't think I had slept that soundly in months.

"It's why I never wanted you to follow that path, his path."

I brushed my hair behind my ears. I didn't want to hear this.

She was going on. "It was why I've worried so much about you."

Bear had jumped up onto the bed beside me and meowed. "Em, he walked away from his family. He walked away from his faith. That's not how he was raised."

I chose not to say anything to this. This is what I heard every time I talked with her. I, too, had "walked away from my family, from my faith," and when you got right down to it, it wasn't the way I was raised either. I didn't need a sermon now. I didn't need her comparing me to my younger twin sisters who were completely perfect in every way.

I took a few breaths before I said, "The police asked me if I thought Ferd was suicidal."

"The police asked me the same thing. I told them given the right circumstances, he could very well be."

"Mom!" I was getting angry now. "He's *not* suicidal. Even you should know that."

"Your uncle. He's been in so much trouble. Trouble with the law. Drugs. Things you know nothing about, Em. Smuggling. Who knows what all? He's lived like a hippie for such a long time he doesn't even know how it is to be normal. And when he doesn't want to face something, he just sails off. That's him. Just off into the sunset. I can see him getting in trouble in Pennsylvania and then just running away."

"Mom, Uncle Ferd would never hurt a soul."

Her sigh was audible. "He was not the perfect person you imagine him to be. That first time he went away to sea? That was him running from a crime. Did you know that? Possession of marijuana. He couldn't face the music. That's why he left. I know him, Em. He's my brother. He's not the man you think he is. You've idolized a fantasy all these years." She went on. She wasn't finished. "The way he carried on—"

I stopped her. "He's in trouble. He's wanted for murder. Something he would never do. You know that as well as I do."

"I know no such thing."

"Mom, hold on. I'm getting another call. If you hear from him, will you let me know?"

We said our goodbyes. No, I didn't have another call. I don't even have call waiting. I just needed to get away.

I sneaked quietly downstairs, not wanting to wake up Barbara. I found a note saying she had to go out, but to make myself at home and there was coffee in the thermos pot on the counter.

I made sure Bear was set up with food and water, and I headed down to the dock. Joan wouldn't be here for two more days, and I had cleaning to do. When I unlocked the door to the companionway and surveyed the damage again, I felt disheartened.

I was coming up with another idea. Maybe today wouldn't be a good day for cleaning it. Maybe there was someplace else I should go. Back at their house, I checked online for Mount Joy, Pennsylvania.

Only one and a half hours by car. Doable. Completely doable.

CHAPTER 8

I easily found Jacobson's Café online. I was even able to get a street view of the place. It looked very ordinary and nice and probably served up a decent home cooked meal. What the heck was my uncle doing there? He often said he had seawater in his veins. He's never used sunscreen in his life even though he's lived on the water, nor insect spray. "You get enough salt water on your skin, it keeps the bugs away. You get enough salt in your system, you don't get sunburned." And how did he get to this place called Mount Joy in the first place? Did he drive? Yes, he has a license, but he doesn't have a car. I didn't get it.

I checked online car rentals, but by this time, Barbara was back and insisted that I use hers. "And you can leave Ferd's cat here, too. If you're on a mission to find Ferd, you need to do whatever it takes. I don't mind cats. I've been acquainted with many of Ferd's 'Bears' through the years."

"Thank you."

****

All of the trouble with my uncle and my mother and my grandparents happened the summer I was ten. Up until then, every summer we went to Maine. Sometimes Uncle Ferd was there and sometimes he wasn't. When he and *Wandering Soul* weren't there, I truly missed him. It just wasn't the same trying to find things to do at my grandparents, when all I wanted was to be on the water. When he was there with *Wandering Soul,* I wanted to sail.

We had been in Maine for two days that summer when I was ten, and we were waiting for Uncle Ferd to arrive on

Wandering Soul. The day he was to sail in was full of sun and promise. All of us, the whole family, would be going on the boat for the afternoon. In the distance, out on the bay, I could see the boat on its way towards us. I watched as the two foresails were doused. Someone, not my uncle, was on the deck and helping to bring down the main sail. My mother looked out at the boat, shading her eyes and frowning. I watched the frown gradually turn into a scowl, then a kind of snarl. Quietly, she said to my father, "We don't need this. My girls don't need this."

As the boat neared us, her body seemed to tense with anger. "We are not staying," she muttered and shifted from foot to foot. "We are not staying for this," she growled through clenched teeth. "I will not have my girls exposed to this. I will not."

"Char..." my father implored.

"Don't 'Char' me. This is not okay." Her words were clipped.

The first thing I saw was her huge orange hat. I had never seen a hat with such a wide brim, except maybe on a Halloween costume. There was a woman underneath all that orange, a woman who was slim and athletic, with a huge smile and a laugh I could hear from where I stood. She had moved to the bow of *Wandering Soul* and stood there, one arm loosely around the forestay and the other hand holding the bowline to throw to us.

Underneath the hat were masses of brown curls. She wore red short-shorts and a loose top. I remember thinking how bright she looked. My mother was just schooling me on things that matched and things that didn't. You never wear stripes and plaids together. You never wear orange and red together. Pink and red don't match, either. I liked it that this pretty woman on the bow of my uncle's boat didn't seem to care about that. I heard her call, "Hey. Hi. You must be the family."

I smiled at her and tentatively raised a hand in a half-wave while my mother, teeth firmly clenched, stood ramrod straight. My uncle, at the helm in cut off shorts with frayed bottoms, t-shirt, and a ball cap was also waving. I couldn't see his feet, but I was sure he was barefoot. To this day, my uncle seldom wears shoes.

"Philip, I'm leaving," my mother was saying. "We are leaving. Right now. We will drive right home to Ohio today, Philip. I mean it. I will not have this."

What was my mother saying? We were going? Why? I moved a little away from her and toward my uncle and the woman. When I go back in my memory, I can't seem to find my grandparents. I'm assuming they were up at the house. By this time, my grandmother pretty much used a walker, and my grandfather spent his time on the porch with crosswords.

As they got closer, I couldn't take my eyes off the woman. She was beautiful. Instinctively, I touched my own poker straight hair. That day, my mother had divided it into two thin ponytails, one above each ear, nothing like this woman's, curly and falling all down around her shoulders and back. When my father and mother didn't run to catch the lines and help dock the boat, Ferd shrugged, and the woman threw the line expertly lassoing a cleat. She hopped off and they tied the boat up by themselves. I noticed her shoes — shiny, red plastic sandals, the kind you could walk in the water with and it wouldn't matter.

I made to run toward them, but my mother grabbed my shirt collar. "Mom!" I tried to wiggle away, but her grasp was firm. With one hand, she held my shirt and with another, one of the twins. My father held the other one.

"We are leaving and we are leaving right now!" she turned and pulled us along.

"But why? What's wrong?" I kept protesting. "Mom? Mom? Mom!"

By this time, we were up at our car.

"Char," said my father. "We should at least talk to your brother."

"Not if he is with that woman. No." She was shaking her head in defiance. "We will get in the car, we will get our things from the house, and we are driving home. We are going back to Ohio."

"Why do we have to go home?" I asked. "Who is that lady?"

My mother turned around in the car and faced me. "She is your uncle's paramour. She is no one you need to know."

I didn't know what the word paramour meant, but I knew it must be bad.

It was two years before we went back to Maine.

****

It took me only ten minutes now to pack the few things I needed. Soon, I was on my way. Halfway to Pennsylvania, it started to rain. An hour and a half later, still in the driving downpour, I pulled up to the motel where my uncle had stayed. Having had to slow down for several black buggies on my way in, I knew I was deep in the Amish country of Pennsylvania.

Why the hell had my uncle come here?

CHAPTER 9

"**W**et out there." Those were the first words that came from the lanky young man in the pinstriped, button-down dress shirt. His sleeves were rolled to the elbows, tie askew, and his long legs were wrapped around a stool behind the reception counter.

"It is," I said.

"We're technically in a drought. If you can believe that. This is what happens. We don't get rain for weeks on end, and then a downpour, which basically washes everything away. Hear that?" He leaned forward, his elbows on the counter.

"What?" I shrugged my bag to the floor.

"Thunder. Severe thunderstorm warnings. Could be hail, even. Hope you're not planning to do any hiking today." He had a very large and lopsided smile, as if his mouth were too big for his face.

"No."

"Sightseeing then?"

"Something like that."

"Need a room? How many nights?"

"I would like a specific room. If that's possible."

"Sure." He eyed me. "It might be. If it's available."

I pulled out my phone. "Can I ask you to look at something for me, first?"

I showed him a picture of my uncle. "Do you recognize this man? I'm told he stayed here."

He picked up the phone and stared down at the picture, his face becoming suddenly very serious. "Are you with the police?" He handed the phone back to me.

"No. He's my uncle. He's missing. I'm trying to locate

him."

"You know what happened here, then?"

"Bits and pieces. I've talked with the police. No one seems to know where he is. I understand he stayed here?"

"He did."

"I'm wondering if I could have the same room he was in?"

He looked through his computer. "Yep, you sure can. Except the police were all over that room. I'm sure you won't find anything. It's been thoroughly cleaned with several rounds of guests since then. How long will you be staying?"

"I don't know. This one night for sure. Maybe two."

"No problem. No problem at all."

"What was my uncle like? Did you get a chance to talk with him?"

"Quiet guy." He turned down the sides of his expressive mouth into a frown. "He never checked out properly."

"That's what I heard. Does he owe you money? If he did I can pay." I pulled out my wallet.

"Oh, no." He put his hands up. "Not that. He paid ahead of time. All in cash. It's just that he left one morning without coming to the desk. We went to his room and he had packed up. He'd paid for two extra nights, even. He left before his money ran out."

"I understand he gave you a copy of his passport."

He nodded. "He said it was the only ID he had on him. I photocopied it and decided to let him pay with cash and stay here, even though that's not our policy." He shuffled some papers. "We usually require a credit card imprint."

I nodded. "How long did he stay here?"

"Around two weeks."

"Two weeks?"

He nodded. "He seemed rather taken aback that I wanted a credit card imprint. He seemed innocent, almost rather naive in a way, if you must know. He said he had never had a credit card. I kept a bit of a watch out for him, too. Made sure he had everything he needed. We recently went through that with my grandparents."

"Went through what?"

"Senility."

I stared hard at him, becoming immediately defensive.

"My grandparents are both in their eighties and have run this motel for sixty plus years. Lately, it was being run into the ground, I'm afraid. I'm a business graduate. I took over this place a few months ago. I've worked with my grandparents on their accounts. I know all about senility." He gave me a smile. "Oh and here's something else. Your uncle specifically wanted to know if the room had a safe. Not all of our rooms do, so I had to find one for him that did. I think he was worried about his passport. I offered to keep it in the motel safe, but he was adamant that the safe be in his room. I remember when my grandparents went through this."

I backed away. My uncle was not senile. I told him this.

"Oh, no. Of course not. I didn't mean that." He put up both hands. "It's just that I know what we all went through with my grandparents."

"How did he get here?" I asked seeking to change the subject. "Did he have a car?"

He said yes.

I eyed him. "It was his car?"

"I assume so."

"Did you get the license number?"

"We always do. The police took it."

"Could I have it, do you think?"

I could see the wheels turning, and then he opened up his computer. "Sure, why not?" He wrote it down and handed it to me. My uncle has lots of friends—I wondered who the car belonged to. I signed the papers and handed him my credit card. He fumbled around in the desk and handed me a metal key.

"This is something that's going to be changed. We're going with coded cards just as soon as I can find a decent supplier."

I thanked him.

"Oh." He called after me. "Just so you know. There was nothing senile about your uncle, nothing at all. Naive, maybe.

I didn't mean that the way it sounded. He seemed quite sharp, actually. Oh, and by the way, my name is Carl. If you need anything."

"Thanks, Carl." I reached for the door handle.

"Oh, and one other thing. I know you're here on a mission to find your uncle, but have you ever been here before?"

I told him no.

"What I mean to say is, I see you're from—" he checked the register, "Maine. Before you leave you should take a detour through the Amish country." He came out from around the counter and handed me a brochure.

"Here," he said. He was so tall and gangly it looked as if he could fold into fours. The brochure advertised something called The Red Barn Gift Store.

"Thanks," I said pocketing it.

"The back of that brochure has a map to it."

"Great."

"It's worth the trip."

"Thanks."

"But not just that place, there are lots of places around that you might find interesting."

"Yeah. Thanks." I said goodbye to Mr. Chamber of Commerce and headed out to my room. It was utilitarian but clean. A largish flat screen TV was attached to the cement block wall, and instead of all the little bottles of shampoo and conditioner, there were only two minuscule bars of soap. Still, it was functional. I've stayed in worse.

I unpacked my few things, wondering why my uncle had come here. I knew Ferd wouldn't expect me to be in this motel and this room, so I wasn't expecting coded messages. There would be no flowered cards asking me to take care of cats and boats. Nevertheless, I checked behind the artwork on the wall, between the box spring and mattress, in the toilet tank. Of course, I found nothing.

CHAPTER 10

When I was fourteen and heavy rains had cancelled our day of family sailing, my uncle told me one of the stories about how he got this boat. I had accompanied him in his dinghy out to where *Wandering Soul* was moored. He had to change the impeller and I was welcome to come along if I wanted to. He could certainly use the help, he said. Since being out on the boat was better than being cooped up in my grandparent's boring house on a stormy day, of course I said yes.

The boat moved gently on the mooring as the rain beat a tattoo on the deck above us. After the job was done, we decided to wait out the rain before donning our rain gear and riding in a wet dinghy back to shore.

He made tea. He always made tea aboard *Wandering Soul*. And with a cup of tea and his pipe, he would regale me with tales of the high seas. I would not only drink the sweet proffered tea, but I would drink in all that he had to tell me.

"What you want," he said pulling on his pipe, "is a good boat like this one." He patted the teak bulkhead.

"Yeah." It was true. Nothing compared to this sleek, dark wood design, the smell of it, the feel of it.

"You want one with long lines, one that sails best on a fifteen degree heel."

"Like this one," I said.

"Like this one." He nodded. "Did I ever tell you how I got this boat? Did you ever hear that story?"

I bobbed my teabag up and down a few times. Truth was, I'd heard many stories from my grandfather and my mother, and didn't know which one to believe.

"I used to crew in the Marblehead," he said, "aboard a boat

called *Sea Witch*. I ever tell you about that boat?"

"Sort of." Lots of times, but it didn't matter.

"In its day, it won that race class a total of five times. I crewed on it four of those races."

I placed my tea bag on a plate. The rain increased. It sounded like hail was battering the sides and top of the boat. I looked up, but since nothing weather-wise fazed my Uncle Ferd, he simply went on talking.

"The owner of *Sea Witch* had just bought this boat. Wanted to race this thing. Wanted to find a race that this one could enter. He found a local race for full-keeled boats. Since he did so well on *Sea Witch*, he wanted this one to win. Except it came way down the fleet."

"How come?"

"Bad crew," he said. "That's all it was, bad crew. People not respecting this boat. Truth was, it was crewed by a bunch of morons. Owner was fit to be tied. Guys couldn't tell their jib from their holding tank." He laughed. "Owner wanted both his boats to win in their classes."

I nodded.

"So, here's what I did. I told the owner I could get this boat to win. He knew my reputation, so he said yes. But you know what I said? I told the owner I'd crew under one condition. If we won the race, I get to keep this boat. Owner says, 'Okay, you can keep the boat provided both boats win. This one and *Sea Witch* in the Marblehead.' Fair enough, I could skipper both. I could do that." He patted the side of the boat as he said this.

"He said he would give you the boat?" I tried a sip of my tea. Bitter. I added another huge dollop of honey.

"Of course. That's how badly he wanted to win. It was a pride thing with him."

I drank the tea. Sweet now, and warm, not too hot. It tasted so good with the wind and rain outside. I said, "And so *Wandering Soul* and the other boat won. And so you got the boat, right?"

He laughed. "Actually, no."

"No?"

"I lost." He grinned at me, winked. *"Wandering Soul* came in third. Third's not bad, but it's not perfect."

"That's too bad."

He gave me a knowing smile. "I knew I wanted this boat. Wanted it more than anything I had ever wanted before. I saw how she sailed. I saw what she could do."

"How'd you get it then?"

"The old-fashioned way. I worked for it. Got jobs, used savings. I earned the money. Then I bought it off the jerk. He was embarrassed that we didn't win, thought he had a stacked crew. He sold it to me cheap, very cheap."

"My mother said you won it gambling."

He had paused, looked down at his tea for several long moments before continuing. "Your mother is a good woman, don't you ever forget that. She just wants the best for you."

When I think about it now, I realize that my Uncle Ferd never said a bad word about his sister. Not one. Whereas my mother was continually berating and criticizing my uncle.

CHAPTER 11

The drive from the motel to the café was short. If it wasn't raining, I could have walked. That's how close it was. I was thinking that Jacobsen's Café might be a nice place for lunch right about now.

I flipped off the car radio so I could practice what I would say when I came face to face with the woman whose husband my uncle had supposedly murdered. Was I crazy for doing this? My mind was reeling and flying apart in a hundred different directions.

Seconds later, I was parked outside Jacobsen's Café. I was wondering whether or not I should turn around, go back to Baltimore, and forget all about this. But, I couldn't. My uncle, my mentor, was in trouble. I sat there for several moments, breathing deeply. I thought about my uncle. He was missing. He was gone. The police were even playing around with the idea that it was suicide. In the end, concern for my uncle outweighed the fear I felt at meeting this widow. Through the years, my uncle had done so much for me, especially my awkward teen years when the only thing I had that was my own was sailing. Now that he was in trouble, it was my turn. He needed me and I wouldn't disappoint him.

I got out, pulled my hood over my head against the rain, and with determined steps, made my way toward the front door of the café.

"For one?" the blonde waitress asked me.

"Yes."

"Do you want a booth by the window or a table here?" I glanced around me. The booths were closer to the back of the building, the part that led, I presumed, to the alley where the body was found.

"Booth. Thanks."

"No prob."

I was shown to my seat by this ponytailed waitress with very red lipstick. Was this Ocean Hollander? No. Her name tag read Becca. She handed me a menu.

In a few minutes, I would head down that hall to the ladies' room and have a look around. Was the alley back there? I guess I would soon find out. For now, I ordered a burger and coffee. I got out my phone and emailed my uncle for the hundredth time. Of course, there was no answer from him. For the hundredth time.

After shrugging out of my jacket, I wandered down the hall to the ladies' room. The mens' room and ladies' room were on either side of a short hallway covered with artwork for sale. Amish buggies were featured, along with farms with red barns and silos. I contrasted this to cafés along the coast where lighthouses and islands are the featured artwork in halls leading to restrooms. At the end was a door marked Staff Only. I decided the door to the alley must lead from this Staff room. Or maybe from the kitchen. I couldn't see where that was. Maybe it was around the other side of the tables by the window. And why did it even matter?

Above the sink and high up on the wall in the ladies' room was a small window. Could you see the back alley from there? While not an advantage in crawling through very small engine compartments on boats to change oil and impellers, my height was certainly an advantage now. I climbed up onto the counter and peered out. Yes, this looked like a back alley. I could see to the back of the restaurant pretty clearly. There were several dumpsters, boxes, plus a bit of debris. Across the alleyway was a cement wall and behind it, a road. I tried to picture in my mind where this was. I got out my phone and took several pictures.

Someone knocked on the door. I flushed the toilet, washed my hands, and went back to my booth. My coffee was already there and poured. I creamed it and went through my phone for messages and email. Not much. And nothing from Ferd. When Becca came and told me it would just be a few more minutes, I showed her a picture of my uncle on my phone.

"Do you know this person?" I asked her.

Her brows furrowed in concentration. "Ferdinand. That's Ferdinand. It has to be." She put a hand to her face. "Are you the police?"

"No. This is my uncle. He's missing."

"I don't blame him for being missing."

"Why's that?"

"They say he killed Ocean's husband."

"You know Ocean?"

"Of course. She works here."

"She here today?"

Becca shook her head.

"I understand my uncle came here to this restaurant. Did you get to meet him?"

"Everybody met him. He was here all the time."

"Really?"

"Most days. Either lunch or supper."

"Seriously?"

"I think he ate everything on the menu at one time or another."

"Wow." I had no idea.

"He struck up a friendship with Ocean."

"With Ocean? Why?"

"Beats me. She's pretty? She has a cute baby? Don't know." She backed away from the table slightly, and I saw something unreadable in her eyes. "But you should talk to Marie. The police told us not to talk to anyone. I just remembered that."

"Who's Marie?"

"Marie Jacobsen. She's the one found the body. She's our boss."

"She here today?"

Becca looked around her as if looking for answers. Finally, "I'll go see."

I checked my phone for email or messages again and drank

more coffee. A few moments later, a pale, thin woman, her hair tied back in a net, approached me.

"You wished to speak to me?"

"You're Marie?"

She nodded.

"My uncle is Ferd Hanson and I'm worried about him."

She stared straight at me when she said, "We're not supposed to talk to anybody but the police."

"But he's my uncle. I'm not here about what he did or didn't do. The family is worried. The police aren't helping us. We don't know where he is. I was hoping to get some answers here. I've driven in from the coast."

"Okay, um..." I could almost see the wheels turning. "I'll tell you what I do know. But," she put up a forefinger, "if I find out you're lying to me and you're really from the news, I will deny everything I said."

"I swear I'm not a journalist."

"And you're not with the police?"

"No."

"I'll tell you what I told the police. If he's missing, I'd look no further than his ranch."

"His *ranch?*" I'm sure my eyes bulged out of my head.

She nodded. "That's where he'll be. If it's a true ranch. It's all he ever talked about, but I have a feeling that too, was part of his scam."

"Scam?" *Ranch? Scam?* I had no idea what she was talking about and asked her to explain.

She frowned. "I knew it," she said. "I knew he was scamming us about that."

"What do you mean, scam?"

She put her hands flat on the table and leaned toward me. She seemed almost eager to talk. Becca came with my burger, and I listened to her story while I added the requisite ketchup and relish from plastic bottles.

Around six weeks ago, Ferd simply showed up in the café one day for lunch. He was very friendly to all the wait staff. That began a pattern. For more than two weeks, he came for lunch and supper every day.

"He practically lived here," she said. "After he met Ocean Hollander — that was it. He sat at her table every time he came in."

"Why Ocean Hollander?" I asked.

"I think he felt sorry for her. Her husband, Stan, wasn't the nicest of guys. No, he was just the opposite, in fact. I can't tell you the number of times she landed up in emergency because of him. Police cars were always at their house. Maybe Ferd, I don't know, maybe he could sense something was wrong there. As I said, he seemed like a nice guy at first. He even started bringing her presents. Little things. Flowers, chocolate. Things for the baby. He seemed so nice. Not one of us suspected —" She paused. "I mean, we should have. Older guy shows up and starts leaving flowers and candy for pretty young waitress..."

This seemed so out of character for my uncle that I was absolutely without words.

"But I figured out that he came all this way not to be nice to people, but to scam everybody. He came to steal money, murder Stan, and then take off with it."

I was stunned.

"That's why he was super nice to Ocean. He was after Stan's money."

I thought about what Ben had told me. I thought about the man who had called my mother. "How much money are we talking about?" I asked.

"From what I hear, around two hundred thousand. Heck of a lot of money for those three bozos. Stan and his moron brother and their lousy friend won it at a racetrack. The three of them were in so many business ventures and shady schemes, and then they finally make it big, the three of them. Except Stan ends up dead, and Simon ends up probably buried in a shallow grave somewhere, and Ronny Joe ends up missing. No one's seen him since this whole thing happened."

"Well, maybe his brother killed him."

She shook her head from side to side. "No one knows what

to think. Maybe Ferd murdered him, too."

I clasped my hands in front of me tightly. "How's Ocean Hollander?" I asked.

"We all try to look out for her."

I picked up my burger, put it down again.

Marie said, "But no matter how she's better off without her cheating husband, what Ferdinand did to her is ten times worse. He comes all this way and butters up Stan's wife just to get at his money? I don't care if he's your uncle or not. He hurt Ocean more than anything with that whole little song and dance he had going here. She recently lost her father, who she was very close to, and to be played like this — "

I looked at her. "Why do you call him a scammer?"

"Somehow he found out about the money they won. Then, he comes here with one purpose — to steal it."

The story she was telling me was so farfetched that I was unable to put together a coherent sentence in rebuttal. It was as if I were standing on a pane of shattered glass.

She kept talking. "Some think that he maybe had something going with Stan and Simon all along. Even Ronny Joe, although Ronny Joe is such a gullible little thing, just follows along with whatever big brother says. I've known the family all my life, and," she pointed at me, "if anyone needs that money now, it's Ocean. She's got nothing." Her voice was harsh when she said, "So, if your uncle stole this money, and you find him, get that money back and make sure Ocean gets it. And tell that uncle of yours never to come around here again. You got that? Never."

I felt like slinking out of there or dropping through the floor, but I needed to know more, much more. "The police asked me if I thought my uncle was suicidal."

She was quiet for a moment. "He may have *seemed* suicidal. But like everything else, that could have been an act."

I swallowed and stared at her. My burger held no appeal for me.

She went on, "He comes around saying he can't live with secrets anymore. That the secrets he's carrying are going to kill him, that sort of thing. I believed him then, but after what he did, I don't believe him now."

I asked her to tell me about the night of the murder. I wondered if her version would differ from what the police had told me. Stan and Ferd had been at a booth by the window, she said, and they were arguing. The argument got quite heated and customers even commented. Then Stan got up and stalked off into the kitchen, presumably to look for Ocean. Ocean wasn't working that evening. By this time, they'd been separated for several weeks, and she had a restraining order out against him. Stan began yelling at everyone in the kitchen. Marie stood up to him, told him to leave. She didn't even want him walking through the restaurant, so she practically pushed him out the back door to the alleyway. A few minutes later, a very angry Ferdinand stomps through the kitchen and out the back looking for him.

"And then it's the next morning, and I come to work early and there's Stan—" She choked. "I guess the police are looking for the gun."

"My uncle doesn't own a gun," I said. "Never has."

"Well, bully for him. He somehow got a gun that night."

"Do you know what they were arguing about?"

She made a sound like a guffaw. "What did anyone fight with Stan Hollander about? Drugs? Money? Gambling debts? All his women? You name it."

I looked toward the door to the kitchen. The whole thing was unfathomable. Finally I said, "Do you think it would be all right for me to talk with Stan's wife? Will she be in today?"

Marie wrote something down on a napkin and handed it to me. "Her address. If you go see her, don't expect a warm welcome."

"Thanks." I scrunched up the napkin and put it in my pocket. "Before I leave, did my, um, did my uncle mention the words *Wandering Soul*?"

"Oh, you mean the name of that phony ranch of his?"

I stared into her eyes not knowing what to think.

She said, "I have another theory. You want to know about

it?"

I nodded.

"I mentioned this to the police, but I don't think they're taking this one seriously. Okay, there was something about him. He seemed too nice, in a way. A part of me doesn't want to believe that he actually came here to scam everyone. So, I got to thinking that he might be one of those online hackers who scam the scammers. There are people who do that—find scams and then set out to scam the scammers. Give them what for. And here's maybe what happened—things just got away from him. Things got out of hand. Because when he mentioned his ranch? That's when things just didn't add up."

"What things?"

"I know a little bit about horses. I asked him a technical question about saddles, and he seemed not to have a clue."

I nodded. Right. He would not have a clue.

"He really didn't seem to know the first thing about ranching. Is he—" she looked at me. "Is he a rancher?"

"No," I said. "He's not."

"Didn't think so."

Before I left, I gave her one of my business cards. She took it and looked down at it. "You're a captain? You said you weren't with the police. What is this?"

"I'm not with the police. I'm a boat captain. Ship captain."

"Really?" She seemed to look me up and down. I get this a lot. People not quite believing that women can captain boats. She placed the card into the pocket of her apron and we said goodbye.

Later, after I paid for my meal, I drove around the café, stopped my car on the road above the alley behind it, and just stood there for a moment or two, trying to quell the shaking in my soul.

CHAPTER 12

Ocean Hollander lived just off the main street in downtown Mount Joy in a big, old house with two square windows facing the front like wide-opened eyes, and a broad front porch, which was paint-flecked and sagged in the middle like a grin. On the porch, there was a stroller, which looked fairly new and decent, and a number of other toys. An overstuffed but slightly dilapidated couch sat under one of the windows. It looked like a comfortable place to sit and have morning coffee and watch the neighbors. Where the doorbell should have been, a few threads of twisted wire stuck out like the veins of a robot. I knocked, hearing nothing from the inside. A part of me felt relieved, but too soon, I realized I would have to come back here later tonight or even tomorrow if I didn't see her now. I had come this far. I needed to see this through.

I knocked again, harder this time, and was about to turn away when I heard movement from inside. Eventually, the door opened a crack by a sleepy-looking young woman with shoulder length dark hair. She wore a lavender tank top over black stretch pants. They hung on her loosely like they belonged to a much heftier friend. She had either just been sleeping or she'd come from a Yoga workout. I guessed sleeping.

"Yes?" She had a quiet voice and dark, sad-looking eyes. I noticed her eyes, so large and brown they were almost startling.

"Ocean Hollander?"

"Yes?" Her voice was barely above a whisper. Something about her face drew me in, was vaguely disquieting, and even oddly familiar. As if I had seen her somewhere before, although I knew I hadn't. She bore little resemblance to the photos I'd seen of her in the online news sources.

"I wonder if I might be able to have a few moments of your time."

"Why?"

I took a breath, but the words I had practiced came out all skewed and misshapen. "First of all, I'm sorry about your husband. I—I'm looking—um—I think you might have information about my uncle. I can't find my uncle. He's gone. He's missing."

"What?"

"I'm sorry." I swallowed. "I probably shouldn't have come. To your house. I've driven all the way here from Baltimore. It's about"—I couldn't get my breath—"my uncle. My uncle is Ferdinand. Ferdinand Hanson. I understand you might have met him?"

Her whole body stilled. I could almost see every tendon in her body seize. She fixed her eyes on me and stared. I fought the urge to turn and run.

She opened the door. "You can come in. My baby's napping. She should be waking up any second. If she cries, I'll have to go get her."

I nodded. "I understand."

I noticed two skinny, deep purple braids down the right side of all of that thick dark hair. I followed her into a living room. Inside, a couple of lawn chairs were set up on the carpet of the front room. No other furniture except for the playpen. A couch is on the porch and inside there are lawn chairs? I wondered at the irony.

"I'm sorry about your husband," I said.

She picked up a baby blanket from the playpen, sat down in a plastic lawn chair, and placed it over her knees as if seeking warmth. I sat in the only other chair. She said, "The no-furniture decor is courtesy of my late husband."

I didn't say anything.

"One day, when I was working, he came and took it all."

"I'm sorry to hear that."

"I got home and it was all gone."

"I'm sorry."

"His brother, Ronny Joe, tried to get it back, but I think it got sold."

I swallowed.

"He's your uncle?" she asked. "Ferdinand?"

I told her yes. I told her that he was missing and I'd come all this way looking for him, but was running out of ideas. "I'm told you met him. Would you have any idea where he might be?"

"Hell might be a good choice," she said. "As far as I'm concerned, the whole lot of them can go to hell. And that includes my mother."

"Oh?" Her *mother?*

"Him and his no good friend. Even his brother who I feel supremely sorry for." She was balling up bits of the blanket between her fingers. Her nails and cuticles looked bitten to the quick. "I recently lost my father. We were very close. He's the person I'm mourning, not my husband. No one will miss Stan."

"I'm sorry about your father."

"My mother and I are not close."

"Does she live around here?"

"No. Up north."

"Your parents were divorced?"

"No, not divorced. My father was a wonderful and special person, and my mother didn't deserve him. She did not deserve him. But he would not divorce her no matter how badly she treated him, and now he's gone. I know what it's like to be treated badly in a marriage."

"You've been through a lot." I tried to sound sympathetic.

"When I first met him, that man, your uncle, I thought he was nice..." She let the sentence trail away.

I wanted to say, "He is nice," but I didn't.

"He's a murderer. Marie thinks he's a scammer. She might be right. He played us all, all of us in the café, and especially me. Just so he could get to Stan and his money."

"What did he do?"

"He pretended to be all nice. Like super nice. Like asking me all these questions about my baby, about Stan. Lots of questions about Stan."

"What kind of questions?"

"Like where does he work? Where's he living? I kicked Stan out, but he kept coming back, kept bothering me, and kept hurting me until I got a restraining order. I told all of this to Ferdinand. I confided in him, and I shouldn't have because he just used that information. Used me. Like all the other men in my life." She paused and then added, "Except for my father."

"Do you think my uncle killed your husband?"

She nodded. "I have no doubt about that."

"The gun hasn't been found."

"Probably that uncle of yours threw it into the Susquehanna."

"The police will find it if he did. They always do."

She looked dismayed at that, and her hands on the blanket stilled. "They don't always find the weapons."

"Most of the time they do." I had no idea if this were true or not.

She said, "He still has it, then. Ferdinand" — She spat out the name — "still has it then. He would still have it." She looked down at her clenched fingers when she said, "He's missing? I'm glad he's gone."

I looked around me at the few toys on the floor. Despite the lack of furniture, Ocean kept a clean house. There was a fireplace along one wall that looked like it had never been used. On the other side, a set of stairs led to the upper level. I decided to change my questions. "What did your husband do for a living?"

She fingered the blanket between her fingers when she said, "Odd jobs. This and that. In and out of work."

"Did he ever work on a ship or an oil rig, like an offshore rig? Maybe on the docks? A longshoreman? Something like that?"

"No, I don't think so. Not that I know of."

How had my uncle come to know about their money? That was the question. I was grasping at straws. It was clear she had no idea where Ferd was, yet I kept asking questions, asking her to think, think about anything my uncle may have said to her, until I heard a cry of a baby from upstairs.

"I have to go," she said. "I have to go. I'm sorry I can't help you anymore. But if you do see your uncle? Tell him to stay the hell away from me and my baby."

On my way out, I laid my business card on her table and said, "If you think of anything else, please call me. I would like to get to the bottom of all of this. This whole thing, coming here, doing what he did, it's all so completely out of character for my uncle. I want to know what's going on."

She shrugged. "Plain and simple. He came and killed Stan for his money. Then he took it and left."

****

My sleep that night at the motel was filled with shadows. I was standing on the road above the alleyway behind Jacobsen's Café, and down below, I saw the bloodied and crumpled body of a man, limbs askew, eyes open. He was looking at me with a kind of strange accusation. I turned away and realized it was not me he was looking at—it was my Uncle Ferd.

He was standing in the doorway of the café holding a pistol. When my uncle came to Jesse's funeral, he had somehow found himself a nice suit. He was wearing that now. I began to yell at him, and when he didn't respond, I went crazy calling to him, "Why did you do it? Why did you do it? Why did you kill that man for no reason?" I screamed at him over and over until my voice was hoarse. He didn't acknowledge me. When I tried to run down the embankment and grab for him, it was like reaching through mist. He simply wasn't there.

I woke up confused and sweaty in the dark room. It was

hot and I got up and adjusted the air conditioner, then went to lay on the bed again until my breathing came back to normal. I fell into a restless sleep until morning.

While I was eating breakfast in the motel's coffee nook, the manager, Carl, came and sat across from me.

"I hope it's been a worthwhile trip for you. Will you be staying another night?"

"No. I'll be checking out in a few minutes, actually. I still haven't found my uncle. But I've got to get home."

"Work beckons?"

"Something like that."

When I got in my car, I saw that I needed gas. And Sheetz might be as good a place as any for a fill up.

CHAPTER 13

The road through Mount Joy was crawling with cars, and it was raining down so heavily, I could barely see the car ahead of me. It seemed fitting somehow. This is the reason I love Maine — not this level of traffic or at least not where I live way out on Chalk Spit. Route 1 in the summer can be like this, but it's only one season. I had a feeling this place was like this all the time. Or maybe there was an accident up there.

Barbara's car was so old it didn't have an outlet where I could plug in my phone and listen to some of my tunes, so I was at the mercy of commercial radio. I shuffled forward inch by inch while I went through the stations one by one.

At one point, traffic was so slow I thought about simply exiting and getting onto the highway back to Baltimore. But I kept in line.

Construction. A flag person stopped me. I texted Ben. Had he learned anything? I smiled a bit when I realized he had no idea I was here. I think that was intentional, though. I knew he would have tried to talk me out of coming here.

How's it going? He texted back.

Fine. I'm in PA.

You're where?

I could hear the accusatory note in his text. Why was I messing around in police business again?

Looking for my uncle.

Find him?

Not yet. You heard anything?

No.

And then in the next text bubble, he wrote, *I have some vacation time scheduled and I have to go back to Montana for a bit.*

Nice. Hope you get some fishing in, I wrote.
It's not that kind of trip. I may be out of touch for a while.
Okay fine. Have a good time, I texted back.
See you soon.

Finally, the drenched flag person waved us on. I pulled up next to the gas pump and filled my tank. After filling it up and getting my credit card receipt, I drove over and parked as close as I could to the entrance. I went inside. I wanted coffee anyway. And to talk with people. Mostly to talk with people. The place was brightly lit and done up in reds and yellows. I found it difficult to imagine anyone trying to rob this place with the number of lights and cameras and concave mirrors it had going for it.

Several people were lined up behind the counter, so I walked up and down the aisles studying the offerings — chips and pretzels, candy and chocolate, gummy bears and gummy worms and walls and walls of cold beverages.

When the line behind the register cleared, I placed my bag of gummy bears and extra-large coffee on the counter. Despite her spiky short orange hair and her absolutely square black glasses, the girl behind the counter looked intelligent and talkative.

"Boy," I said when she rang up my purchases, "sure is raining out there."

"Sure is."

I gave her a ten-dollar bill, and when she handed me my change, I said, "Could I ask you a question?"

"Ask away."

I showed her the picture of my uncle on my phone. "Do you know who this guy is? Have you ever seen him?"

She looked down at my phone for a few seconds before shaking her head, but it was a tentative movement as if she were unsure.

"He's my uncle. He's missing. I was told he might have come through here."

"Sorry. Can't help you." Too quick? Too dismissive?

I pressed some more. "I heard he might have some

connection to the guy who worked here who was killed. Simon Towers."

She squinted her eyes at me. "I don't know a lot about that. It happened here. Out behind us here. But it wasn't a store robbery or anything."

"What happened? Can you tell me?"

"I don't know much. All I know is that one night, Evan — he works here — comes in here at two in the morning and finds Simon dead out back. He calls 911 and an ambulance comes, but by then the body's been moved. It was all pretty creepy and scary."

"The police are thinking my uncle was involved. Is there anyone here who might know more? I'm awfully worried about him."

She pointed to a room in the back next to the restrooms. "You might check in the office with Chad. He's our manager. But I'm not sure anyone can help you. It was quite a shock when it happened."

Someone got behind me in line.

"Thanks for all your help," I said.

"No problem. Good luck with your uncle."

I knocked on the door marked Office and opened it a crack when I heard a faint, "Yeah?"

A young man who looked like he worked out with heavy weights four times a day, every day, 24/7, was seated behind a desk at a computer. His Sheetz sports shirt strained across his meaty shoulders and his name tag read Chad.

I went through my story and showed him the picture of my uncle.

He touched the side of my phone with a finger. There was dirt under his nails. "Him." He was scowling. "So he's your uncle."

"Right."

"He's in a world of trouble, isn't he?"

"Did you get the chance to meet him?" I asked.

"Oh, yeah."

"That doesn't sound good."

He folded his beefy arms across his chest. "Okay. You want to know about your uncle? Let me tell you about your uncle. He came in here angry. He came in here threatening my staff. And I won't have anyone threatening my staff. He said Simon had something that belonged to him, and he was here to get it, and no one better stand in his way. He had someone he had to deliver it to."

"What?" I asked. "What did Simon have?"

"Hindsight says the money. Next morning, Simon is lying dead out back. Then somebody comes and moves the body, the murderer, I'm thinking. You put two and two together. The police know all of this."

"Simon's body hasn't been found."

He pointed at me. "You ask your uncle about that."

"I thought it was Stan who beat him up."

"Well, that's one theory. I don't think the police know for sure."

"I was told it was Stan who killed him and took his body."

"And that's another theory."

"Did you ever see my uncle again? Did he ever come back?"

"Nope." He shook his head. "Just that one time. That one time was enough."

I asked, "So he didn't say where he might go after this."

"You mean did we sit down and have a nice chat over a beer and share our plans for the future? No. He just storms out. Look, if your uncle was mixed up with those three, he's not a good man."

"Those three." I knew who he was talking about.

"Stan, Simon, and Ronny Joe."

"I'm sorry to have bothered you," I said.

He abruptly turned back. "Let me tell you one thing. He was mad, hopping mad when he came in here. If he's lost or can't be found, count your lucky stars."

I handed him my business card. "If he comes in here again, or if you remember something else, can you call or email me?"

"Sure." He surprised me by adding, "Look, I know it might

be wrong of me to say this, but Simon was pretty much of a lowlife. Drugs, drug dealing, you name it. Worked here part time. And to tell the truth, I was this close to laying him off anyway. I'm not surprised that got him killed."

"You think it was drug money?"

He shrugged. "That'd be my guess."

"The police said it was money won at a horse racetrack."

"Yeah. And they all double-crossed each other and now the money's gone."

I sighed. "I don't know how my uncle got involved with these three. He lives on a boat, for goodness sake. My uncle doesn't do stuff like this."

He grunted.

****

Before turning on the ignition, I sat in my car for several minutes, my forehead against the steering wheel trying to bring my breathing back to normal. And then I realized I was crying. For my uncle? Or for me? I couldn't be sure. That Sheetz man was threatened by my uncle. The police thought he was dead, maybe suicide, and my mother knew he could "take care of himself" and she showed no concern for her only brother. She was confident that I idolized him too much anyway. Maybe she was right. Maybe I didn't know the real Ferd Hanson.

I got the car going. I clicked on my left turn signal and exited the Sheetz lot. Just out of Mount Joy, I made a decision. I would go back to the boat. I would take care of *Wandering Soul* and Bear because he'd asked me to. But as for running all over the countryside looking for him? Those days had to be over. It was obvious my uncle had more secrets than could be discovered in casual conversations with strangers.

CHAPTER 14

Before heading home, I made another decision. Maybe I should follow the motel guy's advice and do a little sightseeing. After all, what were the chances I'd ever be back here? I pulled over to the side of the road, scrabbled in my bag for the brochure that he'd given me and plugged the address into my GPS. It wasn't too far. Despite the fact that it was still pouring down with rain, I'd go there. Get my mind off my crazy uncle.

When I exited the highway, I found myself directly behind a black Amish buggy. An orange triangle on the back proclaimed to the world that it was proud and happy to hold up traffic. I got out my phone and took a bunch of pictures. Finally, I found the Amish gift store I'd been told that I "shouldn't miss." It was a humongous cherry red barn covered in hex signs. Out in front, handcrafted rows of slatted wooden Adirondack chairs were getting soaked in the downpour. I call them Adirondack chairs—maybe they have a different name down here.

I parked and raced inside. Instead of one big store, I discovered this space housed a variety of gift shops under one roof. I went up and down the aisles finding vendors of jams and jellies who packaged their wares in little canning jars with cloth covers and pretty ribbons. I passed jars of relish and pickles and sauerkraut, and other stands that sold homemade items, popcorn and kettle potato chips, of which I am very fond. I would grab me a bag or two before I drove home.

It was at the very back of the barn a dozen women clad in either black or deep purple cotton dresses sat around a large square wooden frame with a quilt affixed. Each had a needle in her hand and was making little stitches. They chatted merrily as they engaged in this work. I'd heard the term "quilting bee," but had never actually seen one in real life. I hung back and watched for a while, fascinated by this little sliver of life of which I had absolutely no knowledge.

"That's pretty," I said.

"Thank you," said a hefty older woman who looked to be the matron of the circle. "If you're interested, there are more over there." She pointed with her needle to a wall where quilts of all sizes and patterns were hung right up to the high ceiling. I looked, mesmerized at the sheer beauty and workmanship. Every time I finish a major job, I like to buy a gift for myself. Usually, it's something for my boat. I was planning on a new sail this year, but maybe this time I should get something for my house. A quilt. It's funny. Since losing Jesse there is something inside of me that wants to leave my house exactly the way it was when he was alive.

All of the quilts had names, which was something that surprised me. There was one I particularly liked, a deep blue with stars of various sizes from small to large intertwining one with the next. It reminded me of being way out on a boat at night. When I told them what it reminded me of, they smiled. When I told them I would be living on a boat for the next month, I don't think they quite understood. A younger woman turned to me. "A cruise?"

"Something like that," I retorted but shouldn't have because her idea of a cruise was probably not like my idea of a cruise.

They told me the quilt would be ready in around six months and they'd pack it up and mail it to me.

An hour later, I was walking out with a receipt in my hand after just ordering a quilt to be made for me and delivered to Maine. I'd thought about the ratty spread and decided my bed could use some sprucing up. My bed. It had been two years since my husband had died, but now I was thinking of it as my bed, not our bed. I wondered at that. It made me sad.

Out in the parking lot, I checked my phone. It had vibrated in my pocket while I was in the store. A voice mail from Joan. Even though my introvertish nature prefers texting or emailing to talking, Joan never texts. She rarely even emails. She likes actual talking.

"I have an idea," she told me when we connected.

"Yeah?"

"Why don't you ask Ben to come along for the trip?"

"What trip? You mean the trip on the boat?"

"That's what I was thinking, yes."

"Ben? Our Ben? Our police friend Ben?"

"Yes."

"The three of us? Out on *Wandering Soul* for weeks at a time?"

"Sure, why not?"

I laughed. "Joan, he hates boats. He'd never come. He'd never even consider it. I took him out a total of one time on my boat. He got so sick that after an hour, he demanded I take him to the nearest landfall. He didn't care if it was rocks. He'd climb up over them to get away. That's what he told me. Why on earth would he consent to spend a week or more aboard a skinny little boat with barely sleeping accommodations for the two of us, let alone one more? Plus, I happen to know he's going to Montana."

"Art talked to him the other day," Joan said. "He's not totally sure he's going there. You'd be surprised. I think he's as curious about this whole thing with Ferd as you are. He's even talked to Art and me about it. We're all worried about your uncle."

"Well," I sighed, "first of all, I'm not worried about Ferd anymore. He made his bed, he can lie in it, and second, Ben would laugh in my face if I asked him to come. He'd think I was nuts."

"What do you mean 'he made his bed he can lie in it?'"

I filled her in on where I'd gone and who I'd spoken to and what they told me.

"That doesn't sound like Ferd," she said.

"You're right. It doesn't sound like Ferd. Okay, here's my theory. He's got a doppelgänger, an evil twin." I began humming the tune from *The Twilight Zone.*

"Ferd would not threaten anyone."

"Tell that to Chad at Sheetz. Tell that to Marie and Ocean. I'm tired of it, Joan. I wash my hands of it. Oh, guess what? I ordered a quilt!"

"A quilt?"

"Yeah. From the Amish."

"I bet it's nice."

"It'll be gorgeous when they make it. I spent too much time choosing colors, and please don't ask me how much it cost."

"Don't worry about the cost. It's an heirloom."

"Yeah, something to hand down to all the kids I'm not going to have."

Before we rang off, Joan said, "Would you mind if I asked Ben about coming along?"

"Be my guest. But I know Ben. He'll say no."

After we said goodbye, I swung my car out into the traffic and headed toward Baltimore. Soon *Wandering Soul* would be up in Maine. And then what? I had no idea, no clear plan. Did I just inherit myself a new boat? Where *was* Ferd? Childhood memories danced through my head as I drove south on 83.

Two years after the incident with "that woman," as my mother referred to her, we went back to Maine. "I want to make this completely clear," she told my father when we were all packed up and in the car, "we're going for my parents, not for my brother. I want you to understand that at the outset."

"You're making that very clear, Char."

"I just want it known. If she's there, I want it known."

"Char, it's known. You're parents are at least trying. Give them credit for that."

"I'll try. That's all I can offer."

"Fine."

"I'll try. That's the best I can come up with."

"I said *fine.*"

From the backseat, I said, "You mean that lady on the boat?

The one with the orange hat? Is that who you're talking about?"

My mother's head swiveled around. "I thought you girls were asleep back here."

"I was reading," I said. "What's wrong with that lady?" I was twelve and full of questions.

My mother said, "She's the kind of woman who carries on with men. That's all you need to know."

"Char!" My father's voice was harsh.

I hardly ever heard my parents argue, but when the subject was Ferd, it was the closest they came. When we arrived in Maine, my uncle was there. The orange-hatted woman was not.

The woman wasn't there and no one talked about her. No one asked about her. Least of all me, even though I was dying to know about her. I was almost thirteen and in love with love, and I had seen the woman's face. I remembered her smile, her laugh, the way she pushed forward toward us, waving, as if anxious to meet us. On that day two years ago when my mother had ushered us up to the car quickly, I had hung back, just a little, just enough. I had watched my uncle step onto the dock. He was different then, tall and tanned, not white-haired and stooped, like now.

I raised my hand to wave at him, but my mother slapped it down. "We are leaving. All of us. Now."

Before I climbed into the car, I looked back. The woman was holding the orange hat down by her side and I looked at her hair. There was so much of it. Impossibly long, it hung almost to her waist and glinted in the sunshine. I watched as she stepped onto the dock and affixed the bowline to the cleat. She kept looking from us to Ferd and back again. She wasn't smiling anymore.

My uncle said something. I could see them talking quietly together, her head lowered, shoulders in an attitude of defeat, hands by her side. He touched her face with his hand and then the two were in an embrace, at first tender — I could see that — but then my uncle, with his hand on her back, leaned her way back like they do in dancing. And she laughed, both of them laughed. I could almost hear it from where I sat in the backseat of the car. He got her to laugh when she hadn't been laughing moments before. That's what I remembered. He got her to laugh.

Two summers later, she was gone and I was sailing my little dinghy that he and I had worked on. By the end of four summer weeks, I had that little boat pretty well mastered. My uncle taught me all kinds of things that summer — how to tie knots, how to tack and jibe and anchor. He enrolled me in the sailing school. Even though I was the oldest in the class, I loved it. I did well.

Eventually, I got the certification to teach sailing myself, and that became my high school summer job, taking the bus to Maine each summer to stay with my grandparents and teach in the sailing school. Of course, I sailed with my uncle every chance I got. The orange-hatted woman was never mentioned.

In all of the years, I heard only one short conversation between my mother and my grandmother about the woman. That first summer back, I was just outside the kitchen when my mother said, "So, it's over then?"

"Seems to be."

"He's well rid of her."

"Don't be so harsh, Char. It's unbecoming."

CHAPTER 15

There is a park directly across the street from Barbara and Simone's apartment. It's actually only a bit of a green space with a couple of benches and a few trees for shade. Because of its lack of swings, it's not a park that young mothers wheel strollers into or kids play in. In fact, every time I've been here, I've never seen anyone even sitting on the benches. I did now. There was a man sitting there. He'd been staring fixedly at me since I'd arrived and parked my car. Now that I was getting out, this man in the dark coat was walking toward me with quick steps.

At first, I thought this was Ferd, and I moved quickly. "Uncle Ferd!" I almost said aloud, and then in the middle of the street, I stopped cold. This was not my uncle. I didn't know this man. And yet I did.

Papa Hoho?

"We need to talk," he said.

Obediently, I followed him back to the park bench where we sat at opposite ends. This man was identical to Dr. Papa Hoho, minus the unkempt carroty ponytail, red beard, bushy eyebrows, and huge flowery Hawaiian shirts. This man who sat there, fingers entwined on his lap, had military short dark hair with gray flecks, a clean-shaven face and studious, meant-for-business black glasses.

"You're here about your brother," I said.

"My name is Norman Tomson." He held out his hand for me to shake. His brother had the same pale red fuzz all over the backs of his hands.

"You're his brother," I said. "Twin?"

He gave me a bit of a grin. "Hello, Captain Em."

"You here about Dr. Papa?"

"You might say that."

"What does your brother want?" Those two had to be identical. It was uncanny.

He smiled long and hard at me. "I do not have a twin brother. I am Dr. Papa. It's me, Captain Em. Dr. Papa."

My mouth hung open. "You said your name is Norman?"

"Dr. Papa was my stage name."

My eyes opened even wider. "Your hair."

"I cut it."

"Yeah. Wow."

He smoothed his hair back, such as there was, with the flat of his hand.

"What are you doing here?" I asked.

"Looking for you."

"You look—you look so different."

He grinned and moved his head from side to side in a preening motion. "New show. New me. This is my new look, or more accurately, this is the real me. The old me—the Dr. Papa Hoho guy? He's dead. He's gone. No one wants him anymore. This is me now."

I'm sure he saw the utter confusion in my face.

He said, "You know that meeting with the execs? The reason I had to cut our time on the water short? That was them firing me."

"Oh, Dr. Papa, I'm so sorry."

He smiled engagingly. "Norman. Please call me Norman. And don't feel sorry for me. It's all for the best. I'm going to be launching my own network, my own internet TV channel. I got some backers, even. I even have an online fundraising campaign going." He slapped his thigh. "I'm grassroots, baby. All the way grassroots."

He was getting louder. I realized, while you can change the outside of a person, you can't change the inside. He was the same buffoonish braggart who sat aboard *Townie* talking about seven-figure book deals and how he met Oprah once. I simply let him talk.

"I don't need those high and mighty know it all moronic jerks down at the network," he said. "Nope. Not anymore. Not me." He pointed to his chest with his thumb. "With the web the way it is, this is so easy. Did you know there are some standup comedians who are making more money by people paying to view their downloads and subscribing to their channels than on the comedy circuit? That'll be me. I'm assembling a team. This is the new look I'm going for. Gone is crazy Dr. Papa. I'm now Dr. Norman, Science Man. I wanted to go with Science Guy, but it's already taken."

"Well, I guess congratulations are in order then."

"My new show? It's going to be the supreme slap in the face to the network."

"Oh yeah?" I raised my eyebrows and crossed my legs. It began to drizzle. Dr. Papa Hoho/Norman seemed not to notice. No, he was just getting started.

"Back when I was a kid? No one thought I could do this. I had to learn how to take care of myself. It was the only thing I could do. So I became the conspiracy theorist. The guy in high school who knew everything about conspiracies and wasn't afraid to believe in them, but of course, I didn't. I could read people, though. I do have that skill. I can even tell what you're thinking. Here's what you're thinking, 'I wish this guy would shut up and get to the point?' Am I right?"

Despite myself, I smiled, but before I could respond, he was into his next sentence. He picked up a leaf that had fallen on the bench next to him, fingered it while he said, "That was my 'in' to the world. My ability to read people. Not everyone has that. I've been gifted, you might say. I perfected my mentalism act—did you know that? I convinced people that I had special abilities because I'd been abducted by aliens. I went on the road with that for a while."

"Well, good for you."

"I'm quite convincing. It gets me what I want." He ripped the leaf into tiny pieces. I shrugged, still wondering why he was here.

"You know how I got that show in the first place? Let me

tell you the story." He leaned forward and took on an almost conspiratorial affectation as he pointed the leaf skeleton at me. "Seven years ago, I auditioned for a spot on a reality show. The show was going to feature people who'd been abducted by aliens — you know, follow them through their daily life. See how different we were, if we were different. Well, they never put it on, but I guess the networks saw something in me they liked. They asked me if I had any other ideas. I worked hard, came up with my own show. Those moronic jerks. You know what else they did? They canceled my book contract."

"Norman, I'm so sorry."

"Here's something about me I bet you didn't know. I grew up in the carnival. A traveling circus. My mother was convinced she was abducted by aliens and that was her circus gig. She was pretty convincing, too. My parents? They believed in every conspiracy theory going. How do you think I know so much about them all? And their threat to me when I was a kid? If I didn't do what they wanted, they said the aliens would abduct me and do experiments on me. Put that in your childhood boogeyman arsenal and see what you come up with."

"I'm so sorry." My weird and dysfunctional family seemed normal by comparison.

The rain picked up. I tucked my hair into my hood.

"That's what I've had to overcome in my life. So, what I'm planning to do now is stick it to them all. The circus people. The carnival people. The networks. My parents. I'm going to have a science show where I debunk every theory that I attempted to prove in five years of my network show. I know I made my name by presenting as fact a whole bunch of conspiracy theories. I want to do a double take and now disprove them all. By science. Think of it! It's a perfect show. Former conspiracy theory nut finally sees the light of science. This is the best stab in the back I could give the network, the best eff you I could come up with."

I waited.

He muttered. "Stick it to the man." And then he was quiet. He was looking down at his lap. There was something about his expression that all at once drew me in. Suddenly, I saw not a blustery know-it-all, but a scared child who grew up afraid of being abducted, who grew into a scared young man, and who was now a scared adult. In a way, in a very convoluted way, it was not unlike my own, a childhood of threats and punishments. Both were childhoods of never measuring up to some standard, so finally, you just get up and walk away and say, to hell with it all.

"So," I said searching for something to say, "you're going to disprove alien abduction."

His eyes brightened. "Yes! That will be my second show."

"Well, good for you. What will be your first show?"

He suddenly quieted. "You."

"What!" I looked at him through glasses blurred by the mist.

"I need you. It's why I'm here," he said. "That's why I followed you here." He peered at me and very quietly said, "I know it's your uncle. I know it's your uncle's boat. I've been talking to people." He leaned forward, stared straight into my eyes. "I need to talk to the person who owns that boat. I want to start my show with that boat. That's why I needed to see you." He began talking again about the Bermuda Triangle and all the research he'd been doing lately and how everything about it was bogus. Entirely bogus.

"I told you that, remember?" I said.

"Yeah, yeah, and I should have listened. That's why I need you—" He then began to talk about how things aren't what they seem, and how even though things look a certain way, they might not necessarily be that way. The boat out there in the middle of the Bermuda Triangle was an example.

I interrupted him by putting up my hand. "Wait. Stop. So you did work with my uncle after all—"

"No. I told you no. I didn't put it there, but when it was delivered to me, I figured someone up there" — he pointed a forefinger to the sky—"was finally looking on me with favor instead of a big stick. My show has been on the chopping block for a long time. They don't like me at the network. I'm too brash. I don't fit in. I never did. I got me more sense than two-thirds of them, though. I've been working on an alternate plan for a long time. That's why I need that boat. I don't know how the boat got out there, but I need it. And I need you, Em."

"What do you want with me?"

He pointed a finger at me. "Two choices. You can come onboard with me. I'm assembling a street team of people who will work with me." He lifted up two fingers. "Or, I want an exclusive. This is going to be my Pièce De Résistance. My way in."

"What if I say no to both choices?"

"Then you will miss out on some very important information about your uncle."

"What?" I leaned toward him. "What are you talking about? What do you know? What?"

"Not until I have your word that I get this story." He leaned back against the boards of the park bench and rubbed his nose, a gesture I remembered from our twelve days on a boat.

He folded his hands on his lap and drummed his fingers. "Please, Em. Please consider helping me with this—"

"What do you know about my uncle? First, you tell me that."

"I will tell you only after you agree to work with me and give me the whole story. I know you're just back from Pennsylvania."

"How do you know that?"

"Your friend who owns this apartment told me. I know something about your uncle."

"You're bluffing."

He winked at me. It angered me. "Em," he leaned toward me. "I've got some good people working with me now, people who thought the whole Dr. Papa Hoho thing was a bit over the top, but that's what the TV wanted. The crazier, the better. They have no regard for science. And I want this new show to be science-based. I need this story. I want it to be my kick-off story. To kick off my new show. To prove what really happened to the boat."

"I repeat, what do you know about my uncle?"

He stopped. "Only if you promise to join my team. You join my street team, work with me, and I'll tell you. Think about it. At least think about it."

"Okay. I thought about it. No."

"You're missing out, then."

"How did you know I was here?"

"I've been following you, Captain Em."

"That was you in the silver boat!"

"What?"

"The one that followed me. In Florida and then off North Carolina."

He frowned. "I never followed you by boat. Think about it. I couldn't drive a boat if my life depended on it, and you're the best captain I've ever used. I found out you were in Baltimore and flew up."

"Then, how did you know I was here?"

"I knew that boat was familiar to you. I saw the looks that you and Liam exchanged. I needed that boat. The police called me looking for you. I called Liam. I talked to him. He said you were meeting your friend Joan in Baltimore. I called her. She told me where you were staying. You have some good friends, Em. All of them are so helpful. I know that's your uncle's boat, and I know about what he did in Pennsylvania. The murder. I want that story. If you give me that much, your side of things, I'll tell you what I know about you uncle—what I've been able to find out. Think of it, we could work together."

I stared at him. He had to be bluffing. Of course, he was bluffing. But what if he wasn't? And did I truly even care anymore? Hadn't I just washed my hands of my uncle anyway?

It was raining steadily now and both of us were getting wet. A kid on a bicycle drove past in the rain splashing water up onto us, which made it worse. Norman got up and handed me a business card. "On the back is a link to my new website and also a link to my new YouTube channel. I'd love for you to have a little bit of a look at it and tell me what you think. It's just introductory stuff, maybe five minutes. But already, it's got like two thousand views. Then call me and we'll be in business."

I watched him walk away in the opposite direction toward the waterfront. I shoved the card deep into the bottom of my satchel.

****

The rain outside was steamy and hot, and I sat by the window in Barbara's house and got out my laptop. I pulled Papa Norman's business card out of my bag and looked up his website. It opened up to a gif of a couple of cartoon workmen, tool belts around their middles. One was sawing wood, and one was hammering nails. Underneath it read, "Under Construction, Come Back Soon — but while you're waiting, hop on over to Norman the Science Man's new YouTube channel."

I clicked on the link. There was his face, his clean-shaven face, his slicked back hair and a nice buttoned down shirt. He began by saying, "You may recognize me," and immediately, the screen split into two. On one side was the old Dr. Papa Hoho and the other side was Dr. Norman Science Man. "Yes, that was me, Dr. Papa Hoho. And you may remember that I loved setting out to prove the most bizarre conspiracy theories out there. You may have even called me crazy. Well, you would have been right. I'm different now. You might say I've had a scientific conversion. If you said to yourself after each program, 'that guy is off his rocker. Reptile governments? Alien crop circles?' you would have been right. And let me tell you a little secret, I never believed that stuff either."

He smiled a little for the camera. "I intend to prove over the course of the next number of years—yes, years—that everything I told you before was a lie. All of those conspiracy theories are nothing but hogwash. If you'd like to help me in my quest, please visit my crowdfunding site. The link is right below."

The URL took me to a popular crowdfunding site, and there he was, video and all, attempting to raise twenty-five thousand dollars. So far, he'd raised less than a hundred.

I wished him luck. I sincerely wished him luck.

CHAPTER 16

I grabbed an umbrella from Barbara's closet, checked briefly on Bear, and then walked on down to the dock where *Wandering Soul* was tied. A peculiar kind of weather inversion had taken hold of the coastline. Leaden clouds hung down too close to the harbor like gloved hands reaching for the top of the water. I thought about Papa Hoho. I thought about the Bermuda Triangle and kept on walking. In a weird, very weird sort of way, I felt sorry for him. Raised on conspiracy theories. Raised in a circus. Abusive parents. No wonder he was a bit strange. And yet, he'd pretty much succeeded. How many people get their own shows on network television? He had to have had something going for him.

No one was around. I boarded *Wandering Soul*, unlocked the companionway door, and climbed down below. It wasn't as bad as I expected. Yes, all of the books were off the bookshelf and lay in haphazard piles throughout the boat. The police searchers had also removed most of the things from the cupboards and they lay here and there. They had put nothing back. I could clean up these things. Nothing looked broken. At least, they hadn't destroyed the wonderful teak bulkheads. They could have. Sailors are notorious for hiding things in bulkheads. I started the arduous task of putting everything back. Even though I had no idea where my uncle was, it seemed somehow right for me to put the gardening books back the way he had them.

After I had done a cursory cleaning, I called the police officer, Wayne.

"I'm back," I said, "for my uncle's boat. Did you find anything?"

First thing he said was, "Let me ask you something. Has your uncle exhibited signs of dementia?"

When I finally got my thoughts around that question, I said, "No. Nothing. What about the car he drove?" I asked.

"It seems your uncle bought that car used in Miami. We haven't been able to find it."

I nodded.

He explained to me that one of their theories they were working on was that my uncle had somehow "snapped" and killed both Simon and Stan. Then he came back to his boat and killed himself. "Sometimes this happens with early dementia patients and the elderly. Maybe he was desperate for money."

"My uncle's in his seventies. How would he overpower two strong guys half his age?"

"It's just one of the theories."

"Not a very good one," I muttered. "Did you find anything on the boat?"

"Not really. Nothing that will lead us to where he is. A whole lot of gardening books."

"Yep. That's him."

"Kind of odd for a sailor, wouldn't you say?"

"My uncle has always been a bit of an eccentric. Just wondering," I added, "did you find the money that everyone keeps talking about? Was it on the boat?"

"We expect we may never find that money. It certainly wasn't in the boat."

After we hung up, I went back to cleaning. I took the flowered greeting card and the note out of my computer case and tacked them both up on the corkboard as a reminder to keep on going. Despite what happened in Mount Joy, this is what he would have wanted.

CHAPTER 17

It took me the rest of the day to get the place ship shape and ready and provisioned for the trip home, which would begin as soon as I picked up Joan from the airport tomorrow. A few cruisers who had boats on the same dock came over expecting company, or at least a cheery hello. I wasn't in the mood for either.

One person even recognized the boat. "You crewing for Hanson?" he asked me.

"You've seen him?" I asked. "I'm his niece."

"Really?"

"Yeah."

"Nice to meet you."

"So, have you seen him?"

"Last time was maybe couple, three years ago, in the Med."

I nodded. A dead end.

While I worked, Bear stayed curled up on the settee as if she totally belonged. Which she did.

It was while I began putting the books away one at a time by height that I pulled out the book of poems in which his card to me had been inserted. I sat down on the settee with the slim volume and flipped through it.

It was a book of love poems written by many authors. I turned to a random page. Whoa, I thought, this was certainly racy stuff. I raised my eyebrows, flipped to another. Another erotic love poem. Page after page of poetry like this. I turned back to the copyright date — 1986. Why did my uncle have a book of risqué love poems in among his gardening books? There was no inscription in the front.

I put the book back on the shelf while a shard of doubt sliced its way into my thinking. Why would Ferd put a note to *me* in a book of R-rated poetry? Obviously, there was an answer. When the pirates had come, he'd grabbed the first book his hands came upon, the one that stuck up the most from the shelves.

Another part of me asked if Ferd had wanted me to find a note, wouldn't he have put it in several secret places on the boat that only he and I knew about? The drawer in the Nav table for instance. Or my special place up in the vee berth.

When you are lying in the vee berth — as I used to — when you look straight up, there is a space between the top of the boat and the teak. It was the place I would slide in the current book I was reading or anything else I didn't want found. I went there now. Empty. The drawer in the nav station was also empty.

That's what he would have done if pirates were boarding, right?

If pirates were boarding.

That night, Bear snuggled right up next to me in bed. She wasn't the only one who needed the extra comfort. I tossed and turned. My uncle would never kill himself. He didn't have dementia. He was fit and energetic. He was not an old man. He could still out sail anyone. Years of living outdoors had hardened him, energized him, and kept him young. I reasoned, even if he did decide to kill himself — and I was sure that he hadn't — he would do it quietly and not stage something so elaborate, like put his boat out there floating on the water with the table set and the wine poured. That simply wasn't him.

In the morning Barbara and I drove to BWI to pick up Joan.

On the way, Barbara said, "it'll be nice to see Joan. I haven't seen her in so long. Years, it seems like."

"She's been a great friend to me. Especially when Jesse died."

"How are you doing with that?"

"Some days okay. Some days not. I'm buying a quilt. I

haven't done any fixing up of our house since Jesse died. I wish I could show him the quilt. I know he would approve."

She looked at me sadly. "I'm sure he would."

I sort of chuckled when I said, "Joan has it in her head that it's time I met somebody else."

"Well, maybe it is." She turned to me slightly. "Are you ready for that?"

"I have no idea." I thought about Ben. He was as unlike Jesse as a man could be. "There's this one guy. But..."

"But what?"

"He's married."

The air went out of the car. She flipped her head in my direction. "Are you nuts?"

"Well, maybe —"

"Em, don't even go there. Do not go there. Stay the hell away. You do *not* need that kind of grief in your life right now."

"You're right." I looked out my window. She was right.

Later, as much to change the subject as anything, I told Barbara about Ferd's possible dementia.

She snorted. "Ferd? No way that's him. He's smart."

"Even smart people can get sick. I just have this horrible feeling that somehow he did this, and then maybe killed himself, maybe jumped off the boat. I didn't sleep too well last night —"

"Your uncle swims like a fish. Do you know how hard it is for a swimmer to die by intentional drowning?"

"No."

"Hard. I mean hard hard." The highway to the airport was quite busy. "That's what I've heard. And Ferd wouldn't do that."

"I don't know."

"He has too many friends. Too many people who love him. People all over the world."

"I know." Was this true, though? I was beginning to see another side of my uncle.

By the time we were at the airport, Joan's flight had

landed. Barbara let me off in front. She'd keep driving around and around until we were back. Anything to avoid a parking fee. That's us.

I waited just outside the baggage claim area until I saw her. But who was that with her? *Ben?*

CHAPTER 18

I was stunned.

"Ben?" I said, "What are you doing here?"

"I called him," Joan explained. "I persuaded him to come. I convinced him we needed his police expertise on this delivery."

"You mean on the boat? You're coming on the *boat*?"

"Yes." He grinned at me. "Joan convinced me that I needed to come along for the ride." He wore casual shorts, boat sandals, and a t-shirt with Montana Grizzlies on it. He looked awfully good to me. That big smile of his always got to me. His whole being there got to me. Barbara's warning seemed to fade into oblivion.

He was still smiling. So was Joan. It was as if the two of them were standing in the middle of a big joke.

"You hate boats." I kept staring at his face. "You get sick on boats."

"Joan told me she has an entire arsenal of seasick meds with her."

"I do," Joan said. "I've even got that one you can only get in the UK. Works like a charm. I got a package from some cruisers who were through. You remember the Taylors? On the catamaran?"

I nodded numbly.

"They brought me over a dozen packages."

I wasn't listening. I was simply looking at Ben, and he at me. He carried a small backpack and attached to it, a tightly rolled sleeping bag. When he saw me looking at it, he said, "Joan gave me instructions on how to pack."

Joan laughed and said, "Everything in and out of the bag.

Nothing left sitting around. And no hard-sided luggage."

"Yes, mother," he said turning to her.

I said, "Ben, you sure you're going to be okay? You don't like the way sailboats heel. You told me that."

"I'll be fine. I figure I've been in Maine long enough. Got to get my sea legs some time."

"It's a long trip, Ben. Weeks." My mind was going crazy with the thought. The three of us? On Ferd's skinny boat? What would we do for sleeping, showering, cooking? Had I packed enough food? Water?

Joan said, "I told Ben that any time he wanted to bail, to just say the word, and we'd head into the nearest port and he could take the bus home from there."

"Well," I said. "Wow," I added, and then another, "wow. But I thought you had to go to Montana."

"That got cancelled." Did his face darken just for a moment?

"Well, I'm glad you're here. We're both glad you're here. This is a police matter, after all."

He added, "Just as long as we're within sight of land. Joan did promise me that."

"We will be if there's no fog," I said.

"What?" Ben looked startled.

"You'll be fine," Joan said patting his shoulder. "I've got enough seasick pills to service the entire navy."

"Just as long as there are no ginger concoctions in the mix," Ben added laughing. "I figured out I hate ginger." I smiled at this memory. When he had just moved east, he had to accompany me on a police matter, and we were together for a long day on a big boat in big waves. All the ginger that was served seemed to make him sicker.

Joan said, "I told him we're going to have real drugs on board. None of this natural, organic stuff."

As we waited on the curb for Barbara to come around again, we chatted about weather and fog and oceans and inconsequential things. Because we were out in public, I didn't want to fill both of them in on where I'd been and what

I'd learned.

Barbara and Joan hugged when they saw each other, and she seemed pleased to meet Ben. I like Barbara. She's small and spunky, and with her very short, curly hair, she has always reminded me of a pixie. Barbara is a toucher and a hugger. Joan is not. It's always fun to watch the interaction.

Barbara said, "Wow this could be a party. I should re-evaluate my schedule. I'd love to come along."

"And where would you sleep?" Joan extricated herself from Barbara's pawing embrace.

"Oh, I don't know. Maybe the coach roof? I've done that before, you know."

"I know. We all have." And we had. Maybe I was moving into another stage of my life now, because suddenly, I felt too old for that. I like a bed at night.

"But, alas, work beckons," she said. "I have no intention of crashing the party, but speaking of parties, Simone will be home later today. Should we all go out to eat?"

We all agreed that would be a great idea.

On the way back in the car, Joan sat in the front with Barbara. Ben and I sat together in the back. While Barbara and Joan jabbered, Ben turned to me and said quietly, "The official word is that the police are looking for the bodies of Simon Towers and Ferd Hanson, and into the whereabouts of Ronny Joe Hollander."

"So, maybe Ronny Joe killed his brother and Simon and my uncle."

"Trouble is an alibi for Ronny Joe has come forward."

"What's that alibi?"

"He was with Ocean Hollander."

I raised my eyebrows. "Really?"

"Really. That's why he's been basically ruled out. For now."

"Wow."

After I filled Ben in on all the details of my trip to Mount Joy, he said, "I wish you hadn't gone there."

"I had to. Now," I shook my head. "I don't know what to

think."

"It happens," Ben said. "I've seen it time and time again. Dementia? Mental health problems. People snap. I've seen it all."

"But not with Ferd." This came from Joan who had overheard us. "Art got an email from him."

"Recently?" I asked.

"Month or so ago. Just before you had the Bermuda Triangle gig, but even still, his mind was sharp as a filleting knife."

"Why didn't you say something?" I said.

"Art didn't tell me until yesterday."

"What was in the email?" Ben asked.

"Oh, just that he was in South America." She turned to me. "He said to make sure that I give his love to you."

I leaned forward, touched the back of her seat. "He wrote that? Give his love to *me*?"

She nodded.

"Really?" Wasn't that what people said to you when they were going to commit suicide?

Barbara's old car rumbled onto the exit toward the waterfront.

"What about the money?" I said. "The police don't seem to have any theories about the money, and that's all I heard down in Pennsylvania over and over. Ferd stole their money. Ferd stole their money."

"All they can figure," said Ben, "is that somehow, some way, Ferd learned about their big win and decided to head on over there and steal it. Maybe they bet on the same race. Horse racing. Maybe he was at the racetrack and overheard them talking."

Barbara turned to where we were in the backseat. "Do you know how far-fetched that sounds? This is Ferd we're talking about. Ferd Hanson barely knows the front end of a horse from the back. Horse race? No. That's ridiculous. Sailboat racing? Yeah, I can see that. Horse racing? Nuh unh."

I said, "Sometimes I feel I don't know him at all. Like

maybe my whole childhood with him was a lie."

"Em—" The look Ben gave me was so warm and so kind, if I thought about it, I could burst into tears. I managed not to. "We may find him and he might just be fine."

"But what if he *isn't?* How can I be so mad at him with one breath and with the other, worry about him?"

"Because he's family," Barbara said, "that's why."

Forty-five minutes later, we were at the small house and chatting and drinking beers and talking sailing—or I was attempting to put on a happy face in any case—while Bear lounged her full black haired body long on the back of the couch. "She's coming with us." I pointed at Bear. "Hope no one's allergic."

We spent the rest of the day carting food and other provisions down to the boat and figuring out where we would sleep. Ben would have the vee berth, we decided. Joan would get the quarter-berth and I would sleep on the starboard main settee. Yes, it would be tight, but doable. I showed Ben the one small head. "Think of your standard head on a 747. Now, make it six inches smaller on all sides."

Out on deck, I pointed out the cockpit shower. "He has a hot water tank, but I'll have to hook it up. I'll do that this afternoon. But, showers are still at a premium. This is camping at its finest, folks," I told them.

"What's that?" Joan was pointing to the flowered card I had tacked to the corkboard.

"It's from Ferd. My last correspondence from him. He left it for me on the boat, which is how I know he wants me to take care of the boat and Bear for him."

She untacked it from the board and looked at it, turning it over. "You say he left this for you?"

"He put it in a place he knew I would find it when the boat was floating free out there."

"Pretty card." Ben looked at it over my shoulder.

"It's handmade. Which is typical of my uncle."

"Serioulsy? Your uncle makes cards?" he asked. "I got the impression your uncle is this crusty old pipe-smoking guy."

"He would have gotten it in trade," I explained.

Joan said, "Ferd has a definite soft side." She opened up the note and read it. And frowned.

"What's the matter?" I asked.

"Nothing." But she was still frowning. She took the note and card and went and sat down on the settee, still studying them.

CHAPTER 19

Supper was outside on a deck one floor up and overlooking the Baltimore Harbor. The restaurant we chose featured what were, in my opinion, the best crab cakes in the entire state. We'd decided as a group that we'd spend one last night, the three of us, at Barbara and Simone's before we set off tomorrow for points north. In the meantime, crab cakes and deep fried cheese sticks and beers and live blues on the deck were awfully good. Simone regaled us with tales of her last job. She owns a forty-foot ketch and runs a sailing school for women who are afraid to sail. I'm always surprised at how big the market is for this—women whose husbands love sailing, but anything beyond a ten-degree heel and fifteen-knot winds has them crouching down inside and shivering like scared rabbits, or firmly declaring that they will never again—never, ever—come aboard any boat. And husbands who yell. The biggest problem with scared wives, she always says, are husbands who yell. Yes, sailing seems very romantic to people who've never actually been sailing.

Simone prides herself on her non-confrontational gentleness and thoroughness. She teaches the basics of sailing and then they go out for extended three or four days on the boat. She usually takes five women at a time.

"I never yell at them, you know, but—" she picked up a fried cheese stick and dunked it in a small bowl of red sauce. "I can see why their husbands would—" Then she went on about her latest class and "this one woman" who practically drove the boat straight up onto the rocks.

"In my gentlest voice, I'm like, 'should we maybe turn twenty degrees to port, Margie?' And she's looking at me like 'what's port?' And I'm saying, 'Margie? Remember when we went over the difference between port and starboard?' Then, as casually as I can, I'm fast-walking the hell up the companionway and grabbing the wheel from her."

Ben said to her, "You ever take men on these cruises of yours?"

Simone pointed at me, "Ben, you listen to this gal. She's the best teacher you'll ever sail with. Just follow her example, do whatever she tells you to do, and you'll be a fine sailor in no time. And she won't yell at you, I promise."

I grinned. "Well, I wouldn't go that far."

****

The waters were dead calm when we took off before dawn the next morning. We were so early that neither Barbara nor Simone even got up to say goodbye. We whispered our way out of the house, with Bear and her litter box in tow, as well as all our backpacks and rolled up sleeping bags.

Even though I was pleased to have Ben along, I worried. Would we heel too much? Would that bother him? Would he be sick? Would he be a liability on this trip rather than an asset? If it were just Joan and me, we'd go way offshore and sail day and night. Now with Ben aboard, we would have to stop more often. I wasn't so sure I liked the fact that Joan had promised him that we'd always be within sight of land.

Our first day out proved to be a day of getting used to each other. By happy accident, Joan and I ended up doing the boat management, and Ben decided to take over the cooking and coffee making. Since Ben knew little about sailing, It was a system that would work just fine.

By the third day, the three of us had developed a kind of traveling camaraderie, which often occurs among sailors on a delivery. For the first two nights, we anchored and sat outside under the stars and talked. In the morning, we would wake to the sound and smells of Ben's bacon and eggs frying and coffee and toast made in a fry pan over the flame. "I am a camper," he told us. "I know how to make the best toast ever without a toaster."

By the fourth afternoon out on the sun-drenched water, Ben said, "Man, I could get used to this." Ahead of us, the sun sparkled on the water like scattered sequins.

"It gets under your skin, doesn't it?" I said.

Joan said, "I told you it wouldn't be so bad."

As days passed, it became less about why we were on this trip and more about the journey, which is often the way it is in sailing. Joan put out a hand line and we ran into a school of mackerel, which she cleaned, and Ben pan-fried in butter.

Although I had told Ben that we could stop along the way for showers at marinas, we never did. I'm just as happy not to. I'm what you might call a cheapskate when it comes to paying for nights at marinas when putting down an anchor is just as easy. And way cheaper. The ocean this time of year is warm for swimming. You soap up in the ocean and all you need is a cup of fresh water to wash the salt off. Who needs a hot shower anyway, especially when there are acres and acres of warm ocean?

Bear slept with Ben at night. I got the idea that Bear was used to the vee berth, and whoever happened to sleep there would be a companion to her. We were having a good week — the three of us — a good week. I felt that Ben was opening up, and he'd only gotten seasick once, and even at that, it wasn't the throwing-up kind. I told him later not to feel bad — it had been the type of day that would have even the staunchest sailor heaving over the side. High sea swells as we'd made our way up along the coast of New Jersey had done it to him. The problem with New Jersey is that there aren't a lot of places to turn in for the night. All of us had taken Joan's super-duper UK meds. Maybe Ben should have taken a double dose.

And then it was our first glimpse of the Statue of Liberty, and Ben had been in awe. We'd sailed through the East River under the Brooklyn Bridge and past Manhattan.

"There's Riker's Island." I pointed out the prison island as we motored past. "All police should know where that is."

"Really? Huh." He looked at the high fenced edifice through his binoculars.

And then we were through Hell Gate and up into Long Island Sound without incident. Maybe I could shut out the real reason why we were on this trip.

The closest Ben had come to talking about his past was last night. Anchored at Port Jefferson, under an impossibly large, round moon, Ben had said, "It's been good for me to be here. In Maine, I mean. Here in the east. I didn't think I would like it here. But after what I'd been through, I needed a place of quiet."

"Well, there's no quieter place than this here right now," Joan said staring up at the night sky.

"You know, I think you're right."

It had been uneventful. Fun, even. I could almost forget.

It had been too warm last night and I hadn't slept much. I kept thinking about Ferd, wondering where he was. Joan kept studying the flowered card and note every chance she got, turning it over, turning it this way and that. Something was wrong there, and she wouldn't tell me what she was thinking.

I wondered — did my uncle have a new boat by now? Was that where all his papers and personal logs and journals were? Was he having us all on while he sat on some deserted island, surrounded by pretty girls, sipping margaritas and shining up his new boat that he'd won — or stolen?

I soon realized I was getting further and further away from where Ferd had left this boat. The last time *Wandering Soul* had been this far north was after Jesse died. I thought about Ferd. Worried about him. Sent him email after email that he never answered.

On a fairly regular basis, Joan would take the flowered card from the corkboard and look at it. I don't know why she was so interested, and when I would ask her, she would just shake her head and mumble something.

Once, I said, "Joan?"

"Sorry." She put it back. "Just something funny about it, that's all. Where did you say you found it?"

"In a poetry book."

"Poetry?"

"Love poems, Joan. And pretty racy ones at that."

"Really?" Her eyes narrowed.

"What's the matter?"

"You never said a book of love poems. You just said book. You just found it in a book."

"Does it matter?"

"It changes everything."

But when I asked her why, she said she was still trying to sort it out.

We were in the middle of the Long Island Sound on an absolutely calm and stunningly warm before dawn morning. I was at the helm when I thought I heard something behind me. I got out my binoculars. It couldn't be! It simply couldn't be.

CHAPTER 20

I yelled down in my loudest voice, "Guys, we have company!"

I figured both Ben and Joan were still sleeping. It was far too early, even for them. These were the thoughts that kept me awake.

So, here I was, up before dawn on this morning, the last morning through the Sound. Soon it would be Block Island, Rhode Island, and Buzzard's Bay, and finally, the Cape Cod Canal and home. Not much longer now.

At four in the morning, when I knew I wasn't going to get any more sleep, I'd gotten up, quietly weighed anchor, and got us going. If I could put some miles behind us before daybreak, so much the better.

A quick look through my binoculars confirmed my worst suspicion. As impossible as it seemed, this looked like the silver boat with the lightning zigzag along the side that I had seen in Florida and the Chesapeake.

I called down. "Guys, hey! Can you get up here? Ben, I think it's the same boat, the one I was telling you about. It looks just like it."

He immediately became all concerned as the cop in him took over. "Where?" He climbed up into the cockpit, hair still askew from sleep, and his binoculars around his neck. "What?"

"Abeam us. Over there."

He trained his binoculars on the approaching boat. It was no longer a speck on the morning horizon but was gaining on us. A man stood at the wheel. He was holding something across his chest. A gun? A *gun?*

"Okay," he said quietly. "Go wake Joan up. Tell her she needs to get up here ASAP. Meanwhile, go down below. I know it's not much, but hide as best you can. Climb into the vee berth. There's a folded blanket along one side. Hide yourself in it if you can."

A lot of good that'll do, I thought, but I obeyed his orders. One thing I had learned about Ben was that he was cool-headed and calm during stressful situations.

"Take the radio with you, and your cell. Call the Coast Guard."

"VHF is too public," I said, "no doubt he's got his radio on. I'll use my cell."

"Good thinking. This is why I need your boating wisdom."

Joan was in the head, and I called to her through the closed door, telling her what was up.

Ben's sleeping bag was laid out straight and neat in the vee berth and his clothes were folded to the side. I scrunched myself into the starboard side of the vee berth and covered myself with Ben's sleeping bag. I could smell the smell of him, and I closed my eyes briefly. There was no getting around the fact that I was feeling an attraction to him that I needed to keep firmly in check. Firmly in check.

I was right next to the very small porthole, and if I leaned up, I could see through to the outside. I would keep well away from it, though, knowing how visible I would be from the outside, my face pressed against the glass.

I looked down at my cell. Only one bar of service way out here that was fading in and out. I tried 911. No luck. The boat was beside us now and slowing. I took a chance and glanced out through the small window, keeping my face well away from the glass. I didn't recognize the man who stood behind the wheel, but what he held across his chest made me shudder. Strapped to him was one of the biggest guns I had ever seen. I don't know guns, but it looked to be some sort of assault rifle, a huge one. Completing the uniform were camouflage fatigues, and even in this heat, an army jacket. This had to be the brother who'd disappeared, Ronny Joe —

the one Marie had called a gullible moron.

I clutched the ends of the sleeping bag to me and tried to make no sound. I checked my cell phone again. Still no service.

"Hello!" I heard Ben call cheerfully. "Something we can do for you, captain?"

"Yeah. There's a whole lot you can do for me."

I felt that powerboat nudge up against the side of *Wandering Soul*.

"Hey, watch it there," Ben said. "We nearly collided. You don't want to get that fancy boat of yours all dinged up against this old hulk, do you?"

Ronny Joe, or the man I presumed to be Ronny Joe, was handling the boat very inexpertly. He couldn't seem to get the massive engines on that thing to idle, and eventually, they stalled and stopped. He cursed a blue streak. Joan had flipped ours into neutral. It was dead calm. I'd been motoring.

Ben asked, "Can you put your gun away?"

"I'm looking for someone." His voice was gruff, loud, like he regularly chewed on gravel.

"It's just me and my partner here. Who are you looking for?"

"A woman. And a man. Ferdinand Hanson. And the woman who had his boat."

"Can't help you. Sorry."

"Well, maybe I should come onto the boat and look around. Should I?"

Ben's voice was remarkably calm. "Be my guest. But you'll find there's no one here but us."

"Where is she? I know she was over in Pennsylvania asking questions. Pestering Ocean."

Ben said, "My partner and I picked up the boat in Baltimore. It's a police matter. Would you mind putting down that gun? You're frightening my partner, who also happens to be the captain of this boat."

"She was on that boat. I know she was. Where is she now? I'm coming on. You can't stop me."

My stomach clenched. I glanced down at my phone. Still no service. I kept pressing 911 to no avail. As far as I knew, Ben hadn't even brought a gun along.

"No need for that." Ben's voice was calm. It seemed the rowdier the situation, the calmer he became. "The police searched this entire boat in Baltimore. There's nothing here."

"She stole my money. Her and Ferd. Her uncle. They're in this together."

Ben asked, "And what money is that?"

"Me and my brother. Her uncle killed him, stole our money, gave it to her. Ferd said he was going to give the money to her."

I froze. Ferd was going to give the money to *me*?

"If that is indeed the case," Ben said, "I would advise you to take your story to the police instead of getting all hot under the collar way out here."

I was sure everyone within twenty miles would be able to hear my heart beating. I kept hold of my cell phone in one damp hand and the radio in the other while I stayed absolutely still. Sweat coated my entire body.

"And while you're at it, I would suggest putting away that gun."

"I'm allowed to have it. It's a totally legal gun. I've got the second amendment on my side."

"I'm sure you do, but threatening a police officer with a gun is against the law."

All was quiet for a moment. I thought I heard the man swear under his breath.

"That's right. I'm a police officer. Here, here's my badge, and we're taking this boat to Maine. And I would advise you to put away the gun and head on home. Whatever you're looking for isn't here."

"She has my money..." I thought I heard him whisper "bitch," but wasn't sure. I kept swallowing. My lips were dry.

"Why don't you hand me the gun?" Ben said.

"Okay." He lowered the gun, "I'm gonna go. But if I don't find that money, I'll be back to kill you both." He aimed the huge rifle at Ben and said, "Pow! Remember that. And I'll find that Ferd and kill him, too. And the girl."

A few moments later, after several tries, I heard the silver boat start up and head off toward the shore.

After he was gone, and the engine was just a drone in the air, Joan said, "Ben, you were amazing."

But I kept thinking about his last words—that he would come back and kill us all.

CHAPTER 21

I stood in the companionway unsure whether I should come up into the sun or go back down in the vee berth and hide in there forever. "Is he gone?" I asked tentatively looking from right to left. I could hear nothing.

"It appears so," Ben said. "You can come up. He won't be able to see you even with binoculars. He's too far away. Did you call the Coast Guard?"

I looked down at the radio in my right hand and the cell phone in my left. I felt so befuddled. It was as if all of a sudden, I couldn't quite understand the purpose of such instruments. "I couldn't. No bars on the phone, and I didn't want to use the VHF."

I climbed up into the cockpit and stood there. The water was calm, almost eerily so, like glass, like if you stepped off the boat you wouldn't sink, but would slide across it as if on sheer ice, like we had floated into some parallel universe. Sweat beaded down my forehead, yet I could not stop shivering.

I looked down at my phone. "The money. It always comes back to that money. What if someone random just stole the money from the boat and then let the boat float away from the shore off Florida?" I turned to Ben. "And now he's gone."

"I think me being a police officer was the thing that sent him on his way."

"What if he comes back?" I looked at Ben. "Why didn't you stop him?"

"It was a huge gun." He pulled out his own cell phone from his pocket. When he saw there was no service, he put it back.

I climbed up onto the bow of the boat and held my phone up high. Sometimes up here, you get service. I said, "I could climb the mast. Sometimes there's reception higher up."

Ben looked at me and then up the mast. "You'd do that? You'd climb up there?"

"I do it all the time, Ben. See those metal things all the way up the mast? They're mast steps. They fold out for climbing. I'll go get the safety harness."

This task gave me an adrenaline rush that pushed me forward. Instead of fear, I had a job to do. I easily found the harness behind all of the jackets in the hanging locker. Finding it gave me a momentary pause. My uncle wouldn't have left his harness. Not this one. It had been hand sewn by a good friend.

I got myself into it and had Joan belay me up with the main halyard. I wasn't even to the spreaders when I got a steady bar of service. Up a bit more and I easily got two.

I called the Coast Guard following Ben's directions as he called them up to me. I also called Wayne, the police officer from Mount Joy, and told him that we may have met Ronny Joe Hollander. I relayed the conversation from Ben to Wayne and back again. Wayne took down all the information and couldn't understand why I just couldn't hand the phone to Ben.

"Because I'm halfway up the mast."

"What?"

"I'm halfway up the mast of this sailboat."

"Why are you up there?"

"It's the only place I can get cell reception."

"Oh."

He asked me to tell Ben that he would coordinate with the Coastguard US Sector Long Island Sound. Calls all made, Joan belayed me down, and I put the harness away. Then I started shivering in earnest. I sat in the cockpit looking at the water for a long time while Joan handled the boat and Ben went down and made bacon and eggs.

When he brought them up, I said to him, "Thank you so

much for coming."

"I'm just glad I was here."

"I'm pretty sure that was the same boat I saw three times on this trip, but he didn't approach me until now." I implored Ben, "What if he had? What if he had come up to me with that gun when it was me and Janice? I could have put a young person in danger! Or what if it was just me and Joan? He said he was going to kill us. I heard him say that, Ben." My voice rose at the end.

"It's all right, Em," Joan said. "Ben was here."

"I know, I know, but what if he wasn't? It was the same boat," I kept saying. "How could it be the same boat? It's like I'm seeing things or hallucinating or maybe the Bermuda Triangle is finally getting to me. But I swear that was the same boat. I can't eat anything. I'm sorry, Ben. This whole thing is getting to me. I can't eat anything." My hands were shaking.

"Em," Joan said, "you've been up since way before dawn. You're probably just exhausted. Go down and hit your bunk."

"I should be up here," I protested. "In case anything else happens."

"No, you shouldn't. You're making yourself sick."

"But…" I sputtered

"Go!" ordered Ben.

Finally persuaded, I went and lay down in the quarter berth, but of course, I couldn't sleep. I curled myself into a ball, stared at the side of the boat while images of my uncle sailed in and out of my head.

I was about to drift off when I heard Joan say, "I hope things in Montana work out for you."

And his soft reply, "That's still to be determined."

"I'm sorry you had to miss going out there. I know how much you wanted to go home."

"Yeah…well…crap happens."

I perked up my ears. Joan and Ben were talking about Montana? I leaned up on my forearm. How did Joan and Ben happen to have this level of friendship? It made me feel a little odd. Jealous? Maybe there was a little bit of that. I have always called Joan my "wise, elder aunt" even though she's in her fifties and certainly not old. Joan, who had never had children of her own, seemed to have this motherly air. People confided in her.

"And so you've decided you want to stay in Maine?"

"I think so," I heard him say. Then he mumbled something that I couldn't hear, even though I strained to, and Joan laughed. Then it was quiet. I lay back down. I must've slept because when I awoke, the engine was off. As I lay there, I could hear the sound of the waves against the boat, the gentle creak of the sheets. I stirred, about to rise, when I heard my name mentioned. I heard some mumbling, and then Ben say, "She's very capable."

"I've known Em a long time."

Me? They were talking about me? I listened.

"Extremely. I'm worried about her," Joan said.

"You mean the way she ran off to Pennsylvania looking for her uncle?"

"Wait," Joan said. "Let me fix that jib." Some sailing instructions followed and I lay on my berth wondering if I should go up and help.

"She always does a great job." My eyes widened. It was Ben who said this. He thought that? He thought I always did a great job? He went on, "You sure having the sails up won't make me seasick?"

"Can't guarantee it, but we'll try to keep her steady. We may as well use the sails when we can. Often, sailing is a bit of a steadier ride than motoring, depending on the seas."

"Good, because it was affecting me. Even with those seasick pills, I was feeling it."

I heard more murmuring, and then Ben say, "I think I have a weird stomach."

"Everyone does until they're used to the motion."

A few moments later, he said, "I'm glad she's resting. She needs it."

I heard Joan mumble. "...been through a lot. Her husband's death a few years ago—still going through that,

I'm afraid. He was so young. The whole thing was such a tragedy."

More murmuring that I strained to hear.

And then, a little while later, Joan said, "You're doing well out here, Ben."

"Working on it. I figure if I'm going to stay in Maine, I better learn the ropes."

"They're called lines."

I could hear him laugh. "That's what Em tells me."

I do? I tell him that? I lay back down, my hands behind my head, my head on the pillow.

"Ben, can I ask you something?"

"Go ahead."

"Do you think there's something funny about the card and that note that Ferd supposedly left for Em?"

What did she mean *supposedly*? I listened.

"You mean that flower card asking her to take care of things for him?"

"I've known Ferd Hanson a long time, Art even longer. They sailed together, my husband and Ferd. Ferd would never send a card like that. It's just out of character for him."

"Well, I think lately he's done a lot of things out of character, wouldn't you say?"

"I know. I know they're talking about dementia, but let's play the 'what if' game. What if it's not dementia?"

"Okay."

"If you knew Ferd, you would know that he's more likely just to leave a note." I remained perfectly still on the berth. More mumbling, and then I heard Joan say, "It's not his handwriting. I've seen enough of his log notations to know it's not his writing."

"What do you think the card's about then?"

A pause as I strained to listen. She said, "I keep thinking about something, but it's from a long time ago. I'm just trying to put it together in my mind."

"What?"

"I don't know." Her words were measured. The boat

moved to port, and I could hear Joan adjust the sails. "Sorry. Not paying attention here." Still, I did not rise to help.

She went on, "Em thinks the 'E' refers to her, as in her uncle was sending her a personalized letter. But..." I heard her pause. "The comma is wrong."

"What do you mean?"

"I'll get it for you."

I shut my eyes, kept my breathing steady as she came down below and pulled the card and note from the corkboard. In a few minutes, she was up in the cockpit where I heard Ben mumble something and then her answer, "No, still out like a light. Poor thing. Okay, look at this. See, the comma is in the wrong place."

"Hmm."

"If you are giving a command, you don't put a comma before the name. If it were from Ferd to Em, he would have written, 'take care of the boat E,' rather than 'take care of the boat comma E."

"Maybe that was just a mistake."

"I think the note was *from* someone, Ben, not *to* someone. I think the note might have been from someone with a name that starts with E, not from him to Em. And the flowers. I think I have an idea who sent this card."

CHAPTER 22

I rose quickly. What? Who was it from if not from Ferd? Who was it for if not for me?

I got out of the berth and stood in the companionway. "Hi, guys." I wanted to keep it light. I didn't want them knowing I'd eavesdropped on the last twenty minutes of their conversation.

"Hey," Ben said.

"Hi," Joan said. "You get some sleep?"

"I think so. Just woke up."

"You were sure when I went down a few minutes ago."

"Come on up," Ben said. "It's nice out here."

"Feeling better?" Joan asked.

Why did their words make me feel like a child and they were the parents? "Did the police find him yet?" I asked.

"They're working on it," Ben said. "In fact, I'm surprised the waters around here aren't wall to wall with Coast Guard boats."

I poured myself a cup of coffee from the carafe thermos and went up above into the sunshine and sat down. The card lay on the seat next to Joan.

I looked at it. "What's with the card out here?"

She picked it up and said, "Em, I need to talk to you. I need to ask you something. I think I'm figuring out what's bothered me about this card all this time."

"Yes?"

"It's the comma." She pointed at it. "It's in the wrong place."

She explained it all to me, although I had heard this entire thing when I was supposed to be sleeping. "So, if it's *from* someone instead of *to* someone, who is it from?" I asked.

"Ella." One name said plainly and simply

"Ella," I said the name out loud. Ella. The name came from the deep recesses of my memory. *Ella. Ella.* I said it over a few times out loud, trying to think, trying to remember. The image it brought to me was the woman again, the one with the orange hat climbing down swiftly and easily from my uncle's boat as if she had done it a hundred times.

"Ella." I let the name slide over my tongue. I remembered a long-limbed young woman with sun-glinted, curly brown hair, blown back by the wind. "Ella." The woman that my mother turned her back on, removing us from her presence. The woman who "carries on with men."

"Ferd's friend," I said. "The woman my mother couldn't stand."

"The woman your mother couldn't stand," Joan said.

"Do you think the note's from Ella, too?" I asked, "The one that was in the card?"

"Quite possibly."

I took a long swallow of coffee. The card not being from my Uncle Ferd changed everything. Instead of me taking care of his boat, I was now stealing his boat. Bear trotted up from down below and found a place beside me on the cockpit seat. She stretched her paws on me, seeming to almost sense my confusion.

"Maybe, then, maybe, if the note wasn't for me, I shouldn't even be taking this boat north. I just..."

Joan put her hands on my shoulder. "Em, we still don't know what happened. I'm sure... well, I know that Ferd will love the fact that you're taking such good care of his boat and of Bear."

Bear looked up when she said her name.

I looked down at the card again, and could almost hear my mother's voice, "Your uncle isn't living the lifestyle we want for you."

It was curious that my uncle never married. Every year or so, he would show up with a different woman in tow. Some I liked. Some not so much. But he never married any of them. My mother took them all in stride. She was never thrilled with his choice in women—and that's how she put it—"I'm not thrilled about my brother's choice in women"—but none generated the visceral reaction that Ella did. Through the years, I put it down to the orange-hatted woman being the first.

Once we girls were in the car on that day twenty-seven years ago, my father turned to my mother and said, "Someone needs to tell him why we're leaving. We can't just leave, Char."

"I'll go," she said.

"Maybe I should," he said.

"No. I know you. You'll be too nice to him."

Her car door opened with a squeak, and I watched her stride purposefully back down to the dock where my uncle and the woman were in that laughing embrace. I watched them separate. I watched the woman move aside, away from my uncle and my mother, her head hung low. My mother went to him, close to his face. I remember loud voices. I remember yelling. From the car, I couldn't hear what it was about, but I watched her wild hand gestures.

"Girls," said my father. "Girls, don't bother looking at this. It's just your mother and your Uncle Ferd and you know how your mother is. Just turn around. Your mother will take care of it."

The twins didn't care. They were already deep into their storybooks in the backseat and sharing their little twin secrets. Not me. I didn't look forward. I didn't take my ten-year-old gaze away from my uncle and my mother and the woman. And then, my mother abruptly turned from the two of them and stomped back up to the car. The next two summers were the worst of my life. Going to the public swimming pool, laying my towel down on the hard cement, trying to pretend that I liked going down the slide into the chlorinated water. Trying to pretend I liked the laughter, the noise, the running of feet and splashing. Trying to pretend that I liked the smell of the greasy burgers and fries and blue popsicles melting down your fingers. It wasn't the same as being on the ocean. It wasn't the same.

I scratched Bear's ears as the memories came back.

Joan said, "It was Ella who broke your uncle's heart. He had relationships after that, lots of them. But no one could match Ella. Ever."

I looked at the card and the folded note. "What happened?"

"They were together for a little more than a year. Maybe close to two. They sailed over to Bermuda and then down to the Caribbean and back up. Then she left him."

"She left him?"

Joan nodded. "It broke his heart."

"That's sad."

"She went back to her husband."

The words slapped at me like a cold rag. *Wandering Soul* jerked suddenly as we went the wrong way into a small swell. *Back to her husband.* Joan took the helm. That would explain everything. That would explain why my mother hated the woman so much, why she called her "that woman."

Joan was still speaking. "I didn't know her. She was older than me. Art's age, younger than Ferd. I think Art knew her. What I did hear is that after she had gone back to her husband, they ended up moving away from Maine. For her, your uncle was simply an interlude. For Ferd, she was his whole life. That's what I heard. I think he was expecting her to leave her husband for him. Ferd told Art that she left because she decided she didn't think she could spend her life on a boat. She wanted a house and a garden and a white picket fence and a family. Things Ferd couldn't give her."

I ran my fingers over the card. "And you think this card's from her? But this card looks new. The note looks kind of old, but the card looks fairly recent. Don't you think?"

"That's the part I can't figure out, either. That's the part that keeps baffling me. But I just can't think of anyone else with the name beginning with E who liked flowers. Ella was always growing things. Even on this boat, she tried her hand at putting out a box of pansies. Blew into the ocean at the first storm. Art told me that once."

I stared down at the very small blue zinnia almost as a signature at the bottom center of the card. "It could be an old card," I said. "Maybe he kept it in plastic." But I knew on a boat, even things in plastic become soft over time.

"I can't explain the feel of the card. Unless..." She paused. The wind blew my hair in front of my face, and I brushed it back with my hand. "Unless they are in contact now. Unless they have been in contact all along."

Ben asked, "So, this Ella. What would she want him to take care of? Where does she live?"

Joan shook her head. "Those are things I don't know. I'll talk to Art as soon as I can. He might know."

I kept looking at the card, many thoughts and memories tumbling through my mind. I was thinking about the times that my uncle spent with my husband, Jesse. I would come upon the two of them—my late husband and my uncle, in deep conversation. I liked that. I liked that my husband got along with my favorite family member. Did my uncle tell him about Ella? Did they share deep thoughts like that?

Another memory came to me. It came to me so suddenly and so unexpected that my fingers on the flower card began to tremble. "I saw her, Joan. I saw Ella a second time. I am just remembering this now."

"What?" Joan was at the helm. Buzzard's Bay was just ahead. And our timing had been perfect. We would have a strong current taking us through the Cape Cod Canal. "What do you mean a second time?"

I told her about the first time, when Ferd brought Ella home with him, and how we all had to go back home. "That was when I was ten. But I saw her after that. Two summers later when I was twelve. I saw her again."

"Where?"

"I think it was her. I'm sure it was her."

Two years had passed and my mother, having been

assured that "that woman" was out of the picture, had decreed that we would go back to Maine. The little sailing dinghy was everything I had hoped for. I couldn't think of a nicer welcome back present than to work on that old boat with my uncle. By the end of the summer, I could sail that little dinghy almost to the furthest mooring, almost to the ocean. And it was way out there that I saw her. Or rather, them. Uncle Ferd and Ella.

The rest of my family were on the shore, my mother reading a magazine in a beach chair, and my little sisters down by the water and splashing near the rocks. My father was up with his in-laws on the front porch drinking iced tea and talking politics.

It was my uncle's dinghy I saw first, tied to the back of a trawler. I would know his inflatable anywhere with that characteristic red stripe along the back. I decided to sail closer. See why he was way out here. Closer, I could see my uncle and another person standing in the stern area of the trawler. A woman. The same smiley woman in the bright orange hat I'd seen two years previous. But this time she wasn't smiling. There was no hat, either, but I was sure it was her. There was a stiffness about her demeanor. He would move toward her, but she would back away.

It would take me several tacks to get there, but I proceeded. I tacked away for a while, but when I tacked back again, I saw the two of them. By the expressions on their faces, I could tell they were arguing. I was too far away to hear the words, just the tone. The woman did not look like the bouncy, pretty lady from two years earlier. This one looked sad — weary almost. I luffed off and watched, certain they were completely unaware of my presence. He tried to touch her face. She threw his hand off, a ferocious expression on her face. I don't know what pre-teen wisdom manifested itself in me, but something in her stance made me extremely uneasy.

I turned and gibed my way back to shore and nothing was said about the woman.

"I think it was her," I said now. "She was on a trawler. A

powerboat. Did Ella ever own a trawler?"

"I don't know anything about her boating history. I'll ask Art. Your uncle and Ella had a rocky history. I'm sure your mother can tell you all about it, too. But even now, I think it's a sore subject with her."

"Why," I wondered, "when she sort of accepted all of his other live-in women?"

Joan shrugged. "I have no idea. Other than Ella's husband was a nice Christian man. I think your mother even knew him."

"Ah, that would explain it."

Eventually, I took the card down below. Instead of tacking it up on the corkboard again, I found the book of love poems and put it and the note back where I'd found them. Obviously, I'd gotten the wrong message. Obviously, I'd attributed more to this card than was there. This was not a card for me when I found the boat floating in the Bermuda Triangle. This was just an old letter and note from a former lover. It had nothing to do with the Bermuda Triangle. It had nothing to do with Papa Hoho and with what was going on now. All of this was new, different. And that was old. And now my uncle had turned into a person I didn't even know.

Up above on the bow, Ben was animatedly talking on his cell phone. During my conversation with Joan, I hadn't even noticed that he'd left us and climbed up onto the bow to take a call. Now that we were within cell phone range, it seemed that Ben's cell had not stopped ringing.

Ben called down to me. "I've got something to tell you, Em." He climbed back down into the cockpit. "Some kayakers found a dinghy lodged in some mangrove trees off the coast of Florida. They think it might belong to your uncle. They're sending me a picture of it."

I looked at him and felt my mouth go dry.

CHAPTER 23

"**H**is inflatable?" I asked.

Ben nodded. "According to reports, it's in pretty good shape. Not damaged or anything. They found it about a mile from the shore."

"Seriously?" I stared at him. "On an island?"

"Hold on a minute," he said. "They're sending me that picture now." He looked down at his phone and then handed it to me. "Is this your uncle's boat?"

I studied it for a few minutes before returning it. "It's his." When he came up after Jesse died, this was his new inflatable. He was quite proud of it, too. He'd traded it for some engine work and fish, he'd told me.

"The police are estimating that it's been there for maybe a month. It's not easily seen."

"Do they think it was deliberately placed there or that it floated there?"

"I don't think they've made that determination yet."

"Was there anything in the dinghy?"

"Nothing. No identification. Not even any paddles."

"My uncle had a small outboard. It's not in the picture. It's also not on this boat."

"I'll let them know that."

"It could have been stolen. I bet the mysterious money wasn't there either."

"Right again.

"Still no ID," I mused. "Like this boat. I've never seen a boat so devoid of ID. It's like he wanted to disappear."

"Maybe he did."

I said, "Have you heard if they found Ronny Joe and his

big boat yet?"

"Not yet. Still looking."

"That's heartening. So he's still out on the water with a fast boat he can't handle and a huge gun. Want to hear something funny? If that gun goes off accidentally on that boat and makes a hole in it? It'll sink immediately."

"He'll be found soon, Em. He will. He's not the sharpest tool in the shed. I have a feeling he depended on his brother and his friend a lot. That's the impression I got from what the police have found and from talking to him, too."

I went up on deck to see that we were halfway along Stony Point Dike. Once we were through the Cape Cod Canal, we'd be on what I called my home turf. We could make it home to Portland with a day or two of hearty sailing. And then what?

Ben was up on the bow again and was on the phone. We waved to the people on the shore. A fly landed on the ship's compass. I looked at it for a few minutes before it flew away. The sound of the engine droned on.

The GPS showed that we were doing ten knots over the ground. We'd timed the canal perfectly thanks to Joan, who was such a stickler about such things. I looked out toward the water swirling past us as the engine pushed us on through. We were heading a little to starboard, so I adjusted the wheel and set the autopilot, grateful that my uncle, for all his old-fashioned ways, had installed autopilot. Hand steering a boat for hours can get extremely tiring.

Almost through the canal, I felt my phone vibrate. I pulled it out of my pocket. A text from Papa, or Norman as he was now calling himself. I read the rather long message.

> Anything new on the case? Let me know. We're filming in a week, putting together all the footage we got in Florida plus whatever new I can find. Did you look at my YouTube channel? What did you think? Waiting to hear. I think you'll like the new format. Also, I'd love some quotes from you about how there's nothing to the Bermuda Triangle thing, and how that whole thing with the fog and the WWII pilot

> has been totally debunked. All those things you said
> on the boat - I want to quote you. And I do want you
> on my team. Once you say yes, I'll give you the
> information I have on your uncle.

I frowned as I read it. How dare he hold me hostage this way? And what information could he possibly have?

"Anything important?" Joan asked.

"Dr. Papa wants me to work for him." I grunted out a sigh. "As if—"

I put my phone away. I'd answer it later when my mind wasn't going in a thousand different directions. I watched Ben up on the bow holding onto the front stay with one hand and scowling into his phone. I went down below to fetch myself a bottle of water as Ben returned to the cockpit. I heard Joan say, "Montana?"

"Yep."

"And?"

I waited down below.

I heard him say, "Not good. Not good. Some wounds can't be healed." There was a sadness in his voice when he said this.

Wounds that don't heal. I know about wounds that don't heal. I'm a young widow, after all, with a family I'm not especially close to.

"Don't be so hard on yourself." Joan's voice was soft.

"Kinda hard not to be. With what happened."

After we made it through the canal, we headed across Cape Cod Bay. We could either turn thirty degrees to port and head in to Boston, or we could make a run for it across to Gloucester. The winds were picking up. I knew what Joan and I would do—we'd head across. I told Ben the situation. And he surprised me by saying, "Let's go for it."

"Here," Joan said, coming up from down below with seasick pills and bottles of water. She handed two to Ben. He took them, as did I, as did Joan. We might well be in for it.

For the next little while, we busied ourselves with sails while Ben tried to make himself useful. He was trying—I'll give him that. But by the time we were heeling at twenty degrees, Ben had hunched himself into the bulkhead. The winds were increasing. Waves were beginning to splash over the bow, which is no problem for a boat like this, but it is, if you are seasick prone. Or scared. Or a little of both.

I sat down next to him. "You okay?"

He nodded but didn't say anything, didn't look at me. By now, he had taken on the seasick stance. We sailors all know what that is. You just get quieter and quieter as you hunch against the bulkhead of the boat, not moving and barely breathing, and not talking. Never talking. There's this idea that if you don't move, you won't throw up. We've all been here.

"Maybe I should go down below," he said.

"You don't want to do that. You never want to do that. Worst place to be when you're seasick is down below. It'll just make you sicker."

And it would. Best thing for seasickness? Stay outside, near the stern of the boat in the fresh air, and look at the horizon.

"Go take the helm, Ben," Joan said. "It'll make a big difference."

Joan and I worked around him. We reefed the main and got *Wandering Soul* as steady as we could. Somehow, the hours passed. But that's sailing. You have these long hours of simply sitting there and not doing anything and watching the stars, and reading novels and doing crosswords and tying knots, and then it's utter craziness for a while. An hour before we came to Gloucester, the winds slackened to a nice breeze and Ben came to life. That's the thing with seasickness. It can hit you and you think you are dying—or you're afraid you're not dying—but as soon as the motion changes, it miraculously and almost instantly goes away. Ben said, "Hard to believe I actually come from sailing ship stock."

"What?"

"I do." He laughed. "It's why I came to Maine when the opportunity presented itself. So, I should be more used to all of this."

I simply looked at him.

"My great-grandfather was a ship's captain."

"Seriously? I would have pegged you for an inlander. Cowboy, maybe."

"Nope. Massachusetts. That's why I came back here. Maybe get back to my roots a bit. Even though I'd never been on a boat bigger than a canoe in my entire life, I thought there might be something in my DNA. Now, I'm not so sure."

"I think you're doing really well," I said. "It's amazing how less sick you feel when you're not scared and when you have a job to do. Back there, we had a job to do."

"When we get home, I'll show you the picture of my great grandfather's ship. I have it framed, even. It was one of those old square riggers. I haven't put it up anywhere on any wall. Almost too embarrassed to."

"You should," I said.

We were in lobster pot country now, which meant looking out for lobster floats all along the surface of the water. But, as potential prop tanglers, my uncle's boat with its sea-going full keel wouldn't be too much of a problem if we accidentally sailed over one. Joan and I could have pressed on but decided to call it a day and pick up a mooring at the Eastern Point Yacht Club. Ben promised to make us something to eat. It was calm in here behind the breakwater. Ben handled the BBQ. Steaks. Fried onions and mushrooms. Potatoes. And wine. I decided I'd relax my "no drinking on a delivery" rule. The wine was perfect.

The following morning, Ben got a call. They hadn't found the boat that had approached us, but were sure it was stolen and were checking up and down the coast for reports of stolen boats that fit that description.

"So they don't know where it is," I said. "So he's roaming the countryside with that boat and that big gun."

"He will be found."

"That's what you said before. He's a survivalist, remember? Wearing army fatigues and carrying a gun."

****

Two days later and they still hadn't found him. Neither had they found my uncle. I called Papa Norman and left a message. Maybe it was time to pretend to be on his "team" and find out what, if anything, he knew about Ferd.

Abeam to the port was the familiar flash, every four seconds, of the Portland Head Light. Another hour and we'd be in my own Chalk Spit Bay.

We were almost home.

****

Engine on and sails stowed, we were heading toward Jeff and Valerie's dock. I'd called Jeff a few hours earlier to make sure I could tie up. He was standing on the dock, ready to receive our lines. I pulled in right behind the *Valerie J*, Jeff and Valerie's big lobster boat. Jeff and Valerie had moved my little sailboat, *Wanderer*, up and had tied her against the *Valerie J*. There was plenty of room to maneuver.

"This is much appreciated," I said to Jeff as I handed him a line. "I'm going to take her out to my mooring just as soon as I unload everything."

"Keep it here as long as you like. This dock is strong enough for the Queen Mary."

It felt good to be home. Bear had taken up residence on the bow and was watching the goings on with high-pitched meows. Liam was there, and I asked him to catch Bear if she jumped off. Liam and Bear had sailed this boat in Florida, and so they knew each other.

Several neighbors came down to watch, people I didn't know. This was the middle of summer, so Chalk Spit Island was crowded with tourists. In the summer, the population of my little island triples.

I live at the very end of a tidal island near Portland, Maine. It has a lot of summer cottages on it, but year round people are few and far between. Next to me is my elderly neighbor, EJ, who busies himself cooking chunks of meat and whittling and woodwork and spending time on his HAM radio. I tell him, for a man his age — which has to be into his 90s, although no one is quite sure — he has too many hobbies. It's EJ who takes care of my late husband's aging dog Rusty when I go on trips.

On the other side of me is a summer rental. Closed up during the winter, it was now bustling with life. I couldn't keep track of the children who were running hither and yon. Next to them are my good friends, Dot and Isabelle, elderly sisters, who EJ and I dub the "bickering sisters." Despite their continual arguments, these two love each other and keep me well supplied with tuna casseroles and neighborly gossip.

Next to Dot and Isabelle are Jeff and Valerie, whose son Liam accompanied me on the Bermuda Triangle trip, and to whose dock we were now affixed. Liam had captured Bear and put on the makeshift collar that I had made of macramé out of line on the boat that was kicking around. When I have nothing to do on boats, I like working with rope. If it weren't such a large tome, *Ashley's Book of Knots* would always be in my kit.

Isabelle was down on the dock to greet us. Dot, however, had stayed up on their porch and was watching us through her binoculars. I waved cheerfully to her, and she went inside.

"What's with Dot?" I asked her sister.

"Oh, you know Dot. Dot is Dot. Her knickers are in a knot most of the time. Just ignore her."

I closed up *Wandering Soul* and carted all of my stuff up to my house. Liam carried Bear. I had no idea how this little cat would get along with Rusty, but I wasn't prepared to find out. I'd close Bear in my bedroom with her food bowls and litter box, and then I'd drive Joan and Ben into Portland.

I checked the tide on my phone. We were in luck. The tide was going down, and if we hurried, I could drive them across and then back before the tide was back rising again. We loaded everything into my car and headed into the city.

On the way, Ben asked me, "Are you going to be okay in your place alone?"

"Sure. You saw all the neighbors there. This is summer. People come and go all day and night there."

He nodded, but his expression was grim. If I was even the little bit afraid, I didn't want him to know.

I dropped Joan off first. And then it was Ben and me. He came and sat in the front seat. I wanted to ask him about Montana. I wanted to ask him about the trip he was supposed to have taken. I wanted him to tell me what had happened there. I wanted him to talk to me like he talks to Joan, but I couldn't think of how to start so all I said was, "So you had a great-grandfather who was a sailor. Cool."

"If you have a minute when we get to my house, I'll show you the picture."

"Okay. Sure. I'd love to." Yes, I'd have to hurry. Yes, I didn't want to miss the tide. But I also wanted to be with him, even though Barbara's warnings echoed in my ears even now.

Ben's small house was basically a three-room cottage. It's several blocks from the water and I guess it suits him. He says it does. We'd divvied up the food from the boat, and I carried in one of the boxes for him.

Inside, he said, "Let me go get that picture. I want you to see it. "

"Super."

He had one of those door mail slots, and his mail from the weeks had accumulated all over the floor right inside the door. I decided to help him by picking it up and stacking it on the small table next to the door. I was in the middle of picking everything up when I saw a thick padded envelope. Across the envelope was scrawled in black sharpie. "Return to Sender." I picked it up and looked down at it. The person it was addressed to was Cindy Dunlinson and an address in Montana.

Cindy. His wife.

As quickly as I could, I piled it all on top of it on the table.

"Just getting your mail for you," I said by way of explanation when he stood there, looking from the mail, and the envelope on top to me and back again.

He said, "Here it is." He handed the picture to me, but something had gone out of his voice. "Proof that I'm not as bad as everyone thinks I am."

"You're not." I tried to keep my voice bright as if I hadn't just seen a returned envelope from his wife. I made myself look down at the photo of the whiskered, bearded man with a captain's hat, suspenders, and a pipe, standing at the helm of a big wooden boat.

"Are you impressed?" He smiled.

"Very," I said. "You should take this and put it on your office wall down at the police station. That should impress all your co-workers. Show them you really do have sailing blood in you. And you do. You did very well. Nothing to be ashamed of..." I was aware that I was talking too much and too fast. I clamped my mouth shut.

On the way home, my cell phone vibrated. I looked down at it. A Mount Joy, Pennsylvania phone number. Since I was driving and eager to make the tide, I let it go to voice mail.

CHAPTER 24

I didn't listen to the voice mail until I was home and safe and had poured myself a well-needed glass of wine. I kept thinking about the envelope I'd seen and wondered what Ben was doing at this precise moment. I could picture him on his couch, head in his hands, as he examined whatever the contents were. Or maybe the envelope would have set off another flurry of phone calls, like the ones he had a few days ago on the boat. Or was he calling Joan for solace and advice? Maybe that was a good thing. Maybe I shouldn't be so jealous.

"This is Marie. From Mount Joy?" I heard when I listened to my voice message. "Can you call me? It's important." She gave a number. I called it.

"It's about Ocean Hollander," she said.

I took my wine and went and stood beside the window and looked outside. It was early evening, and the kids from next door were still chasing and calling at each other down by the water's edge. Even though Marie's words were anxious, my thoughts kept going to Ben.

"Yes?" I said.

"I kept thinking I should either call you. Or call the police. Well, I did call the police and all they did was give me the runaround."

The *police*? "The runaround about what?"

"She's missing. Ocean is gone. She didn't show up for her shift. We called. No answer. I finally had Tim from the kitchen go over to her place — so many things have been happening and they're freaking us all out. He came back and said the place was all closed up and her car was gone." Marie's words were coming out like breathless sputters. "I know where her key is. She gave it to me once. She thought I should have one. We worked out a safety code. She and I did. If she was being beat on, that is. So, Tim and I both went. But here's the scary part. The part that totally creeps me out."

"What?"

"Well, first of all, she was gone. And inside? Inside, it was like two people were going to sit down for supper, and then they got up and left. There were two plates set at her table with glasses of wine. Half full. And pots on the stove with food in them. But to me, it's just plain weird. Two place settings. Like who was going over there for supper and what happened to them all of a sudden?"

I admitted that it sounded weird — a bit too familiar to me, as well.

"You don't know where she is, do you? She's not there with you, is she?"

"No. Why would she be here?"

"I don't know — I just thought — "

"She's not here."

"You said you had a police friend? You do, right?"

"I do."

"Would you, I mean, could you ask him to look into it? I know the police here want to talk with her some more. I don't know why, though. But maybe if there were another police friend who knew about it, we could find out why they want to talk with her so much. One of the officers came in here, to the café. His tighty-whiteys were all in a knot because he said he specifically told her not to leave town. I didn't know what to say. So, do you think you could talk to your friend?"

"I will. But he's up here in Maine. I'm in Maine now."

"I said to the police, why are you so anxious to talk with her when the murder's been solved? They told me themselves they thought Ferdinand did it."

I said, "I know she has family up north somewhere. Could she have gone there? Maybe she was distraught about her husband dying."

"She wouldn't go there. Not in a million years. She and her

mother do not get along."

"And her father passed away recently, too," I said.

"Yes, that has been weighing on her. No, she would never go to her mother."

"Just curious. How long has she lived in Mount Joy?" I asked.

"Long time. She grew up here basically. When her father died, her mother moved away. Then Ocean met Stan. Worst match possible, but I had this feeling she just married him because she wanted a husband, wanted some stability."

"Why would her mother leave her and move away?"

"The two were never close, mother and daughter."

"What about Ronny Joe? Could she be with him?" Is that where Ronny Joe was now? Had he gone back and gotten Ocean? Kidnapped her for some reason?

"Stan's brother? He was always crazy about her, gaga-eyed over her, but she couldn't stand him. She'd never go off with him in two million thousand years." She paused. "It's so unlike Ocean to go away without leaving an email, voicemail, anything. She just doesn't do that. She's very conscientious. I think something's happened to her, and the police just think she's running away from more questions."

"Well, all I can say is if I hear from her, you'll be the first to know. But I don't think I'm on her Favorite People list. When she found out Ferd was my uncle, she practically booted me out of her house. I haven't seen that kind of anger in a long time."

Marie said, "I've never known Ocean to raise her voice. Losing her father was a real blow to her. It changed her."

"How long ago did he die?"

"About four years."

"That's a long time to mourn for a parent."

"I guess."

"Well, Marie, all I can say is if I hear from her, I'll call you right away."

I stood beside my window looking out to a bay that was darkening. Knife blades of black cut through the light. I closed my eyes briefly and took a sip of my wine.

I sat on my couch and Rusty came and sat beside me. I heard meowing from behind my bedroom door and remembered Bear. I guess there was no time like the present to introduce the animals to each other. Bear got her back up, while Rusty just sniffed at his new housemate. But since no fur was flying, I decided that maybe they would, in time, become friends.

"Well, Uncle Ferd," I whispered, "even if the note wasn't for me, I'll take care of both your boat and your cat for as long as you're away."

****

I'd just gotten through my second cup of coffee the following morning when Joan called. "Art told me something. He said you should maybe talk to Dot."

CHAPTER 25

"**D**ot? Why does he think I should talk to Dot?" I put my coffee cup on my kitchen counter.

"She and Ella were friends. They sailed together."

"What?" I went into the living room. "Are you serious?"

Bear had jumped up high onto the top of my bookshelf and was hissing down at Rusty, who was whimpering up at her. I took my coffee cup out onto my front porch and stared down at the water in the early morning light. "Are you sure you have the information right? You're talking about Dot? Dot from Dot and Isabelle? My *neighbor* Dot?"

"Yes."

"My neighbor Dot isn't a sailor."

"I'm just telling you what Art said."

"Art knows her? He knows Dot?"

"He says he does. Not well, but he knows her."

"Joan, I've known Dot and Isabelle ever since Jesse and I moved in here. If she was a sailor, she would have told me. She's never mentioned anything about sailing. Or knowing Art. Or my uncle."

"All I'm doing is telling you what Art told me. He said to me, 'Get her to go and talk to Dot.'"

Through my big front window, the sun was glinting through the trees.

Joan went on, "Here's what Art said to me, and I'm quoting, 'Ask her to find out if there was more between them.'"

"Between who?"

"Between Dot and your uncle."

"What!"

"That's what Art said."

"Dot and my uncle? Like a relationship? Is that what you're saying?"

"I'm just telling you what Art told me."

"My mind is totally blown." I left my animals to their own devices. I sat down on the wooden chair on my porch. Next door, the summer children were already running down to the water's edge. One house over, Dot and Isabelle were on their front porch, coffees in hand, surrounded by all their flowers and gardens.

Flowers and gardens.

Did Ferd's garden books have something to do with Dot's flowers?

"Do you want to know the rest of the story?" Joan said.

"Do tell."

"Art says that Dot and Ella were friends, and it was through Dot that Ella and Ferd met. Your uncle left Dot and went off to be with Ella. Ella and her husband had been married close to ten years before she left him for Ferd. Art says it caused quite a stir. This was almost thirty years ago. Believe it or not, Art suggested that Ferd might even now be over at Dot and Isabelle's — that maybe he's hiding out there."

I simply could not move. I did not know what to make of any of this. I said, "Okay. I'm going to go over there right now, see if what you're saying is true. Joan, how could I not know this?"

"You were just a girl. I was younger, too. And I didn't know any of it until just now."

My *neighbor* Dot? One half of the bickering sisters? In the years I've lived here, Dot never said she knew my uncle. Not once. And nothing about sailing. Not ever. All the times I'd said to her, "Dot, you should come out sailing with me. You'd probably like it." What she would say is, "Oh, no, not me. I'd fall over backwards into the water. No, I'm better up here on my porch just admiring you."

How could I simply not know this?

I went inside and got Rusty. I scuffed on my flip-flops, and the two of us took off over to Dot and Isabelle's.

Dot's first words to me when I walked up on their porch were, "Where's your uncle? What's his boat doing down there?"

Isabelle asked, "Is he visiting with you, Em? Staying with you?"

"That's my question for you guys — is Ferd here?"

For a moment, Dot seemed unable to say anything. Her mouth worked, but no words came out. It was like she was staring at some long forgotten memory. Isabelle finally said, "What are you talking about, dear?"

I repeated my question. "Ferd's missing. The police are looking for him. I was told he might be here. At your house. Hiding out."

"Told by who, dear?" Isabelle's voice was as pleasant as ever, yet there was terseness behind her words.

"Joan's husband, Art," I retorted.

Isabelle's mouth hardened further. "That is absolutely ridiculous."

I stared at her. Isabelle was always the soft one, the nice sister while Dot was the eccentric one, the "say whatever's on my mind" one. Today I saw a different side of Isabelle.

"Why would he be here?" Isabelle asked attempting to change her expression from harsh to sweet. "Why would you ask such a question of us?"

"He's missing. Missing and feared dead," I said. "Maybe even dementia. He's wanted in connection with a murder," I added. "Another theory is that he's committed suicide."

"No!" Dot looked down at her tightly clasped hands, and suddenly, I knew every word Joan and Art had said was true.

I leaned against the porch railing. "My uncle is missing. Someone was killed. You guys need to tell me about Ferd. And about Ella. I need to know all of this. I know some things, but I don't know whether I should believe the gossip."

Dot was still as stone. I had always thought the sisters knew about my uncle from his brief visits with me and Jesse, and from my characterizations of him. "I have this crazy uncle who lives on a boat," I would say. "He's such a sweet old guy." Why had they never told me they knew him? Never. Not once. Not even a hint.

I stood on their porch in amongst the hanging baskets of pansies and petunias, the planters of lavender and cosmos and marigolds and blue zinnias. I told them what happened—from finding Ferd's boat off Miami, with the crazy conspiracy guy, to finding out Ferd was wanted for questioning in connection with some murder that occurred in Mount Joy, Pennsylvania.

At the mention of Pennsylvania, Isabelle started coughing and got up and went inside.

"What?" I called to her. "What do you know about Mount Joy?"

"Nothing." Isabelle put a hand to her neck. "Just a tickle in my throat."

"I don't believe you." I got up, made to go inside, but Dot touched me. "Don't."

"Why not?"

"This is a sore subject with her."

"Why is it a sore subject with her? Dot, you know Ella. You and your sister both know her. Who is she? Art said you knew Ferd from a long time ago. And that you and Ella used to sail together. And that you and Art were maybe more than friends a long time ago."

Isabelle came back, wiping her hands on a dishtowel. "Dot," she cautioned, "we don't need to dredge up ancient history. No one needs to go through all that again. You, least of all."

Dot leaned forward, sighed, and placed both palms of her big, strong hands on the knees of her wide red pants. With her green plastic clogs, she looked like a scowling Christmas elf sitting there.

Isabelle continued fiddling with the dishtowel, white with embroidered pink edges. "I'm going in to make more coffee. Em will want coffee. Right, Em?"

"Yeah." Dot's tone was cold. "You go and make your

bloody coffee. That's what you always do, isn't it? When life gets too much, you go in and make coffee."

I heard a small whimper out of Isabelle, and I said, "Dot?"

Lots of people would be uncomfortable with the amount these sisters bickered, but underneath it all, there was a layer of respect and love. They were sisters, after all. Their bickering had always seemed over inconsequential things— the right recipe for tuna casserole, the right sherry, how strong the coffee was or wasn't, or which type of flowers would look best in the hanging baskets for the summer. This time, things seemed different.

"Dot?" I said when Isabelle left. "What's going on here? Did you and my uncle know each other?"

"A long time ago, I may have. Yes. I may have."

"You may have."

She shrugged, but there was something taut and rigid about her.

"I didn't mean to start anything between you and Isabelle," I said quietly. "I don't know, and I don't mean to pry. I'm just worried about my Uncle Ferd, is all. Do you have any idea where he might be? The police think he's dead, maybe killed himself. I don't know what to think."

She looked away from me when she said, "That moronic Art should have kept his frigging mouth shut."

"Nevertheless, he didn't," I said.

Dot said, "Ferd can take care of himself."

I decided to try something else. "Tell me about Ella."

"What do you want to know?"

"Who was she?"

She looked at me. "There's a whole lot of polluted water under that particular bridge, Em." She leaned her head back and laughed at her own analogy.

"I thought you lived on this island your whole life."

"Ah, Em, you don't know everything. And how would it come up in casual conversation? Oh, by the way, you know your uncle who you never see or hear from? Well, he and I were lovers once. Bloody hell."

"Dot!" Isabelle had returned to the porch. "Watch your language."

Dot stared hard at her, and I found it difficult to stifle a smile.

"There's a lot about your uncle you don't know," Isabelle said turning to me.

"Apparently." I directed my remarks to Dot. My mother had told me this. So had Joan. "You and this Ella person were friends once?"

"Friends?" Dot said derisively. "Is that what you call it?"

"I don't know what to call it," I said.

"And you think your uncle is here?"

"I don't know what to think."

"Go ahead." Dot opened up her hand in a gesture of welcome. "Be my guest. Go ahead. Look through the house. Ferd isn't here."

"You going to go and see Ella?" Isabelle asked.

"Well, since I have no idea where she lives or who she is, no, I won't be visiting her." I asked, "Do either of you know where she lives?"

Isabelle stood behind the wooden chair and placed her hands on the back of it. "Dot, Em's only concerned for family. He's her family. She doesn't care about what went on that long time ago. And if we know where Ferd is, we have to tell her."

I looked expectantly at the sisters.

Isabelle said, "If we know, we have to say. The address, it might be in with the photo album. And the letter. Dot, did we ever have the address?"

Dot stood. "Isabelle, don't show her the photo album. Not now, not ever." Dot got up, and walked down the stairs toward the water. "As far as I'm concerned, you can burn that damn album," she called back. "I don't know why the hell you've kept it all these years. As for the letter, that's long gone."

"Dot!" Isabelle called. "Language!"

Dot made a dismissive gesture with her hand and kept on

walking down toward the bay.

"I'm sorry," I said quietly. "I didn't mean to dig anything up. I didn't mean to stir up any old stuff. I should go. This was a mistake..."

Isabelle put her fingers on my shoulder. "She's had a bit of a bad time of it. Ever since she saw his boat down there earlier. She thought he'd come back. For her."

"For her?"

"She lives in hope."

****

On the way back to my house, I looked down at Dot. She was sitting on a rock overlooking Ferd's boat and running a blade of grass through her arthritic fingers.

Later that afternoon, I decided to take *Wandering Soul* out to the mooring. I was pulling in the aft line on *Wandering Soul* when I heard Dot call my name. I looked back to see her hand raised. I waited and she came down to the dock. She said, "I think I may know something about Pennsylvania."

CHAPTER 26

The scowl was gone. She looked earnest, even fearful. "I didn't want to mention it in front of my sister. This whole thing is a sore spot with Isabelle."

"Yeah?" I climbed aboard *Wandering Soul.*

"She wants to protect me. Always has. It's an older sister thing. I was the younger one, the wild one. Are you, um, are you taking the boat, Ferd's boat, out for a sail?"

"Nope. Just to the mooring."

"Would you mind if...if I came along?"

"I'm just going out to the mooring. Not that far."

"Still, I'd like to come." She wiped her mouth with her hand. "If it's all right, that is."

"Hop in, then."

She pulled in the aft line and climbed aboard like a pro. "I saw his boat when he was here for Jesse's funeral, but I didn't go inside it then. It's been years." She stood in the cockpit with a kind of awe. "Years," she said again.

"Dot, I didn't know you sailed. Why didn't you ever tell me?"

"There's a lot you don't know about me."

"So I'm learning."

I tied the line from the inflatable I'd bought in Miami to the stern cleat and turned on the engine. Dot climbed up onto the bow. I stepped back onto the deck and threw her the bowline. She caught it and coiled it like an expert. All I could do was shake my head at the whole thing.

"Like riding a bicycle. You never forget." She climbed back into the cockpit.

"All these years I've lived here. We could have gone

sailing, you and me."

"I thought it might be too painful. Even after all this time."

The ride out to the mooring took mere minutes, and in an instant, Dot, up on the bow, fetched the mooring pendant with the boathook. She called back to me, "You want two lines on this?"

"I don't have any more spliced. I'll add a second later. Weather's pretty calm. One should hold until I can get out here again."

"I don't mind helping with this boat. If there's anything you need..." She looked at me expectantly. She held onto the front shroud, her arms leathery from so much sun. I looked at her, and for the first time, I saw a sailor's strong body and not a single woman on the far side of middle age who puttered in a garden.

"Well, I don't know," I said. "Sure. We could even sail together if you wanted. I have no idea what I'm going to do with the boat anyway."

I sat down in the cockpit and said, "You said you know something about Pennsylvania. You wanted to talk to me about it?"

She came and sat across from me, looked down at her green rubber gardening shoes. "Mount Joy. It's where Ella and her husband moved after she went back to him. After Ferd."

I was silent for a moment trying to figure out what this meant. "So Ferd may have gone to see her there?"

"She doesn't live there anymore. Not since Samson died. Her husband. He was a university professor."

"You kept tabs."

She looked away. She pulled out a folded piece of paper from her pocket and handed it to me. "This is for you. You can do with it whatever you want."

I opened it up and looked down at it. It was an address for a place in Concord, New Hampshire.

"Ella moved there after her husband died."

"You really did keep tabs."

She gave me a bit of a half-smile, and I remembered back to when Jesse died more than two years ago. Ferd came and tied *Wandering Soul* out on this mooring and stayed a month. In my stupor, in my pain, I would walk down by the water, and when I looked up at Dot's and Isabelle's house, there would be Ferd and Dot sitting together up on their porch, side by side, talking. At the time, I thought the sisters were just being nice, showing hospitality to my eccentric uncle who'd come all this way.

She said, "My niece, Isabelle's daughter, helped me find where she'd moved to. She's a whiz with the computer. But she is sworn to secrecy not to tell her mother that I was looking for Ella."

"Why did you want to know where she was?"

She shrugged, drummed her fingers on one knee. "I can't explain it. It's just something I needed to know. Maybe there would be a time when...I don't know."

"When what?" When Ferd would go back to her?

"When we could be friends again."

I regarded her for a moment. "Isabelle mentioned a photo album and some letter." I asked, "What's that all about?"

Dot sighed. "There was a letter. I threw it out. I don't really know what photo album Isabelle is talking about. If it's the one I'm thinking of it's basically pictures of me and Ferd and Ella and Samson. Of Ella and Samson's wedding. Trips we'd taken, sailing trips, that sort of thing. Things I did not want to see. My sister, she was there for all the fallout. She was there when Ella, pretty, little, much younger than me, Ella stole Ferd away. She was there when Ella went back to Samson. She was there when I went chasing after Ferd. Not—I may add—one of my finer moments. She begged me not to go after him, but I was sure he still loved me, that Ella meant nothing to him. She was so young. I was sure he would prefer someone more mature, more his age. But, of course," she paused, "that didn't work out. We were together maybe a month after that, and then he dropped me like a ton of cement blocks into the ocean."

I kept staring at her. "I'm just amazed that I never knew this, never even had any inkling. Ferd didn't tell me. All the time I'm living here with Jesse and my uncle never told me."

She smiled when she said, "There was a time that had your uncle asked me to go off with him, I would have gone anywhere. I would have just up and left. I would have traveled the globe. I didn't care." She looked away from me. "But love is an elusive thing."

Wandering Soul was moving gently on the mooring. The wind had moved the boat in such a fashion that from where we were seated, we could see the houses along the shoreline. The children from the summer house were down on the one sandy spot with shovels and buckets, wading in the water with bright plastic sandals.

"I had no idea," I said.

"You weren't meant to."

"Tell me about Ella... if it's not too painful."

"You mean my friend Ella? She was a lot younger than me, maybe ten years younger. Our families knew each other. I used to babysit for her, if you can fathom such a thing. But even though there was such a vast difference in our ages, she looked up to me. She wanted to learn how to sail, so I took her. I taught her everything. I think I was like the older sister she never had, her mentor. I was even maid of honor in her wedding. Did you know that? Maid of honor. Honor. What does that word even mean, honor?"

I waited.

She picked a spot of gardening dirt off her pants. She looked down through the companionway and into the cabin of the boat and motioned with her hand. "Can I go down below? Would that be all right?"

"Sure."

I followed her. "It's a bit of a mess right now," I said. "We just got back from a long trip."

There looked to be tears in her eyes as she slowly walked around the cabin touching things—the teak bulkhead, the oil lamp that hung on the wall, the ship's clock, the brass barometer, the galley stove, the gardening books. She stood for a long time in front of the gardening books.

"These are new," she said.

"I suppose."

"He didn't have these when I was with him."

"I suppose not."

"I love gardening, you know."

I said, "Maybe these books are in your honor then." I wondered if this was a lie. Joan had said the one thing Ella missed was her garden.

She looked pleased suddenly. "Do you think?"

I shrugged.

It was a while before she said, "No, that was another thing she stole from me."

"What's that?"

"Gardening. I taught Ella everything she knew about that particular subject, too."

"I'm so sorry," I said.

But she was still standing there, touching this, touching that. "It is so like how I remember it. This boat. This galley. He made so many meals here. I cooked, too. Fish. He caught fish. Or we would buy lobsters from the boats. We used to laugh. Oh, how we laughed. Your uncle was so funny. We would sit right there—" she pointed, "and go through an entire bottle of red wine in an evening, the two of us..." Her voice trailed off.

I waited.

"There was a time," she went on, "there was a short bit in all of the time we were together that I knew he loved me. Just for a while. It didn't last. It was maybe all of a couple of weeks." She paused. "But we had it. For that short time, we had it. I've thought about this through the years. Maybe he decided that he wanted to try to love me. It worked for a while. A matter of weeks. But then he came to realize that you can't make a person love you, no matter how you try. It just won't happen. And he didn't love me."

She hastily wiped her eyes with her fingers. "Em, I want

you to promise that under no circumstances will you tell Isabelle one word of what I'm telling you here. Not that I'm standing here blubbering like an old fool. Not that I'm even here on the boat. She's gone to town. She doesn't know I'm out here. Remember when Jesse died and Ferd was here? He and I talked for a long time then, and Isabelle was totally against that. She thought I was in for a world of hurt again. But even after so many years, he was still in love with Ella."

"I would never share your secrets."

She went on, "I've built up a persona for myself all these years. I never married. I still am the family 'wild child' in lots of ways. That's what my family thinks, and you never live that down. I've had my share of lovers, but I never married. Do you want to know why?"

Not knowing quite what else to do, I nodded.

"It's your damn uncle's fault. He ruined me for anyone else. You want to hear the whole story?"

"If you want to share it," I said.

Dot and Ella's family were friends, she told me. The families grew up side by side in a small coastal town in northern Maine. "I had four older sisters of my own, but she became like a younger sister. Following me around, following in my footsteps, but I didn't mind it. I was kind of flattered by it, if you want to know."

Because they lived on the water, the girls took to sailing. Dot had a small sailing dinghy and taught her young charge how to sail. Samson was another family friend. One big happy family. She laughed aloud when she said that.

The families knew each other, and Samson had been Ella's on-again-off-again boyfriend all through high school. "She would tell me that she liked him a lot, a very lot, but didn't know what love was. She kept asking me for my advice, being her 'older sister' and all. She kept wondering if what she felt for Samson was love. She would ask me, 'Should I marry him? Is this what love is?'"

Dot couldn't advise. Dot thought Samson was a sweet man and that Ella was lucky...if what she felt was love. Even on the day of her wedding, Ella had said, "I think I should call it off."

But no one did anything that scandalous in those days. Although what Ella did later would be far more scandalous than merely calling off a wedding.

An entire decade after Ella and Samson were married, Dot finally met someone—Ferd. They met in a café where Dot tended tables. "He was sweet."

She told me that they got talking. He'd just come up from Boston on his boat. "And the next thing I know, we're sailing together on his new boat. This boat." She slapped the seat beside her with a hand. "And I'm rapidly falling in love. Of course, I was dying for my friends Ella and Samson to meet him. I think I had a bit of jealousy for Ella. She was younger and pretty, and basically seemed to get everything she wanted. I had never met anyone quite like Ferd Hanson. He was strong, worldly wise, and oh, so good looking." She turned to me. "Your uncle was a looker. Still is, for that matter."

"And you were close with Ella and Samson?"

She nodded. "I introduced him to Ella and Samson. We all went sailing. We four were good buddies. Oh, we were such good buddies. I thought everything was just about perfect. And then the next thing I know, Ella has left Samson without a how-do-you-do and he's heartbroken. And off she goes with my boyfriend down to the Caribbean on *Wandering Soul.* And I was heartbroken."

"How long were they together?"

"Almost two years. She broke his heart when she went back to her husband. And Samson, dear sweet Samson, he took her right back. Ella left three heartbroken people in her wake."

"And you haven't seen her since."

Dot said no.

"And yet you've kept tabs."

"Right. She and Samson had a child after that. So I guess they were cemented together then. There are times I want to forgive her, and there are times when I never want to see her again for as long as I live."

After Ella left Ferd, Dot went running back to him. Dot could never measure up to Ella, however. The two were together for just a few months "before Ferd sailed off into the sunset without telling me where he was going. I think I need to leave this boat now." She stood up on shaky legs.

"I'll row you to shore. Let me just lock up."

In the dinghy on the way in, she said, "And despite how much scum water is under that particular bridge, despite how he treated me, I'm worried about him. Same as you."

"Everyone says he can take care of himself. My mother says that. Joan does, and Art, too. But I'm not so sure anymore. Do you think he's with Ella now? Could that be it?"

Dot sighed. "Em, you have the address now. Do with it what you want. I don't even want to know. I just want Ferd to be safe."

CHAPTER 27

Back at the house, I flattened out the piece of paper Dot had given me and looked up the address online. I easily found it. I even tried a "street view" and was rewarded with a house that was so surrounded by lush and pretty gardens that it looked like something on the front cover of an English country cottage magazine. It was the type of house where you would be served afternoon tea and scones on wrought iron tables set out on the newly mown grass. I looked at it from all the directions and aspects that the computer feed would allow. Ella's house? The house of my uncle's lover?

I mapped it online and saw that it would take around two hours to drive there. I tried to find a phone number, or the name of the person who lived at that address, but came up with nothing. I knew there was a way to learn these things online—some database somewhere—but I didn't know where that was. I could have asked Ben, but I was quite sure if he knew I was planning to take yet another wild goose chase road trip, he would try to dissuade me.

Heck, was I actually thinking of driving there? Yes. Was I just going to walk up to that flower covered house and ask if my uncle happened to be there? Yes. I'd check the tide and leave tomorrow, first thing. If all went well, I could be there and back in one day. At most, two, but I was sure I could easily find a motel. Should I call this Ella person first? No, I wanted the element of surprise on my side. What if I drove up to her house and she wasn't even there? What if she was on vacation? No, I still wouldn't call her. I had to take my chances. If she wasn't there, she wasn't there.

I hiked on over to EJ's, and when I told him I had some

business in New Hampshire, which may take me a day or two, he offered to look after not only Rusty but Bear as well, despite my protests that I could take Bear with me.

EJ was wearing a set of old-fashioned heavy-duty looking headphones around his neck. I figured he'd been hailing people on his Ham Radio. Behind him, a gigantic stockpot was bubbling away on his stove.

"I remember your uncle. Why do you have his cat, may I ask?"

It dawned on me that EJ had no idea what was going on, so I filled him in on everything, beginning with finding my uncle's abandoned boat floating off of Florida. I also told him about the accusations against my uncle, the money, and the man who'd been chasing me. I also told him about Ella and Mount Joy.

I thought of something. "EJ, you didn't know my Uncle Ferd, did you? It seems like everyone around here knows him and his life except for me."

EJ said no. "I met him at Jesse's funeral, but I think that might be all. He struck me as a nice man. Knowledgeable in the ways of the sea."

"Just one other question. You haven't noticed anyone here have you? Like at my place when I was gone? Looking for me, maybe? The police think he may be suffering from some sort of dementia, and I wondered if maybe he was confused and showed up here looking for me or something."

"Can't say I've seen anyone. No one at all. Wait a minute —" He went to his fridge and got out a plate. "I barbecued a couple of chickens here the other day. I would love your opinion of this new recipe."

"Thanks, EJ." I took the proffered plate. "Smells delish."

"Sad when old people get dementia," he said.

"Sad, yes," I said to EJ, who had a good fifteen years or more on my uncle, but was still sharp.

At home, I realized I was hungry, and my two animals and I ate part of the chicken. I needed some cat food for Bear. I was pretty much out of the stash of kibble I'd taken from the boat. I found a couple of cans of tuna in my cupboard and gave her half of one. Tomorrow, on my way home, I'd stop in and buy some proper cat food for her. For now, EJ's barbecued chicken and tuna would have to suffice.

I spent the rest of my day out on *Wandering Soul*, cleaning up and sorting through things. It was blisteringly hot on the boat, and I must have gone through gallons of drinking water as I worked. I was still looking for that money. Of course I didn't find it. If this truly was my boat now, at some point, I'd take down all of the gardening books and replace them with my own. But for now, it seemed sacrilegious to do so. I left them, but first, I went through them one by one—looking for what? Some clue that these belonged to Ella? Some clue as to where Ferd was? None of them had names in them. None of them whispered the answers I wanted to hear.

In the evening, I thought about calling Ben and asking his advice, or even telling him where I was going. I decided against it. For now. I remembered again the returned envelope I had seen at his house. He was probably sitting there and dealing with his own garbage about now. Maybe he didn't need me calling him. I opened my laptop and was about to go into the Montana news story about him again. My fingers were on the keyboard. Maybe there'd been some new developments I should know about.

No. That was his story. He would tell it to me if and when he was ready to. I clicked away from those links.

Ella was married when she took up with Ferd. That was the problem. That was the scandal. Those were far different times, I argued to myself. People were more scandalized by everything back then. This wasn't the same, was it? Yes, Ben was married, but he was obviously separated. Especially, if he asked me out those two times in a row a year ago. What was that all about? Plus, he even had a son. Somewhere, there was a son.

It was overcast the following morning when I dropped my animals off at EJ's and drove across the tidal road and down I-95 toward Concord. I hooked my iPhone to my car and listened to music. I hit the 101 just after Portsmouth. I kept seeing Ella's face. She was a beautiful woman back then, tall, and lithe with a generous mouth and high cheekbones. When I was a girl, I had been drawn to her. Back then, I had this idea she would be friendly and fun. I wonder what she would look like now.

If I was able to even find her. What kind of fool drives two hours to see someone who might not even be there? But maybe she would be. Maybe my uncle was there, too. Then what? I would cross that bridge when I came to it — the bridge which spanned all that dark and dirty water.

Before noon my phone GPS led me right to the address. I recognized the place from the street view. The house itself was a one-story home with a screened-in front porch and many windows. I had never seen such big window boxes. The color of the petunias underneath them was such a deep velvet that I immediately wanted to walk up and run my hands over the petals. Hanging baskets of tangles of colors were everywhere. A white wooden archway, covered with vines, opened up to a flagstone path which led to the front door. I got out of my car and stood under the archway and knew instantly why my uncle collected gardening magazines and books. This place was a treasure. The houses on either side, with their manicured, mowed lawns and rectangular gardens along the front, looked squat and ordinary compared to this place. A child would love this house. A child would call this a fairy house.

The sky above was clear and blue, making the gardens look even more resplendent. Even though it was early fall, the place did not have that late summer, overgrown look that gardens sometimes get, as if their tenders have, by now, grown tired of the daily ordeal of weeding and keeping things in order. I walked up the path, marveling that even here tiny flowers grew between the stones. I knocked on the front door. No response. I tried to peer through sheer curtains on each side of the door, but the sun was too bright. For a moment, I thought I saw a blitz of movement inside, but when no one answered again, I figured it was a trick of light.

I backed down from the porch and saw that a side path led around to the back of the house. I took it, again in awe of the multitude of flowers. The house had a basement with small windows and window wells. I bent down. Perhaps there was something to see inside, but the windows were covered in a chintz cloth. At the rear of the cottage, I made my way up the back steps to a screened-in porch. I tried the door. Unlocked. On the porch, were two white wicker chairs in a comfortable seating arrangement with throw blankets laid across them. Between them was a cedar table with a couple of magazines. Gardening magazines I noted. I knocked on the door. Again, no answer.

I went back down the steps. The yard, which was small, but well-kept, housed a shed and a tiny greenhouse. The door of the shed hung open and I went to it. Perhaps she was in there gathering her garden tools together. I stood in the doorway. It was the cleanest, most organized shed I'd ever seen. On two walls, floor to ceiling wooden shelves contained baskets and containers, fertilizers and seeds, and pots of all sizes as well as a collection of garden decorations — gnomes and turtles and big ceramic colorful mushrooms. I never knew there were so many shapes and sizes of trowels. Everything was labeled. The other two walls held longer implements, rakes, shovels, edgers, and hoes, all hooked up to the wall. It was the kind of place that made me want to go home and immediately start organizing. I ventured inside but saw no evidence that anyone was camping out here.

Back outside, I walked over to the tiny greenhouse. Since I could see into it, I noted it had the same level of cleanliness and organization as the shed. Shelves of small starter planters were there, plus some pots of flowers and veggies in raised beds on the counters.

I went back to the rear door and knocked again. Still nothing. I decided to leave a note and shuffled around in my bag for some sort of piece of paper. If I were as organized as Ella was, I would have brought along a pad of paper for such eventualities.

I started a note on the back of a grocery receipt when I heard, "You looking for Ella?"

To my right and over the ivy-covered fence, a large woman, a pink plastic visor atop her head, and wearing a blousy, flowered muumuu, was holding a trowel.

"Yes," I said making my way down the steps and toward the fence. "Do you happen to know where she might be?"

"She'd be at the church."

I looked at her. "The church?"

The women nodded. "She's there most days." She had a fleshy face with big, bright red lips.

"Can you tell me which church?"

When she told me, I wrote it on the paper.

"Not far," the woman said. "Just up the road a bit."

"Thank you." ◆

She looked at me curiously. "If you don't find her, who should I tell her came by?"

I hesitated. "Ferd's niece."

"Ferd's niece." She repeated the words.

"Yes."

"Okay, I'll tell her Ferd's niece."

"Thanks, and you can tell her I'm looking for Ferd."

"Ferd?"

"Her friend, Ferd."

"Okay. Ferd." She came and touched the ivy on the fence that separated the properties. Her fingernails were the same color as her lips and she wore lots of rings, at least one on each finger.

"Do you know Ella very well?" I asked.

"No one does."

"Can I ask you something? I'm wondering if you've seen anyone around here. He would be an older man. Gray hair. Little taller than me. My Uncle Ferd. He might be here."

"Haven't seen anyone by that description around here. She doesn't get too many people dropping by."

"Oh, yeah?"

"Kind of keeps to herself. You a friend of hers?"

"I've never met her. She's a good friend of my uncle's. So, she doesn't have a lot of friends dropping by? No family?"

The woman shook her head. "None that I've ever seen. She's kind of a loner."

"Looks like she spends a lot of her time in her garden."

"Yeah, all of her time."

"It's beautiful."

"Puts the rest of us to shame. Kind of a sad thing, she is. Or at least that's what we in the neighborhood think. Won't come to neighborhood potlucks, that sort of thing."

I asked, "Do you know why she would be so sad?"

"Husband died. That's what she told me. When he died, she moved here. Don't ask me why, though. She doesn't have any people here. You ask me, it's because she's wanting to keep herself to herself. If you want to do that, what better way than to move into a town where no one knows you?"

Unless you're running from something, I thought, but didn't say it. "Guess that's true." I wanted to get more out of her, but she was already backing away.

"Well, I hope you find her."

"Thanks."

****

A church? What would she be doing at a church? A few moments later, I had my answer. For several minutes, I sat in my car admiring the church grounds with awe. It was like her house, only more so. The stone church was an old one, probably a heritage building, and the grounds around the steepled structure were completely decorated with flowers, shrubs, arbors, paths, fountains, cement benches, pots of flowers, and more pots of flowers.

I got out of my car and walked completely around the building. The church itself was a marvel. Entirely made of stone, its many stained glass windows reflected the sun on this bright day. I knew it would be glistening and lovely inside. I got out my phone and took several pictures. The place was alive with color and fragrance and sound—bird songs and the whirring of insects. All the way around the church, in and out of the pathways, and I didn't see Ella. I saw no one, in fact.

Back at the front door of the church, I took hold of the brass knob and pulled the heavy door, expecting it to be solidly locked. It wasn't. It opened soundlessly in my hand. Quietly, I stepped inside. It was cool and dark in there, and my rubber-bottomed sandals made no sound on the wooden floor. It was as I expected, dim save for shards of bright sun shimmering through the patterned glass. I didn't see anyone. Didn't call out. To make any noise in this place would be to ruin the stillness. It would be irreverent. Ornate wooden tables in the foyer were stacked with pamphlets and papers, church bulletins and the like. I saw a poster about collecting blankets for the homeless and one advertising a mission trip somewhere overseas for teens. I touched nothing.

When my eyes adjusted, I moved forward toward the sanctuary and stood at the back. It had been a long time, a very long time since I'd been inside any kind of a church. I half expected some vicar to breeze out of the front and walk down in full robes to give me a hearty country smile and handshake. But I continued to be alone.

The sanctuary was every bit as beautiful as the outside—all dark wood and smelling like the finest old boat. Hard, narrow wooden pews faced forward to an altar area with throne-like chairs and behind it, a huge organ with pipes that reached to the ceiling. Wood and light. The place was wood and light.

It was then that I saw her. Halfway up on the right sat a woman, her head bowed, brown hair, flecked with gray and pulled into a knot at the nape of her neck.

Slowly, quietly, I made my way down the aisle. A few rows away from her, it occurred to me that coming upon her so suddenly might startle her unnecessarily. I forced myself to make a noise as I walked, coughing slightly, adding a bit of a heavier step.

She wore large sunglasses, even in the dimness of the church. When she turned to look at me, I could see her cheeks were wet. She had been crying?

"Oh!" she said when she saw me. "I thought you were the pastor."

"Sorry. I'm not."

I recognized this woman immediately. I saw in this woman the same young woman who came bounding off my uncle's boat laughing, one hand on her huge orange hat. She took her sunglasses off and wiped her cheeks with a handkerchief. "I cannot come in these church doors, into any church without crying. I never have. Can you? Churches do that to me. All churches do. It's so beautiful in here."

"It is," I said looking around me at the dark wood, the stained glass, the ornate designs. "It's a beautiful place. The outside gardens are beautiful, too."

"I only come in here when no one is here. I can't come through these doors when services are on," she said.

"You have a real gift. Gardening."

When she stared up at me, it was as if I had seen her face before. In a dream, maybe. A cloud must have covered the sun, because suddenly, the sanctuary was bathed in gloom.

I asked, "Are you Ella?"

She nodded. I could see that her fingernails were garden-dirty on her plain hands. "And you're her. I wondered how long it would be before you came. The niece."

I had no idea what to say to this. I had so many questions. I kept thinking of Dot's assessment of this woman.

I swallowed. "He's missing."

"I know."

"You know?"

She drew in a breath. "I read the papers. I know."

How did she know this? "It was in the papers?"

She nodded.

It was in the papers? I had Googled just about every article out there and hadn't found my uncle's name. I was about to ask what article when she said, "Emmeline."

"Me," I said.

"I remember you. A bit. From that time. When you were a girl. On the dock. That time."

I looked at her. "I saw you two years after that, too. On the back of a trawler. With my uncle then, too."

Her lips became a thin line. "That meeting. It didn't end well." She took off her sunglasses and paused before continuing. "Your uncle spoke of you constantly. You were his favorite. He was so proud of you."

"He taught me a lot," I said. "Everything I know about sailing. And a lot I know about life." I moved to sit down in the pew in front of her and turned so that we faced each other. "Dot thought my uncle might be here. With you."

"Dot!" The name caught her off guard, and she clasped her hands together tightly in her lap.

"Dot lives two doors down from me," I said. I wanted to ask her so much. I was practically brimming with questions and with sentences I couldn't say. I pulled out the flowered card from my pocket and handed it to her.

She looked down to the card in her hands. She examined the front, the back, and read the inside message. From the front, I heard a sound like the cry of an animal. I looked ahead to the door of the vestry.

"The pastor," she said looking toward the front of the church. "He, um, he brings his cat with him sometimes."

"Oh." I handed her the inserted note. "This was in it."

"Where did you get all of this? Where was it? Did Dot have these things?"

"It was in Ferd's boat. The card looks recent. Is it from you? Are you 'E'?"

She didn't answer my question. Instead, she asked me, "What do you mean it was in Ferd's boat?"

"It was in the bookcase on *Wandering Soul*. At first, I thought it was addressed to me—that the E was for my name and that Uncle Ferd wanted me to take care of Bear, his cat. Or his boat. I have both his cat and his boat now."

She made a noise like a start. "I don't understand. He's not on his boat?" She seemed bewildered.

"I have his boat."

"And Bear? You have Bear?" She stared at me for several seconds. "I know Ferd was missing, but I thought—" Her lips moved and she scratched a place on her neck. "I thought he'd taken off. On his boat. Where did you get his boat?"

"I found it floating in the Bermuda Triangle. Abandoned."

"What?" She leaned toward me and in her lap she fiddled with the arms of her sunglasses. "What do you mean?"

I told her the entire story. Why not? I began with the crazy Dr. Papa and told her about finding the boat abandoned and the table set for two. I told her about finding the note and taking the boat home. I told her about Ferd's murder charge, and when I mentioned Mount Joy, she visibly bristled. I stopped and asked her, "What about Mount Joy?"

"I have no idea why he would go there."

"You lived there," I said. "That would be a pretty good reason, I should think. Maybe he didn't know you'd moved."

"I have no one in that place anymore."

"I went there. To Mount Joy. No one knew where he was. I didn't find him there. There's also something about money. Do the names Stan Hollander or Simon Towers mean anything to you? The police are thinking that Ferd murdered both those men."

"Wait." She put up a hand. "Ferd did this? He killed people? Why? And now he's gone?"

"That's what they're saying."

She looked down at her hands in her lap and said quietly, "I don't know anything about that. I don't know where he would be. Believe me, I don't."

I picked up the card, put it in my bag, and said, "So, you've been in contact with him? This card and note were from you?"

"Before—before all of this. Yes. I sent him the card. I needed him to take care of…" She paused as if searching for words. "Of Bear. My cat. Yes. It was my cat. I named him Bear. In honor of—in honor of all the Bears that Ferd had. I had a friend drop her off with Ferd. That was the purpose of the note. I never saw him. I haven't seen him in years." During this whole speech, she hadn't looked at me once.

She relaxed her hands and ran them over the knees of her pants, which were dirty from kneeling in the dirt. I could sense that she wanted to talk, to tell me something, yet could not find the words.

I heard it again, the sound from the front of the church. We both looked up. She made to rise, "I should check on the cat. Sometimes he needs tending to. Mostly, he wanders around the gardens, but sometimes he gets in through a basement window. It always ends up being my responsibility."

She stood for several seconds before the noise abated and she sat back down again.

I nodded. The sanctuary brightened at once with a shaft of sunlight.

She paused before saying, "It was such a long time ago..." Her voice trailed off. "I haven't been on a boat, any boat, in a long, long time."

I waited. This woman was lying. I could tell from the way she wouldn't look at me square on, from the way she kept picking at her dirt-encrusted fingernails. Maybe she was hiding Ferd even now. Maybe my uncle, wanted for murder, had come running up here, knowing she would take him in and hide him for however long he needed. Maybe that was the sound we were hearing from the front.

As I sat there, I was beginning to put the pieces together. He knew I was going to be in the Bermuda Triangle. He knew what I was doing there. So he ditched his boat knowing we would find it. Maybe he was hoping it would get more press, get on TV. He had taken his dinghy, and ditched it on that island. How he got from the mangroves to the shore, I hadn't figured out. Maybe he'd towed a small boat behind him, a kayak or canoe, for instance. Had gotten to shore, gone over to Mount Joy to pick up the money that Simon or Stan owed him. Gambling debt? And then, when Stan was killed — no, I couldn't believe that he had killed him — he took off up here to hide out at Ella's. That's why she was acting so strangely. I thought about the shadows I'd seen through the windows of her house. Ferd was there. He had to be.

But she had seemed genuinely surprised when I'd told her I had sailed his boat up the coast. "What about the note?" I said. "The one folded inside?" I pulled it out. "Please don't try to find me? I had to leave?" I read it out loud. "I thought that had something to do with his leaving. But it was you, wasn't it? You wrote this when you left him. This note is close to thirty years old."

She nodded. "I took the chicken's way out. When I knew I had to leave, I simply wrote a note and walked away."

"He kept the note all these years." I looked square at her. "He's at your house, isn't he? He's there right now."

"Of course not." But did she say it too quickly?

"If I call the police, they will come and search your house because he's wanted for murder."

She reached forward and touched my hand. Her flesh felt cool, smooth. "He's not at my house. I wish to God he was. I wish to God I knew where he was. He wants nothing to do with me now. Some hurts are just too deep."

She leaned back and said, "Let me tell you something about my time with your uncle. We were together for seventeen months. It was the happiest time of my life. It was the saddest time of my life."

"Why the saddest?"

"I knew I had to eventually leave him and be with my husband. My husband deserved so much better than me. He was a very gentle person. A good, good person. But..."

"But what?"

"I never stopped loving your uncle. Not for one day."

****

Outside, the sun was receding, and the closer I got to the coast on my way home, the cloudier and foggier it became, and the murkier and grayer became my thoughts. I was still pondering that woman and why her gaze so pierced me. She seemed so intent. What did it mean? It was at this point, some forty miles from home, that I got a phone call. I let it go to voicemail. It was Ben.

"Em? Call me. It's urgent."

I pulled over and did just that.

"Em? It's about Norman Tomson or Dr. Papa Hoho. He's dead."

CHAPTER 28

"**D**r. Papa Hoho?" I held my cell phone tightly in my hand. "Norman? Are you kidding me, Ben? How — ?"

The phone reception screeched in and out, but I thought I heard the word "suicide."

"Suicide?" I remembered the loud buffoonish man who was all set to make his debut with his own online channel and his many, many online subscribers, and his crowdfunding site, and how well his online money-raising campaign was going, and how he was working on "changing his brand" and how he even had a whole bunch of fans supporting him. But, *Suicide*?

"Suicide?" I said again.

"Word was he was losing his TV show. He tell you anything about that?"

"He did, as a matter of fact, but I got the idea it wasn't a bad thing. He had cut his hair and had this whole new image thing going on. Ben, he seemed all right then, like he was really all right with everything. I never would have thought he would kill himself. Never in a million years."

"That sometimes happens with suicidal people. They clean themselves up. It's like they are preparing for it. I've seen it time and time again."

"How did he — um — do it?"

"Gunshot."

"Oh."

"Here's the odd thing. He died in Pennsylvania. Same town you and your uncle were in. Same town where those two men were murdered."

I felt a chill go through me. I turned off my car's AC. "He

was in Pennsylvania?"

"Yes."

"He wanted me to work with him. He came all the way up here to find me, to ask me. He also said he had some—some information for me about my uncle that he would give me if I helped him on his new TV project. I called him once and left a message. Ben? This is so sad. Do you think he was killed because of what he knew about my uncle?"

"What did he know about your uncle?"

"I never found out. He wouldn't tell me unless I joined his—whatever-you-call-it—street team."

The reception cut out for a moment as the sudden downpour increased. I watched a bicycler come peddling up the road in all the drench.

"Where are you, Em? Are you home? I hear rain."

"I'm on the I-95. I should be home in another couple of hours. I was over in New Hampshire."

"What were you doing there?"

"I was visiting Ella. Remember the woman that Joan told us about on the boat? The long ago friend of my uncle's? The woman with the letter 'E' name? I thought maybe Ferd was there—"

"Em!"

"I had to see if he was there."

"Was he?"

"No."

"I thought you said you'd given up on all of this."

"I guess not quite. Ben? Do you want me to stop in and see you before I head back home? I brought my laptop with me, and I'm sure I can show you Papa's online TV channel. He sent me the link to it, plus the link to his crowdfunding site."

"Message me the links, and I'll get them to Mount Joy. And coming by? I don't think that's necessary. It's pretty straightforward."

I turned on the windshield wipers.

"Okay then." *I don't think that's necessary.* So, he didn't care if I came by or not. Or was I reading way too much into this refusal? Quite possibly.

Just before we said goodbye, he said, "Em?"

"Yeah?"

"Just thought I'd tell you this one thing. I'm really glad I came along on the boat trip. It may have turned a corner with me as far as sailing is concerned. Anytime you need a sailing partner, let me know."

"Great."

On the way back to Portland, I listened to a lively political debate on the radio. Anything to get my mind off Papa and my uncle. And Ben. I passed that same poor cycler along the side of the highway who was peddling along. I tried to slow down, but I'm sure, when I passed him, he got even wetter.

My animals were happy to see me when I finally got home, and EJ, true to form, gave me another tinfoil wrapped plate to take home. I knew what it would contain, some form of meat, and some form of potatoes. EJ only eats meat and potatoes. He really and truly only eats meat and potatoes. I don't know how he survives, but he is nearly ninety and still going strong. I've long decided that he has a different constitution than the rest of us. I thanked him and left.

In my own home, I settled my animals in, poured myself a glass of wine, and opened up my laptop. There was an email from Marie at the café. Ocean was still missing. The police figured she was with Ronny Joe, a fact that Marie totally didn't believe since Ocean hated Ronny Joe with every fiber of her being. That's how Marie wrote it—every fiber of her being. She wrote, "If Ronny Joe kidnapped her, then she's probably okay. That's the part I keep thinking about. He would never hurt her."

I wrote back to her that I had no idea where she was.

Next, I went to Norman's website.

It wasn't there.

I manually typed it in.

Still not there.

I went back into my history and tried to log in that way and got the proverbial 404 Error. I tried his YouTube channel.

It, too, was down. Oh, the video was there, with his face, but when I clicked on the right facing arrow to watch it, the notice came across the screen that the video had been taken down. It didn't say why.

It was the same at his crowdfunding site. He was simply not there.

I googled Dr. Papa Hoho, and while Rusty and Bear and I picked at the tender and succulent slices of paper thin beef EJ had sliced for me, I found myself reading about the life of Norman Tomson, AKA Dr. Papa Hoho. What he'd told me was pretty much the truth. He was born into a family of entertainers. His parents performed a mentalism act at fairs and campgrounds. Never making it big, Norman, an only child, grew up in relative poverty. When he was ten, his mother was "abducted by aliens." She played that up big, self-published a book about it, and the whole thing became her "act." No wonder Papa chose the occupation he did. He had a gold mine of conspiracies to choose from.

It was after midnight when I finished my meal, poured myself a second glass of wine, and discovered in my spam folder an email that gave me instant pause. It was from Norman Tomson.

CHAPTER 29

Dear Em,

They are following me. If you get this, it's not aliens this time. I always blame the aliens because it's what's expected of me. They think I know something. And I'm not paranoid. Please, if you get this in time, take this to the police.

Norman "Papa" Tomson.

It was dated three days ago. I read it again. Then, just to make sure it didn't magically delete itself, I made a copy of it and sent it to myself again as well as forwarding it on to Ben. "Sorry about the late hour," I wrote. "I just noticed I got this. It's from three days ago. It was in my spam."

Ben's phone call woke me early in the morning.

"So he tried to contact you?"

"Three days ago. His website is gone. All of his online presence seems to be gone. Do you still think it's suicide?" I asked him.

"I don't know. Are you by any chance coming into Portland today?"

"I could be." *Of course I could be. I'll come now.* Right now. How soon do you want me? "When?"

"Any time."

"Let me take care of my animals and get a bit organized. I can be there in maybe an hour."

"Oh, wait. No can do. I've got a meeting this morning."

Of course you have a meeting. "Okay then," I said.

"How about for lunch? I can be free around lunch time."

"Sounds good." *Sounds real good.* "I'll be there later then."

"And bring your laptop, if you don't mind."

"Wait. The police don't want my laptop, do they?"

"Oh, no. I've got a tech here who might be able to get into your history. But he can do it in minutes, I think."

"Just as long as I don't have to leave it overnight."

"No, nothing like that. You can be here while they have a look at it."

"Okay."

"Something else you need to know. The police found that powerboat, the guy who approached us out on the Sound? The boat was found beached right in front of a high-end home near New London, Connecticut. The prop was pretty mangled. Stolen boat. Looks like he aimed the boat toward the shore and gunned it. The guy whose boat it is—he's furious."

"What about the people who live in the house? Did they see anything?"

"No one was there. It was a summer home owned by some rich people."

"Ah." As a coastal sailor, I know about this. There are many very wealthy people who own glorious summer homes on the waterfront, and they spend maybe one week in them per year. If that. Sometimes they're staffed by maids and groundskeepers all summer. Sometimes not. Sometimes they're just pretty much abandoned.

"Where did the boat come from?" I asked.

"It was registered to someone in Miami. It was stolen right from his yard—boat, truck, trailer and all."

"So he towed it."

"Right."

"And put it in the water at various places on the way up?"

"It would appear so. A couple of marinas reported that, and even said they helped him since he seemed so clueless about his boat."

"Wow."

"They'll find him. He's without a boat now."

"Yeah, but he does have that big gun of his. And if he's

into living on the land, he could last for months."

A few hours later, Ben and I and his tech expert, a young man who wore a black t-shirt with a sitting penguin on the front, looked through and around the inside of all my messages from Papa. I guess the police thought that if they could find out where they were sent from, they might get a handle on whether it was really suicide and what he was doing in Mount Joy. He also wanted to see if he could find a time stamp on the email Dr. Papa had sent me. The techie reminded me a little of Jason, Dr. Papa's cameraman. He wanted my computer overnight, he said. He thought that Papa's email had left a "trace" on my computer and he wanted to check it out more thoroughly.

I looked at Ben. "You promised."

"It'll only be for one night," he said. "This guy's good."

"If you say so." At least I had my phone plus the thumb drives with most of my important files. With that and my computer in hand, he walked out.

Ben said, "So, are you ready for that lunch? I have a few things I want to run past you, if that's okay."

"Sure." I was used to this. This is what Ben and I did. When he had a police question for me about some aspect of Maine life, or things nautical or boating, we went for lunch. There is a café directly across from the police station that we frequent. This time, however he said, "It's a nice day. Let's head to a different place."

"Fine with me."

When we were stopped at a red light, he said, "How are you doing, Em?"

"Scared, a bit. Worried. I have my uncle's boat, and I have no idea where he is or what I'm supposed to do with it. I've met two of my uncle's former lovers in the space of three days and my head is spinning. I'm getting email from dead people, and then—oh yeah—and then there's this guy with an assault rifle looking for me because my uncle told him he gave me this so-called money."

The place Ben chose looked like an ordinary house from

the outside. It reminded me, in a way, of Ella's cottage with its flower boxes under each window.

"Pretty," I said.

Inside was crowded with lunch goers. There was even a short line at the door. We were shown a table smack in the center of the room. I would have preferred a place closer to the edges, but that was not to be today.

"Crowded today," he told me. "It's usually not like this."

"Good food?"

"You'll see."

"Hey, Ben," a slim blonde waitress grinned at us as she handed us menus. "Coffee, I presume?" she asked.

"Always," he said. "You know me."

Ben introduced us. "Em, meet my friend Jill."

His *friend* Jill? I mustered up a smile and she grinned at me. Her name badge read Gillian. She *knows* him?

"I'm actually Gillian, but he," she poked Ben in the shoulder, "he likes to call me Jill or Jilly. I guess he has an aunt with that name who used to be called Jilly." Her bracelets clinked.

"Nice to meet you." He'd never told me about any aunt named Jilly. "I'm Em," I said. "Short for Emmeline. I'm also named after a long-lost aunt somewhere." I tried to keep my voice light and airy because, after all, was this woman here, this waitress, the reason Ben and I hadn't gone out on any more adult dates? And why was I noticing that she hadn't looked at me—not once—during this entire exchange, but kept her eyes firmly fixed on Ben? Who was I kidding? I had no claim on Ben. All I did was casual work for the police station now and again. Ben could go around getting poked in the shoulder by women named Jill, and share deep secrets with people named Joan, and get returned envelopes from wives named Cindy. It had nothing to do with me.

When she left, I said, "Good friend of yours?"

"I'm in here a lot. We live next door to each other. She brings me over food. Stuff they're throwing out. I think she feels sorry for this old bachelor by himself."

"Right." *Bachelor*. I rooted around for a tiny round plastic cup of cream for my coffee and ended up spilling it all over my fingers and the table. I quickly wiped them up with a napkin. I would need to be more careful in the future about where I placed my heart.

Ben leaned toward me and over the table. I wished he wouldn't look at me with those eyes of his. Maybe there is only room in a life for one true love. I had mine in Jesse, my Jesse, who has been dead for more than two years, murdered as it turns out, which is how I met this man across from me in the first place.

"I'm worried about you, Em. You seem distracted. Maybe you need to leave the rest of all of this to the authorities."

"It's my uncle," I snapped. And then more quietly, "*My* family." I scrounged around the little bowl for more creamers, but they were all of the flavored variety and I hate flavored cream. Hate it!

"Em. What's wrong?"

"There's no cream! How can there be no friggin' cream?"

"Jill?" He called with a smile. She immediately brought more cream. And while she was at it, we ordered. I couldn't think of anything I wanted so I chose the special, which happened to be fish and chips.

After she left, Ben took out his notebook and asked me a few questions about sails. It was for a case, he said, and I nodded and felt like no one ever wanted to be my friend. All people wanted were things from me. Information for a case. A few hours on my sailboat. No one ever tells me anything unless I pry. My friend Dot has had an affair with my uncle, and I'm the stupid, little person who's the last to find out anything. I answered Ben as best I could. It wasn't Ben's fault I was a total wreck. Well, maybe it was.

Jilly came out with our meals. After depositing them on our table, she put a hand on Ben's shoulder. I stared at her pink fingernails.

And then he was asking me questions, and I was answering them as best I could until lunch was over and we were walking back to the station.

"You're awfully quiet," he said.

"I told you. I'm worried." How many times was he going to tell me that? I just wanted to get home before the tide. I glanced toward the waterfront. Fog was coming in, slowly, surely, stealthily.

I was sitting in my car getting ready to head home when my cell phone rang. I glanced down at it. Marie from Mount Joy. I didn't feel like talking to her. I didn't feel like talking to anyone. Nevertheless, I answered it.

"Em? Ocean is still missing. I wondered if you'd heard from her."

"I got your email, Marie. No, I haven't heard from her, but I would have no reason to."

"Oh, I just thought—"

"What do the police say?"

"They don't think she's been kidnapped. They think the house was all staged to look like a kidnapping with the dishes and food out and everything."

"Marie, I really don't know what's going on. And my friend Ben doesn't either." I felt an impatient sharpness come into my tone, and I tried to temper it. I didn't have the tide on my side. It was coming in and to make it, I needed to get going now.

"Well, I'll tell you one thing. If she's with Ronny Joe, first of all, he wouldn't hurt her, and second of all, she would never run away with him. She thought he was a bit of a dope. The police are looking for Ronny Joe. Seems he stole some big boat somewhere. That's the news we're getting."

"Yeah. I heard something about that."

"The three of them. Survivalists. Simon and Stan and Ronny Joe. And they believed in all that conspiracy theory shit. Ronny Joe was supposed to be on some stupid TV show about it. He told us about that the last time he was here. You ask those idiots, the zombie apocalypse is just around the corner."

I sat very still and held my phone. "What TV show?"

"What?"

"What TV show?"

"I don't know. Nothing ever came of it. But you should've heard Ronny Joe bragging about it. Made no sense to me, him being on a TV show when two out of three of them are dead."

"Do the police know this? About a TV show?"

"No. I don't know. What difference does that make?"

"Just trying to put two and two together."

"The police keep thinking she went up to see her mother, but I can't see her going all the way up to New Hampshire and I told them so."

I couldn't move. "Her mother lives *where*?"

"New Hampshire."

"Really?" I became very still. Now, I really *was* trying to put two and two together.

"Yes. Why?"

"What is her mother's name?" I said.

"What?"

"What is the name of Ocean's mother? Is it Ella?"

"Ella? I think so. I only met her a time or two. Ocean never had much to do with her mother. Even when her parents were living here. Her mother always struck me as a rather cold woman."

"And her father's name is Samson." I was remembering Ella's eyes and why they seemed familiar. I had seen them in the daughter. Did Ferd know that Ocean was Ella's daughter? He must have. I was thinking about what Ella had told me. All of it was starting to make sense.

Ella wasn't in love with Ocean's father, but stayed with him for the sake of the baby. Could Ocean have picked up on that all of her life, that her father loved her dearly, but her mother only stayed with her because of some motherly duty? That her love lay elsewhere? Ocean seemed to have such a close relationship with her father. It had been mentioned time and time again how she missed him. Yet, Samson died four years ago. Odd that she would be mourning him to this extent still. I wondered about that.

I was remembering something else, too. The sound I heard in the church. Ella had said it was the minister's cat. What if it wasn't a cat? What if it was a baby? Ocean's baby?

"Marie, keep me informed. I gotta go. I have to make the tide."

"The what?"

"The tide. On my road."

"Oh."

My thoughts still spinning, I headed out onto the highway and, eventually, the gravel road that led on over to Chalk Spit. I would need to hurry and pray my car didn't break down in the middle of the tide road. Right now, there was maybe an inch of water across the road and the tide was coming in. If the tide was going out, that would be another story, but coming in? Not good. How many times do I chide people for doing just this, chasing the incoming tide across the road?

Since cutbacks had shut down the ferry, more and more cars were getting caught on the road and more and more, the Coast Guard had to come and rescue them. In a kind of weird irony, the news was even saying the government was now spending more in Coast Guard rescues than it ever spent in running the ferry. I looked at the water. If I gunned it, I'd make it across. I was a local. It's only stupid tourists who get caught. I was tired and all I wanted at this point was to be home.

Halfway across the road, with the tide rising by inches around my tires, and a dense blanket of fog, I saw a figure. A man was out in the middle of the tidal road. Right in my way. Water was already swirling around his ankles. A veer to the left and I would be on rocks. A veer to the right and I would be in the churning water which was coming up more quickly than I had calculated. I had no choice but to stop. He held a gun across his chest. An enormous gun.

I shuddered.

CHAPTER 30

This was the man who had followed me. This was the man who had stolen a sleek, silver boat with lightning zigzags along the side. This was the man who had followed me out on the water, kept following me, kept showing up. This was the man who had rammed said boat up onto the shore making a royal mess of the thing. This was the man who had accosted Ben and Joan (and me!) out on *Wandering Soul*. This was the man who had threatened to come back and kill us all. This was the man with the big gun.

For several minutes, I simply sat there, foot on the brake, motor on. The only thing I could think to do was to put my car in reverse and back up. I looked over my shoulder. Behind me, an ever-deeper fissure of tide water was making its way across the road. The mainland side of the channel was the deepest, and I had successfully driven over it. I didn't want to go back. In twenty minutes, it would be too deep to drive through. That's how fast the tide comes in once it starts.

I made sure the car was locked and in gear and I sat there, my hands on the wheel and my foot ready to hit the gas. The consequences of driving on ahead and on up to solid ground were not good. That man there could shoot a hole in this car with that cannon of his. I was sure it would splatter pieces of the car and me all over the incoming tide. Maybe he would step to the side and there would be an opportunity to gun the engine and slide past him. I reached for my cell phone, but down in this gully there was no reception.

He sauntered around toward me. The gun seemed to get bigger the closer he came. He motioned for me to roll down the window. I looked straight ahead, and with one movement, I revved the engine and sped past him. If I could make it up the hill and onto the road, I'd get that call into 911.

The blasts were like nothing I'd ever heard before. The back window shattered and a wall of water sprayed up behind me. I screamed and lost control of the car and it swerved into deeper water and sputtered. I kept my hands on the wheel while I attempted to manhandle it back up onto the road. Mentally, I checked my body. No pain anywhere. No blood that I could see or feel. I hadn't been hit. That was good, but when the car coughed and stopped, I realized the car's engine must be flooded — literally. Shaking, I checked my cell phone. One bar of fading in-and-out service. I tried 911, but the connection died before it could get through.

The fog down here on the tide road was like waves of cold smoke. If I got out of the car, maybe I could disappear into the fog. I know these waters and rocks and paths. I know which rocks are good to step on and which aren't. He may have survivalist training, but I had something else. I had local knowledge. I turned and saw him walking toward me through the fog, clad in his fatigues and boots. Boots. Hmm. Leather boots on slick rocks. I might have the advantage after all. I took my chance and ran up the tide road. Almost there. Almost there.

The blast deafened me even more. The pain to my ears was intense and my hands flew immediately to them, as I stumbled headlong into the water. Had he shot my head? Were my ears bleeding? Was I going to die? It took me awhile to realize that the pain was from the noise, not from being hit. I felt my face. I felt my nose, my eyes. I opened them. I could still see. He was standing above me, a formidable figure in his camo and aiming the barrel of his gun directly at me.

"What do you want?" I finally managed. I could barely hear my own voice.

"You know what I want. The money." Even through my diminished hearing, I could tell his voice was gruff and harsh.

"I don't have your money."

"Liar," he spat.

The cold salt tide was rising all about us. I groped to get up, placed my hand on a slick piece of seaweed, fell again. Aside from a few bloody scrapes, I wasn't hurt. He hadn't shot me, he'd shot the gravel beside me. Instinctively, I knew something—as long as he thought I had his precious money, he wouldn't be killing me any time soon. I glanced over at my car. The tide was swirling around the chassis, and the car was actually floating sideways a little, driver's door opened.

As best I could, I said, "We have to get out of here." I pointed toward the water coming in. The shore on either side was obliterated by the fog. My hope was that someone had heard the gun. How could they not have? He aimed the large rifle at me while I leaned up on my forearms, trying to get my balance. "The tide. Even your big gun will not stop the tide. I have no idea where your money is." My ears still hurt. I rose all the way and stood up shakily. "I don't know anything about your money."

"The money your uncle took and hid on his boat and then left floating down in Florida for you to find. He knew you'd be there, you know. All that money. It's mine. He told you where it was. Ocean told me he stole it."

"I don't know where my uncle is. I'm looking for him just as much as you are."

"Lying bitch. You're in this together."

"The police searched that boat and there was no money. I've searched that boat and there is no money."

"Your uncle has it."

"I haven't seen my uncle in years. I don't even know where he is."

"Don't play stupid with me. Okay, here's the thing. I know you have a dog. And a cat. You're going to take me up to your house, and I'm going to kill your dog unless you tell me where the money is. If I kill your dog and then you don't tell me, the next will be your cat. Oh, and if you don't lead me up to your house? Off goes your foot. And maybe a couple of your neighbors. That kid who went on the boat with you—"

I choked, swallowing down bile. I knew he wasn't kidding.

He would do this. He would actually do this. I said, "Listen, I really, really don't know anything about any money. You have to believe me."

He laughed. I hated the sound of it.

I closed my eyes briefly. The pain in my head was worsening. "Okay," I said thinking, thinking. "The tide is coming in, and it's coming in fast. There's a lot of fog. We have to make it up the road here. You need to follow me because I know the path. But before I take you to my house, you have to tell me one thing. How did my uncle get involved with you creeps?"

"You tell me."

"I don't *know*. Was it a gambling debt? Did he owe you some money from a debt? Is that where the money came from? Did you and your brother work on an offshore rig or the docks? Is that how you met Ferd? You were gambling against Ferd and lost? Was that it? Was Ferd at that famous horse race, whatever?"

"We won that money fair and square at the track. Fair and square. And that stupid old man just shows up one day and starts making trouble for Ocean. Starts making threats to Stan. To me. Guy's a jerk. Old men jerks are the worst jerks. Then he takes the money. Runs off."

"Where did he supposedly get this money from?"

"Simon was the one picked up the money. It was supposed to be three ways. Simon had it. He double-crossed both of us. I never trusted Simon in the first place. I told Stan that. He told me I was nuts, but I knew there was something wrong about him."

"So you killed Simon. So, that doesn't have anything to do with my uncle."

"No. Wasn't me. I didn't beat up that little twit. It was your stupid old uncle who did that."

"I thought Stan killed Simon. Or the two of you together."

"Wasn't me."

"So where'd you bury his body?"

"I don't know. You'll have to ask your uncle that."

"But you killed Stan."

"Wasn't me, either."

"Right. You were with Ocean. She's your alibi."

"I been helping her with her house."

"You two pretty cozy there? That why you killed Stan? Get him out of the way? Take the money for you and Ocean?"

"Ocean never got the money. Stan had it and Ferd stole it off him. Ocean told me this. She hated that old man. Said he came around bothering her. Said the money was in her kitchen, and after Ferd left, it was gone."

"Ocean is missing, by the way." I stopped to look at him. "She with you?"

Maybe it was a trick of the fog, but there came across his face a look so painful and so sad and so beautiful that all I could do was stare at him. And then the moment passed, and he was a grizzled and mean fighter.

"She's missing? She's gone?"

"Yep."

"My brother didn't deserve her. He didn't treat her well. He beat her. I never would have. I would have treated her well." His voice trailed off. "I would have. All I wanted was to protect her. He deserved to die. He didn't deserve Ocean. It was me with Ocean in the first place. And then he comes along—"

"So, you *did* kill him."

"I *didn't!* I wish I did, but I didn't."

"He beat her up pretty regularly, I understand," I said. "So maybe she killed her husband. Is anybody thinking that?"

He hit my side with the gun so hard that I nearly fell over. "Don't ever say that about her! Don't ever goddamn say that. She wouldn't ever—it was—it was—your uncle. That man—"

I righted myself and stared at him, at the gun, his full camo outfit, which almost seemed like a Halloween costume on him, like he was a little boy dressed up and playing a part.

"Ferd didn't kill him," I said. "The police don't even think that anymore." I didn't know why I said this when it might not be true. I guess I just wanted a reaction.

"They don't?" He stopped for a moment. There was a confused look on his face.

"Nope, they don't. They're still looking for the real killer."

He was quiet as he looked at me, his mouth working as if to say something. Then he stopped. "He has the money, though. I know that."

"He doesn't," I insisted.

"Lying bitch."

The water was up to our knees and rising quickly. "Listen," I said. "We have to get out of here. The tide—"

"Not until you promise to take me to the money."

"Okay, listen, follow me." I was coming up with a bit of a plan. "The tide is tricky here," I told him. "Once it reaches a certain height, it goes faster. It's not the rising tide that will kill you. It's the currents. Come with me. We'll head up to my house and get all of this straightened out."

I began walking, leading the way with him close behind.

"Just one more question," I said. "Did Dr. Papa contact you about his show?"

"Yeah. That was his name."

"What did he want?" I asked carefully.

"He came to me, wants me to be on some stupid TV show. About our survival camp. You ask me, he was fishing. That was all, he was just fishing."

"Fishing for what?"

He grunted. "He had some information about your uncle."

I stopped. "What information?"

"Dunno."

"You killed that TV guy." I could hear the water lapping against the rocks now. "You made it look like a suicide. He wrote me an email. I know it was you!"

He backed up, looked at me square on and shook his head from side to side. "He wrote you an email? Said I was going to kill him? That's not true. That's not the way it was."

"How about you tell me 'the way it was' then?"

"I didn't even know he was dead. He's dead?"

"He's dead." A wind was coming up, too, which wasn't a good thing. We needed to climb up the road and make it to solid ground. I told him this. "I know the way up when the tide is like this."

Except I didn't lead him up the trail toward the road. Instead, I headed on down a treacherous path that ran parallel to the road. As I walked, things were starting to come together in my mind. Ella was Ocean's mother. Maybe that flowered note which read, "Please take care of her," was meant for Ferd. Because Samson was dead, could Ella, knowing that her daughter was married to a wife beater, be imploring Ferd to take care of Ocean for her? And then Ferd, learning about the windfall, had tried to steal it? Maybe he wanted simply to give it to Ocean. I remembered Marie's words, *If anyone deserved the money, Ocean did.* If that were the case, why did Ocean have such a visceral reaction to Ferd? Or did Ferd kill Stan, and then the potential of all that money became too much and he decided to keep it for himself? I still couldn't get my head around Ferd doing something like that.

Or maybe Ocean wasn't the innocent that I thought she was. The poor, abused wife? Maybe she was the abuser. Could that even be possible? She certainly seemed angry enough.

I thought about the name Ocean. Who names a child Ocean?

Someone who loves the ocean or someone who at one time loved the ocean, that's who.

As I led Ronny Joe down the wrong path, I was adding piece after piece to my theory. The water was flooding in harder and higher now. I was fine—cold, but fine—with my rubber bottomed boat sandals, which are made for the most slippery surfaces possible. I'm used to walking on wet boat decks and wet rocks. I've been walking on slick rocks all of my life. Ronny Joe behind me was not. I heard him stumble several times. Good. Up ahead, I would seize my opportunity. Up ahead, things would change. Up ahead, we would climb up onto a flat and very slippery rock. I would go left onto the road, but he would not.

Meanwhile, I needed to keep him distracted with conversation. "So, you stole that boat. How did you get away from both the police and the Coast Guard?"

"I have survivalist training. I'm good at hiding out in the woods."

"I imagine you are." In the distance was the foghorn. All we had to do was walk in the direction of the foghorn. My ears were still hurting from the gun blast and the foghorn was hazy in my ears.

"Why aren't we walking up to the road?" he asked.

"Can't do that," I improvised. "Tides in too far already. It's already too deep there, and that's where the current is the fastest. Just follow me. I know these trails like the back of my hand."

When we were finally standing on that big flat rock together, with one motion, I pushed him, and he fell forward into the murky water. I heard him sputter and curse.

I ran. But my plan was not to run up toward Chalk Spit and home. I ran back toward the Portland side, even though the road on that side would be covered in water and nearer to the shore was a current that would be running swiftly by now. I knew where to go, though. I needed to get back to the Portland side where I'd get cell reception at least. I knew I could do it if I was careful. My phone was secure in my zippered pocket. I hoped it hadn't gotten too wet.

I could hear him hollering and cursing and floundering on the wet rocks. The cover of fog was my advantage, and I made as little noise as possible. Other people have tried this. Tourists often do, get stuck, and have to be rescued. But while I laugh at the stupid tourists, I'd done it myself enough times to know which rocks were safe and which weren't.

I did not stop. I did not turn around to gloat. I did not turn around to see where Ronny Joe was. Even five minutes could make a difference with the tide.

When I reached the other side, I heard a loud splash. And then another. It sounded like Ronny Joe had climbed his way up onto the Chalk Spit side and was dislodging rocks on his way up the incline. So much for his survivalist training. He thought I'd gone up that way. Good. Let him think that. I heard another splash, and then quiet. Had he fallen into the water? I didn't look back. I didn't stop. I kept moving.

When I finally reached the shore, I collapsed with relief against a tree and caught my breath. I pulled my cell phone from my zipper pocket. One bar. Before I could hit 911, there was a breath behind my ear.

"Keep walking."

I gasped. It was Ronny Joe and he was covered in dirt and mud and seaweed and muck. The rifle was gone, but now he held some kind of handgun. I could feel his foul breath in my ear. "Keep walking."

"Wha..?"

"No more tricks. You forget who you're dealing with."

"Where?"

"My camper is here, and then, when we can, we cross to your house. Your dog and cat are waiting." He sneered.

I slipped on a rock and nearly fell, but it gave me an idea. I still had the fog, and I had one more chance. Only one more chance. There was a place where this path led to a rocky outcropping over the water. My one hope was with the fog we wouldn't be able to see the water below. It wasn't a cliff per se, but an incline, but it might be enough. It just might be enough.

We kept walking, his gun nudging me on. When we finally reached that bit of an outcropping, I faked-tripped and fell to my knees. Moaning in phony pain, I picked up a rock, the sharpest one I could find, and hid it in my right palm.

"Get up!" he yelled.

"I hurt something." I gave it my best shot. "Ow. Ow. I did something to my ankle. You're going to go on without me."

"Get yourself up, damn you."

"I told you, I can't. I think I've broken something. Ow. Ow." I rubbed my ankle.

"Get up."

"I'm trying." I really didn't have to pretend to be crying. By now, I was sobbing with fear. "I did something to my ankle and I can't move."

"Well, you're going to have to, bitch."

I started to rise, fell forward onto him as if I had lost my balance. He reached toward me to steady himself. As he did, I threw the sharp rock straight into his face and shoved him backward. Surprised, he was off balance and went stumbling off the incline. He had no choice but to let go of the gun as he scrambled for bushes and roots to break the fall into the water. I scampered up onto dry ground, up, up. I kept running, running, much faster than I had the first time. Finally, I was on the road leading back to Portland. I kept on running. At first, I could hear him growling and cursing at me. As I made my way further and further down the road, his cries became fainter and weaker. I did not stop.

Not wanting to talk out loud, as soon as I had a clear cell phone connection, I texted Ben.

Walking toward Portland. Ronny Joe shot a hole in my car with his AR. I think it's sinking in the channel between Chalk Spit and the mainland. I pushed him into the current, but he could be right behind me.

I thought that would get his attention.

It did.

CHAPTER 31

WHERE ARE YOU? He wrote in all caps.

Using my cell phone's compass app, I texted him my lat/long.

He wrote, *ON MY WAY!*

A new text bubble appeared. *Seek shelter. Bushes. A cave. Anywhere along the side of the road. Don't stand out in the open. We know where you are. We're coming.*

I waded for some distance into the waist high brush at the side of the road. I was vexed to discover that I had chosen a marshy place and my sandaled feet sunk to my ankles before stopping. I didn't want to think about what kinds of microorganisms called this place home. I squatted down and out of sight. I didn't hear Ronny Joe. I was quite sure he was still in the water where I'd left him. A few broken bones to immobilize him wouldn't hurt, but so far, he'd proved to be very resourceful. If he did manage to climb up and find me, he might not have his gun. I'd seen it go flying into the bushes, hadn't I? It was so foggy, I found it hard to remember.

Seconds later, the bugs found me. I have heard of people, sane men and women, who have been driven crazy by mosquitoes, deer flies, and other assorted biters. Did I have anything resembling insect spray with me? I often carry it, since our Maine mosquitoes can grow to be the size of hummingbirds. I felt my pockets. No such luck today.

I tried to go into some sort of Zen state as I squatted in the mud and waited. I kept asking myself what is better — being dead or being eaten by bugs and feasted on by leeches? Surely, this was better than being shot to pieces.

Maybe. But not by much.

I found it difficult to move my thinking away from Lyme and West Nile and to Ronny Joe and Papa and Ocean and Ella and my uncle. Finally, I did manage a kind of quietness as I stayed perfectly still. It's amazing what the human body is capable of enduring. I thought about the flowered note. Maybe my uncle was in the midst of this whole money thing because Ella had asked him to "take care" of Ocean. Maybe he went to give the abusive man a "talking to," their argument got out of hand, and he ended up shooting Stan. Where did my pacifist uncle get a gun, though?

I was trying to put together bits and pieces of the puzzle when I heard a movement in the brush behind me. I flattened my entire body down into the mud and waited. Something slithery crawled across my neck. I fought the urge to jump up and run screaming.

The rustling disappeared, and when I turned my head and looked up a small deer had cocked its ears back and was regarding me. For some strange reason—known only to the universe—seeing such a beautiful animal gave me hope. I smiled just a little through my pain. My eyes filled with tears. I stayed this way, my cheeks wet from my crying, until I heard the wail of police sirens. They stopped precisely where I had told them. I heard someone yell, "Em! Emmeline Ridge! Are you in there?"

Like a crazy person released from chains, I jumped up and stumbled out to the road waving my wet, mucky hands in big huge motions. The first person who saw me was Ben, and despite the fact that I was slick with wet, covered in black sea muck, and that several leeches had decided that my dermis was lunch, he came right over and wrapped me in his arms and wouldn't let go. He held me tight and kept saying, "It's okay. It's okay, Em. I'm here now. It's okay. Don't cry."

Nope. Back that train up. That didn't happen. Ben wasn't even there. It was a female who was rushing toward me from the police car. Several other officers pulled up, parked, and got out, but it was this young woman who clambered right into the brush toward me.

"Don't come in," I yelled. Already, my face felt bloated from bites. "It's gross in here. I'll be there in a minute."

Several other police cars sped past me, and I knew they were heading toward where I told them Ronny Joe was. A piece of the wet marsh was plastered in my hair. I threw it off and shook my head like a dog. Pieces of grunge dislodged, fell to the ground. I stood before her, all mucky five foot nine inches of me, soaked and dirty and wet and barely coherent. It was then that my body began its uncontrollable shivering.

Her first words to me were, "Em? Emmeline Ridge? Are you okay? I've got some blankets in my squad car. Come on. We need to get you out of here. I have some coffee in a thermos. Come with me." She indicated the police car. "I've got a towel in the back. You can dry off. We'll take your statement once you're comfortable."

"I'm filthy," I said.

"Don't worry. There's been worse back there."

Which was something I didn't want to contemplate as I climbed into the backseat. She handed me a towel the size of a dish cloth, and I proceeded to try to wipe off my face and hair and arms and legs. Despite the gray police issue blanket around my shoulders, I was cold and shaky and could not keep my eyes from tearing up. "Where's Ben? Where's Ben?" I kept asking.

"He's gone after the assailant," she told me.

The police officer climbed into the driver's side of the police car and turned to look back at me. She seemed gentle and kind and had one of those pretty, high-cheek boned faces with deep-set eyes. Her hair was pulled severely off her head and into a short ponytail. "You've been through a lot. Would you like some coffee?"

I said I would, and she poured some into the thermos lid and handed it to me.

"My name is Lisette, by the way."

"I'm Em." But, of course, she already knew that. I was having trouble forming coherent thoughts. I was having trouble breathing. But now I was safe, safe. But for how long?

I was quite sure any minute now, Ronny Joe's big face would appear in the car window, and that gun would be aimed directly at us. "My car," I said.

"Your car?"

"He shot my car to pieces."

"Em? Are you comfortable to talk about what happened yet? I'll be recording it."

"Sure. I'm okay. Let's just do this."

A radio transmission interrupted our discussion.

"We got 'em!" It was Ben's voice. "We've arrested him. Read him his rights. Taking him in now. Still looking for the rifle. If you have Em there, we're going to need for her to tell us if she saw where it dropped."

Lisette handed me the radio, and as best I could, I described what had happened out there on the trail.

"Be careful," I said. "I think I saw the rifle fall into the water, and I think the handgun is in the bushes. But be careful. Those currents will be pretty bad by now."

"We're on it." A slight pause. "Thanks, Em."

"You're welcome."

"Em?"

"Yeah?"

"You okay?"

"Peachy."

Another officer climbed into the passenger side of the police car. It was someone named Jeffrey who I had met once before.

"Hey, Em." He leaned over the seat and patted my shoulder. "You done good."

I nodded. Tears kept falling out from the sides of my eyes, and I felt incapable of stopping them. Even though it was a hot evening, very hot, I was chilled and shivering, and quite sure that this was the first symptom of West Nile. All the way into the police station, I was scratching and scratching. On deliveries, my first aid kit is well stocked with Benadryl. You never know when some otherworldly creature was going to bite you. After a long and very hot shower, I was going to need a double dose tonight.

I accompanied Lisette and Jeffrey into the police station, looking, I was sure, like Swamp Thing of the Deep. Jeffrey and Lisette let me clean up in the ladies' room where I removed the worst of the gunk. Then they led me into a room and took my official statement. I had to go over everything—from visiting Mount Joy to what happened today. In great detail. I tried not to scratch too much. Jeffrey left and then came back and told me that Ronny Joe had admitted to everything.

"What do you mean everything? What everything did he admit to?"

Lisette pushed an errant strand of brown hair behind her ears.

He went on. "Ronny Joe killed Stan because Stan didn't give him his fair share of the money they won."

"I thought he had an alibi—Ocean."

"Turns out maybe not."

Something didn't feel right. "What about Papa Hoho?"

"What about him?"

"Do the police still think it was a suicide?"

She looked across the table at me.

"Never mind," I said. "Is it possible to speak with Ben?"

"He's with Ronny Joe. But you're free to go."

I simply looked at them, from one face to the other. "Free to go where?"

"Home."

"How am I supposed to get there?"

Lisette looked at me until recognition dawned. "Yeah. I guess you don't have a car. I can drive you."

I sighed. "I'll call my friend Geoff about getting me across the channel. Ferry doesn't run anymore."

She stood there and looked at me sadly. "I don't know how you can stand to live over there."

"I love it," I said.

Geoff used to operate the government ferry across the channel. When the ferry was shut down, he lost his job and now operates his own channel boat on an "as-needs" basis for a donation. I gave him the reader's digest version of the events, and he said since I no longer had a car, he'd pick me up in his Boston Whaler, and then drive me home from there with the truck he keeps on the other side.

"I thought I heard gunshots earlier. That was you?"

"Yep, that was me."

Just before I was getting ready to leave, Ben came into the room, my computer under his arm.

"Em! So sorry I wasn't there when they found you. I wanted to be."

"That's okay."

"I've got your computer, you'll be happy to know."

"They find anything on it?"

"Not really. Just that Dr. Papa's websites were systematically taken down one by one. The forensic people have determined that Tomson did this prior to killing himself."

"But he wrote me that email. Did they find where that email came from?"

"The motel in Mount Joy. Looks like he stayed in the same one you did, and your uncle."

"Really?" I thought about that for a few seconds. "Ronny Joe said that Dr. Papa wanted him to be on the show."

"He's denying that now," Ben said. "He says he never met Papa Hoho or whatever his name is. The only thing he is admitting to is killing his brother."

"What about the gun he used to kill Stan? Where is that gun? Is he going to give it to you?"

"He says he threw it into the Chesapeake."

"That's convenient," I said. A little *too* convenient? "Stan was killed with a small caliber pistol, a woman's gun. I can't see Macho Man Ronny Joe using such a gun, can you? He's all about his huge weapons, the bigger the better."

"Nevertheless, he confessed to that killing. We have his written statement."

"What about my uncle? Where is he?"

"We are also questioning Ronny Joe about your uncle. We

think he may be responsible for your uncle's death, as well."

"But, but… maybe my uncle isn't dead…"

"Em…"

"And Papa Hoho?"

"Suicide, Em. That was a suicide and has nothing to do with this."

"And the guy from the gas station. The one whose body they can't find?"

"Ronny thinks that his brother killed him and put the body somewhere. We'll find the body."

"Where's the money? In all of this, where is the money?"

"Em. It's over. As far as the police are concerned, it's pretty much over."

But was it?

CHAPTER 32

I stood there, holding my computer under my arm and saying, "But there are still so many unanswered questions. Ben, you have to admit that."

"They may all be answered in time."

"Or might not be."

"Sometimes, in police work, when you get a gift horse given to you, you just accept it. Ronny Joe has confessed to the murder of his brother, and the time lines fit. Also, he knew certain things about the murder that were withheld from the press."

"But—"

He said, "Finding the bad guys is more important than finding out why they did it."

"No, Ben, you don't believe that. You have always told me that motive is the most important thing, and that when you find the motive, you find everything. You said that to me, Ben." I was aware that my voice was getting high and whiny, so I stopped talking. I simply stopped and stood there while I tried to get my thoughts under control again.

"The motive will come," he explained. "The motive will reveal itself in time. And it will be entirely different from the track you've been going down. Maybe your uncle being there was entirely random. Wrong place, wrong time."

"No. No, no, no... This all, all of this has something to do with Ella and her daughter, Ocean, and my uncle. The money is also a part of it, but I can't figure it out."

"Em, you need to stay out of it now."

"Ben!" I protested. "This is my uncle! It has to be connected. All of this. There has to be a motive."

"You want a motive? Money."

"That mysterious money that no one can find," I said. "That mysterious money that seems to have disappeared completely."

He nodded and sighed. "Here's a lesson. If you win more than two hundred thousand dollars at the track, don't get it in cash."

"Cash?"

"Yes, apparently, cash. Or, so says Ronny Joe. He says that Stan came with two bags of cash, laid it on Ocean's table where it was stolen by Ferd. The story is that Ocean was upstairs changing the baby, and when she got back downstairs, Ferd was gone and the money was, too. That's her story, and Ronny Joe confirmed it."

I sighed.

Ben went on. "They're looking into the possibility that your uncle may have been at the same racetrack on that day. They're trying to find witnesses. Maybe he overheard Simon on the phone to his friends telling them about the win. Your uncle might have been desperate for money and saw his chance."

"But that's not true! He specifically went to Mount Joy to help Ella's daughter."

"We have no proof of that, but from what we've been able to piece together, your Uncle Ferd was known to gamble. He's never had a real job, has he?"

"He doesn't need much. He lives a different sort of lifestyle. He does odd jobs."

"Still. Maybe he was in some trouble and got in over his head."

"But a horse race? He doesn't know anything about horses."

"He has been known to gamble, though. You told me that yourself."

"He plays cards. Cards are a different story. All sailors play cards. It's what they do. Sailors do not bet on horses."

"We think Ronny Joe found and confronted Ferd about the

money. Ferd said the money was on a boat floating out in the Bermuda Triangle. Then Ronny Joe kills Ferd and disposes of the body, steals the powerboat, and goes searching for the money."

"But the money wasn't on the boat. The police searched it. We were on it. I looked everywhere."

"Vandals could have found the boat prior."

"Ben, I'm just not buying this. Ronny Joe told me something different. He told me he's always been in love with Ocean and that Stan regularly beat her up. Maybe he killed Stan because of that, so the two of them could take off together."

"That never came up. He didn't mention that."

"Do you think I could talk to Ronny Joe for a minute?"

"That's not possible." I could feel his sigh. "Em, these people lie. It's what they do. You know your problem? You get taken in by people. You believe what they tell you when they are mostly lying."

"I still don't buy it."

"It's not for you to either buy or not buy. It seems to be enough for the police right now. They're hoping in time he'll lead them to where your uncle's body is and Simon's."

"Maybe they're both alive."

"That's not looking very likely."

And then Lisette and I were in the car and we were driving to the landing. She tried to make conversation, but I was silent. She even asked me about sailing, about the work I do as a captain, but I was tired, tired and buggy and itching all over. Half way there, I got out my cell phone and wrote another email to my uncle.

Hey, Uncle Ferd. You can come out now. Someone's confessed to the murder that they wanted to talk to you about. I have no idea why you were in Pennsylvania, but the police have found the real killer. Hey, did you by any chance go to the Seven Oaks racetrack?

Minutes later, in Geoff's Boston Whaler, it was too dark for me to see over to where my car was buried in salt water. I wondered what my insurance would say when I called them in the morning. What if they didn't cover it? That would be my luck. I didn't have any money for a new one. I had a bit in the bank from the Papa Hoho job, but I needed that to live, as in buy groceries. I wondered if it was possible to cancel that quilt order.

The fog had still not lifted. Instead, it seemed to have gotten more caul-like once I was on Chalk Spit Island. I didn't feel like talking much to Geoff who was driving me home in his ramshackle pickup truck with the door that didn't shut and the window that wouldn't roll up. As a result, I was cold. In the middle of a fall heat wave when everyone else is walking around in shorts and I'm cold.

"So," he said trying to make conversation, "you had some guy with a gun chase you down the tide road?"

"Yeah. Something like that."

"Man. What are the chances?"

"Yeah, what are the chances?"

"They caught the guy?"

"Yeah."

"Some loony, I take it?"

"Yeah, total looney tunes."

When he dropped me off, he said, "If you need anything, you be sure to let me know, okay?" Then he slapped the seat.

I decided I needed a shower even before I ventured over to EJ's for my animals. I threw my dirty clothes outside on the porch in a pile. I'd deal with them later, if at all. Maybe I'd take them out back and burn them. I stood under the hottest shower imaginable until I started feeling normal. I washed my hair three times. I didn't look at the drain. I didn't want to see what sort of debris, be it plant life or animal, that circled down and out. When I was satisfied I was finally clean, I examined my face in the mirror. It looked like I had a good case of the chicken pox. One cheek was puffed out to twice its size. Boy, if I were trying to make a good impression on Ben, I had sadly failed. I popped a Benadryl before I went to go and get my menagerie.

EJ was kind, and I sat in his kitchen, with Bear on my lap

and Rusty beside me, and between tears, I told him everything. He offered me a glass of red wine and I declined, telling him I'd just taken a Benadryl. It was kicking in, and so I needed to head home to bed.

"You can use my truck any time," he told me.

"Thanks, EJ."

"Except you'll have to get a boost. The battery's dead. Jumper cables are in the shed."

"I'm sure I can manage that."

He gave me a tin foil covered plate of pulled pork to take home with me.

In the morning Isabelle woke me from a sound sleep when she knocked on my door. I answered it in my sweats and t-shirt, my eyes bleary. She was carrying something in a cotton store bag.

"Em?" Her normally flawless gray upswept bun was loose, and pieces of it were down around her face like little gray shoelaces. It looked like she hadn't slept much, either.

"Isabelle, you okay?"

"Oh, Em, I didn't know you were home. I didn't see your car. Thought I would take a chance. Oh, my gosh. Look at you. Are you okay? Your face —"

"I had a run in with some mosquitoes."

"Well, my oh my, you must've walked right into their nest."

"Yeah."

"Dot doesn't know I'm here. She's gone into town. Can I come in? I want to show you something." The cloth shopping bag contained what looked like a couple of old photo albums. "Tide's come up so I know she won't be back for a while. She's so..." Isabelle looked away from me. "She's so distraught about Ferd missing. She's been not quite herself since *Wandering Soul* got moored down there. I think it's brought everything back to her. I tried to talk to her, but she changes the subject. I heard her pacing all night. All night, Em. I don't even know where she is now — I don't even know if she was in her bed at all. I heard her car starting up, and then this note on the table." She thrust it in my direction.

Doing errands. Back soon.

I said, "Maybe she's doing errands and will be back soon."

Isabelle shook her head. "She never do that. She never just leaves. Neither of us does. If we're going to town, we always tell each other, because nine times out of ten, we've got appointments and end up needing to go together. This is unlike her." She looked away from me. "So unlike her."

Since she had asked me not to, I didn't tell her that Dot had been aboard *Wandering Soul* with me. Isabelle ran a hand through her white hair. "I was married at the time, and Dot and I weren't that close. She was so much younger. And her life was so different. I was busy. I had small children to care for, three under the age of three. I knew she was going through something but couldn't be there for her."

"I'm sure she understands that."

"Our parents were gone. Both of them died when Dot was just a teenager. She didn't have a mother to go to during those years when you're emotionally all at sea. And Dot was. Dot wasn't like the rest of us sisters. The rest of us were married, had children, the whole package. Dot was different. All she wanted to do was sail—"

It made me so sad to know that I had only just learned this, and I told this to Isabelle.

She was quiet. "It hurt her too much. How do you get over your sweet little friend—and Ella was such a sweet, little friend. How do you get over that person going off with the love of your life for a year and a half?"

I nodded. "Dot never married."

"I don't want to offend you, Em. I know how close you and Ferd are, but he didn't treat her well."

What do you say to something like that?

She sat down on my couch and placed the cloth Rite Aid bag on the coffee table in front of us.

She said, "Maybe I'm wrong in saying that about Ferd, but back then, I never got the feeling he truly loved Dot. It was like when he needed a sailing buddy and no one else would go, he'd call on Dot and she always jumped to say yes. Even I could tell the feeling wasn't mutual. The way they would be together, her hanging onto him for dear life, and him always moving just a bit away. I spoke to her about it time and time again, but she was convinced she could make him love her. It's not that simple, I told her. At the time, I thought his only love was the sea and there was no room for any woman in his nomad life. I thought that was the problem. But I was proved wrong when Ella came along."

I felt my eyes sting with tears.

She paused in the telling of her story. "Do you even remember Ella at all?"

"I just saw her a couple of times. Never spoke with her. I heard about her, though. My mother was in a fine state over Ferd and Ella's living relationship."

Isabelle laughed. "Your mother hated Ferd. Your mother was quite incensed. She knew Samson, I think, from some church convention thing or something."

I felt my teeth clamp together. "When Jesse died, and Ferd was here for a month, I used to walk by and see him and Dot on your porch a lot talking."

"They were very kind to each other during that time. But, I think it hurt Dot, even then, to have him here. She would never admit this, but I still think she held out hope. By this time, Samson had been dead a year. And when Ella and Ferd didn't immediately hook up again, I think my little sister still hoped. Maybe she still does. I think she keeps hoping he'll just sail up and take her away with him."

"Why didn't Ferd and Ella get back together then?" I wondered. "It would have been the perfect end to a love story."

She sighed. "I don't know why." She reached for the bag. "I want to show you something. Did you know that Dot was in Ella's wedding?"

"I think I heard something about that." Dot had told me this.

"I have some pictures I thought you might be interested in

seeing." She pulled a large blue photo album out of the bag. Photos were arranged underneath clear plastic sleeves. The very first page was the bride and groom. The inscription read Sept 4, 1977. I recognized this young bride. This was the woman I had seen on Ferd's boat when I was a girl. I knew her face immediately. I knew that smile. She was the woman with the big orange hat who had climbed off the boat and smiled at all of us. She was the one who had looked so lovingly up into the eyes of my handsome uncle.

And here she was looking into the eyes of this other man, this young man Samson. He was tall and there was an endearing quality about him. I think it was his rather large ears that did it.

My gaze went back to Ella, and I ran my finger across her face. I recognized in this picture the woman I had seen in the church with the lined face and hair pulled back and sunglasses. The more I looked at her pictures, the more I came to understand that Ocean was her daughter. The resemblance was uncanny, the dark hair, the slight lift to the eyes.

Page after page, we perused the album. I turned a page and there was young looking Dot in a bouffant gown with puffy sleeves, her hair piled up on top of her head and styled with flowers. Isabelle said, "Dot caught the bouquet, you know. But it was a long time before she met Ferd." Dot had that long lanky athletic build, a sailor even then, with her tanned face and well-defined arms. In the photo, she looked slightly uncomfortable in such a prom-like bridesmaid dress.

"I've met Ella and Samson's daughter. Ocean."

Isabelle looked at me.

"It was her husband who was murdered. They were looking for Ferd in connection with his murder. But now I guess her husband's brother confessed to killing him."

I told her the whole story, how as soon as Ocean knew who I was, she wanted nothing to do with me, wanted me out, and accused Ferd over and over of murdering Stan, stealing her money and playing on her emotions, scamming her.

Isabelle asked, "You think Ferd went to Pennsylvania

looking for Ella's daughter?"

"It has to be the case. Ella left him a note asking him to please look after her. So I'm thinking now that Ocean's father's dead, Ella reached out to the only person she knew and asked him for help in dealing with an abusive husband. From what I gather, Ella and her daughter are not close."

"Maybe that comes from not ever being fully in love with your child's father."

We went through the entire album. It included quite a bit more than just the photos from the wedding. There were some of Isabelle and her family, her daughters and her husband, which we skimmed. Family picture after family picture. She took out an envelope of photos from the back of the album and spread them out on the table. There were many more pictures of Dot. Of Dot and Isabelle. Of Dot and Ella. Of Dot and Ferd.

I picked up one that was so telling. Dot and Ferd were standing very close together on the bow of *Wandering Soul*. Dot is looking up at him straight into his eyes as if she just wanted to see into his soul. Instead of looking at her, his gaze is focused away as if peering into the future. If I looked hard enough, I could even see a bit of a frown on his face.

One envelope contained a few photos of me on my bright red sailing dinghy, and then the one of me, nine years old and behind the wheel of *Wandering Soul*. Even then, I loved that boat.

I asked, "Where did you get these?"

She shrugged. "When they finally separated for good, Ferd gave Dot a bunch of pictures. I think these were among them. I have one more thing I want to show you. And Em, I only wanted to show you these things so you have a better understanding of my sister. Of what she's been through."

She pulled out a folded piece of paper from a yellowed envelope. "After it all happened, Ella wrote a letter to Dot when she went back to her husband. Dot immediately threw it out. I retrieved it and kept it all these years. Dot would absolutely kill me if she knew I was showing it to you. I don't know how, but maybe it might help you locate your uncle, and that's the most important thing. Not any of this stuff. It's such old scandalous garbage, but Ferd is still missing. I have no idea why I kept this letter the whole time. At first, I think it was to protect her. If that scoundrel ever came back, I could show her the letter."

She opened up the letter and handed it to me.

CHAPTER 33

Dot,

I won't begin by writing Dear Dot. I'm sure you would throw this letter into the garbage can if I dared to call you "dear." Maybe you will do it anyway. I'm not even sure why I'm writing, but I feel the need to explain myself, but most of all to apologize. And wonder if we can still be friends? Somehow, I doubt it.

I need to explain myself first, not that explaining will help. Not that it will make you understand.

Who knows the way of the heart? I just know that when Ferd and I saw each other, something very deep happened. It was like we had known each other all of our lives and were just now finding each other. It was like we were two broken parts finally fitting together. Or like water after a long drought. Or seeing someone from a dream.

I stopped reading here and looked up at Isabelle. No wonder Dot had thrown this letter into the trash.

But I can't go on with that. I fear I will cry too long and too hard for all of this to make any sense at all.

I know it will do nothing now to ease your pain, but what I need to do for you, for Ferd, for myself, is to apologize. I am so, so sorry, dear Dot. You have been my mentor and now my friend forever, the older sister I never had, and I have betrayed you in the most horrid of ways.

I was married. I shudder when I think of that, because not only did I betray you, but I also betrayed dear Samson, who I have also known for my entire life. I deserve all of the comments and gossip and scandal that come with this territory. All of it.

I left Ferd because I needed to go back to Samson because of the baby, my dear darling daughter. We have to be a family now. Samson will be a good father and I will do my best at being a good mother, although I fear I'm not very good at much of anything.

If I could erase those eighteen months of my life, I would in a minute, Dot. But maybe I wouldn't. I think of Ferd and I know a weak part of me wouldn't. I know you will probably not want to speak to me again, and we shall part. Some crevasses are too deep to bridge. This may be one of them.

Samson and I have moved to a place called Mount Joy, PA. He has a job there now. Or close by in any case. We will raise our daughter there. I am going to bury myself in the church and in finding forgiveness and being a good mother and learning to love Samson as I have loved Ferd. I will plant flowers around my house.

At the bottom is my address if you want to write to me, but I will leave that decision to you. If I never hear from you again, I will understand. And I hope you find happiness and love or at least contentment.

Once a long time ago, your best friend and little sister.

Ella

I read it through a second time more slowly and something clicked like a thunder in my head. I suddenly knew. Oh, the letter didn't state it outright, but it was there between the lines. She and her husband Samson had been married for ten years without children. Now suddenly they have a child?

I folded the letter, placed it in its envelope, and handed it back to Isabelle, who had already closed up her albums and put the scattered photos into their respective envelopes.

"It's funny I'm here," I said. "Funny that I would just happen to live here, two doors down from my idolized uncle's long-time-ago lover."

"Not so strange," Isabelle said without looking up. "You remember how you met Jesse in the first place."

"Through Joan and Art."

"Well, Art was friends with Dot and Ferd, and Art knew Jesse when Jesse was a boy. Took him under his wing sailing a lot. Jesse and his family spent all their summers out here on Chalk Spit. And Joan was your friend. Dot and I grew up here, too."

"Everyone just one big happy family," I said.

Isabelle shoved the letter deep inside one of the albums.

Out in front of my house, *Wandering Soul* was rocking gently on her mooring. "I have to go," she said. "I have to get this up and hidden away in the attic before Dot gets back."

After she left, I went out and sat on my front porch with a coffee. I stayed there for a long time, looking at the water and wondering at the circles and spheres of life. If you throw something far out into the universe, eventually it will come back, either for good or to hurt you, to haunt you. Some religions call it Karma. The religious tradition I grew up in calls it "reaping what you sow."

I needed to go back and see Ella. If my theory was correct, Ferd might be there. One problem—I didn't have a car. I needed to take care of the insurance matter. I went into my office. In all of my confused pieces of paper and file cabinets, which are actually cardboard boxes, I managed to find my insurance information. With a deep sigh, I sat down at my makeshift desk, a piece of plywood on cinder blocks, and phoned them.

It was going to be less of a problem than I thought. They needed to see the police report, they told me, and if all was copacetic, they'd write the car off and I could get any car I wanted up to the blue book value of my old one. Until it was completely settled, they would provide me with a rental.

Really? Truly? This is great. Thank you very much.

In the afternoon, Valerie from three doors down was driving into Portland and gave me a ride to the car rental place. A little while later, I was driving out with a cute, little bright green Nissan Sentra. I wouldn't leave until the following morning, so in the afternoon, I decided to bring *Wandering Soul* back to the dock. I still had more cleaning to do. I couldn't keep my mind on things, though, and by later afternoon, I'd packed a quick overnight bag, and by the following morning, I'd dropped my animals off with my sweet neighbor, EJ. I warned him that I might be overnight and was that okay? "Certainly. Certainly," was his reply.

I was on my way.

I may not have family who understands me, but I have neighbors who look out for me and give me food and companionship and rides to town when my cars get covered with water. On my way in, I toyed with the idea of calling Ben but felt uncertain. At a roadside stop, I made a quick call to Marie, and before I could ask whether Ocean was back, she practically screamed in my ear, had I heard the news? Ronny Joe's been arrested and confessed to everything! I told her, yes, I had.

"But I find it weird," she said.

"Yeah."

"I don't think Ronny Joe would have done that."

"Why's that?" I asked.

"He just wouldn't. He was afraid of his own shadow most of the time. Would barely go hunting. You almost got the feeling he was scared of those big guns he carried around."

Well, I begged to differ. The gun he shot at my car was very real. The bullet that landed beside me in the water was very real. "I'm not so sure about that."

"Well, it's true. If he carried a gun, it was just to show off to his big brother. And he was so gaga-eyed over Ocean. Followed her around like a puppy dog. Kept saying his brother didn't deserve her."

That's what he'd told me. "But he confessed to murder," I

said.

"I just don't think he would have done it. Just how I feel."

"What about Ocean?" I said. "Is she still gone?"

She told me yes, and that the police were beginning to take it seriously. They had figured she was with Ronny Joe, but now they didn't know where to look. "They still think she just ran off, but she's never done this before," Marie insisted. "Even when I would beg her to leave Stan, she wouldn't."

"Maybe she's afraid." I was running on my own theory.

"What's there to be afraid of now that Stan's gone?"

"Ronny Joe? Who knows?"

"Ronny Joe would never hurt her. Never. Could she be with..." She paused, "...your uncle?"

"That's impossible. She practically kicked me out of the house, told me that my uncle was probably in hell, and that was fine with her. No, she has to be somewhere else."

"Well, everyone has run out of ideas."

Maybe not, I thought. Maybe not.

CHAPTER 34

A few hours later, I was parked beside the church. She was there — Ella was, kneeling in the brown dirt along the side of the building. Her back was to me and she was cutting flowers with long-handled scissors and laying them out in a basket beside her — zinnias, cosmos, geraniums, daisies. She was humming, something low and tuneless. When I approached her, she turned and faced me.

"Sorry," I said, "sorry for startling you."

Since the day was overcast, she was not wearing sunglasses. The brim of her denim gardening hat was narrow enough that I could see into her eyes.

"Your daughter has your eyes," I said.

Without comment, she turned back to her garden, her shoulders stiffening. She cut a few more red flowers and placed them with shaky hands into the basket. The humming had stopped. I watched her pull out a few small weeds. I just stood there. I was in no hurry. A blue flower head had fallen to the ground next to the basket. She picked it up, held it in her palm as she rose to full height and stood before me.

"Ocean," I said, "she is very like you. The same hair. The same eyes. Same smile. When I did see her smile. Which was only once."

"We don't smile much," she said. "Neither of us do."

"She should. She's young and beautiful. She has a lot going for her. You have a lovely little granddaughter."

"Yes."

My height over her gave me the advantage, and I determined I would not leave until I had some answers. "It's good she resembles you rather than her father."

Her eyes narrowed. Her mouth opened as if to say something, but I got there first.

"You were fortunate in that regard. If she looked too much like her father, I imagine that would have been difficult for you all those years."

"I have things to do." She backed away and turned toward her garden. "We have rain coming. More rain. Don't you feel the fall in the air? I need to get these flowers arranged for the church service. I need to tuck the garden away for winter."

Without hesitation, I said, "I'm part of your family, Ella. We are related."

Her back was still to me.

"Ferd," I said. "Ocean's father is my Uncle Ferd. That means that Ocean and I are cousins."

She turned back toward me, the short stem end of the blue flower between her thumb and forefinger. She twirled it ever so slightly. "How?" She swallowed visibly. "How did you find out? Did—did Ferd tell you?"

"I haven't seen my Uncle Ferd in years, so no, it wasn't him. It was a guess." I paused. "How could you and Ferd have kept this a secret all these years?"

She pulled off her hat. Underneath, soft brown hair flecked with gray was clasped loosely in back. She brushed her hair behind her ears with her garden-worn fingers. Very quietly, she said, "Nobody knew."

"Well," I commented, "he kept that secret pretty good, too."

"No. I mean nobody knew. Just me. Not even Ferd."

I took a step back. "Ferd doesn't know? Really? He doesn't know he has a daughter and a granddaughter?"

"He knows now. So does Ocean. I told Ferd a few months ago, Ocean more recently."

I looked at her.

She went on. "It didn't go well. The telling. With either of them."

"Did you expect it would?"

She moved her head from side to side. "I don't know what

I expected. Maybe a bit of grace after all this time. My daughter had a very close relationship with her father. With Samson."

"And Samson never knew and now he's dead."

She cast a glance down to her basket of cut flowers. "Samson must have guessed. For one thing, the timing of the birth of our daughter was all wrong. We had tried for ten years to conceive—"

"He never confronted you about it?"

"That wasn't Samson's way. Samson was a good, good man. Maybe he did know. And maybe he didn't care. He doted on Ocean. I think he accepted her as a gift. It was never mentioned. It never came between us. He loved us both."

"And you? Did you love him?"

"In my own way, I did. I tried to love him, I mean, but..."

"But?"

"I could never love him the way I loved your uncle—you may as well know that—I could never love Samson with that wild and reckless passion that Ferd and I had. That craziness. Your uncle, he was quite a bit older than me. Maybe that was part of what attracted me to him." She gave a very small smile and I saw in that face the smile I'd seen on the young woman in the big orange hat who stood on the bow of the boat laughing. I remembered the way he came to her on the dock. The way he kissed her and they laughed afterward. She went on. "We were so crazy. The two of us. So crazy."

"You left him. First you left your husband and then you left Ferd."

"I needed a solid home for my daughter. And only Samson could provide that. He had money. A job. Stability. A house with a picket fence."

"But not love," I said.

She looked down.

"Why did you marry him in the first place if you didn't love him? Why stay with him for ten years if you didn't love him?"

"It seemed the right thing to do. Those years. Back then. A

young woman had to be married. Divorce was a scandal. It wasn't like today. Samson's family and mine go way back. It may sound funny and unbelievable, but it was sort of expected that we marry. He was the only boyfriend I'd ever had. But..." She gazed into the far distance, "I didn't know what real love was until I met Ferd."

"Ella, we're — we're family. Ocean is missing, and Ferd is somehow involved in this whole thing. Two people have died. Make that three. Ferd, himself, may well be dead. He's my uncle. And maybe all of this has something to do with what happened so long ago."

"Let's go sit down then. I'm just so exhausted from carrying all of this."

"I'm sure you are."

It was overcast and slightly windy, gusty more than windy. The breeze felt good, though, after all the heat we'd had lately. I followed her to a cement bench and we sat and faced each other. She put her little denim hat on again, and twirled the blue flower between her fingers, round and round. In the garden was the song of birds.

She began talking. "Dot taught me how to sail. Dot taught me...all this, too." She swept her arms around her.

"Gardening," I said.

She nodded. "Samson and I had been married around ten years when she told me she wanted me to meet her new sailing buddy, Ferd."

Dot told Ella that he was a man she could easily "fall in love" with and she wanted Ella's opinion about the whole thing. The attraction between Ferd and Ella began when the four of them went on a weekend sailing trip. Two nights aboard *Wandering Soul*, the four of them.

"Close quarters," I said

"Very close quarters."

She licked her lips. "We were just two couples sailing together. The four of us went out a lot of weekends. Usually, we'd anchor somewhere, swim, and eat. Lots of eating. Maybe a bottle or two of wine." She paused, rested her chin on her hands for a minute as if conjuring up an old memory. "Or we'd head up to Freeport. The four of us gradually began doing more and more together. And it..." she paused, "it just happened."

I stared sharply at her. "Things like that don't just happen. 'Oops, I'm having an affair now. How did *that* happen?'"

She pulled the brim of her hat down as a sudden shaft of sunlight broke through the cloud cover. "You're right, of course. It was a conscious decision. On both our parts. The way it happened was it got so that Samson didn't like sailing so much. Said it made him sick. Plus, he worked all week. So did Dot. But I had the bug. I wanted to learn to sail better, so Ferd took me. It was Ferd and me. Because of the difference in our ages, no one suspected it was anything other than Ferd teaching his girlfriend's young friend how to sail. Dot even used to joke about it."

Several times, she wiped her eyes as she relayed her story. Sailing together turned to talking together and talking together turned into sharing the deep ponderings of their souls. The deep ponderings of their souls — she used those exact words — gradually turned into an affair.

"Samson was heartbroken, of course." She swatted at a bug that had landed on her wrist. "I was so young and stupid. Dot was devastated. I was so in love, I didn't care. I remember she came to me and told me she never wanted to see me again as long as we both walked on the same planet. I think that's how she put it. I wrote her a letter after that but never heard from her again."

"I read that letter."

"What?"

"Isabelle saved it. She showed it to me yesterday. Along with pictures of Dot as your maid of honor."

For a long time, she simply looked down at the zinnia twirling between her fingers. "My wedding." She paused. "I don't remember what was in that letter. Ferd and I took off one morning leaving two broken hearts in our wake. Ferd's entire family was against him. Especially his sister —"

"My mother."

"We were together for almost two years." Her voice faded off.

"So I've heard."

"Two years is a long time."

"Then what?"

She told me as soon as she discovered she was pregnant, she knew she had to leave Ferd. Like the prodigal daughter — or the prodigal wife — she decided to go back to Samson. She would beg him to take her back. She had no idea whether he would or not, and she certainly didn't deserve it, but she had to try. As soon as her pregnancy became known, she would have to stay with Ferd. And she couldn't. She just couldn't. Ferd couldn't know. He absolutely could not know.

Three weeks after she knew she was pregnant, she and Ferd were on the dock in Camden, Maine, after having sailed over from Bermuda. This was her chance to leave, her only chance to leave. In a day or two, they would be heading south. It was now or never. While Ferd was up talking shop with the marina guys, she packed up her things and walked off the boat and into town and stuck out her thumb. She got a ride to Bangor where she caught the bus to Pennsylvania.

"My child needed to be raised on solid ground in a house with flowers and a fence and a dog rather than traveling the seas with no address. I needed ground under my feet, not water. My child needed to be raised by someone with a salary. I needed that for my child far more than I needed Ferd. I needed my child to go to a real school, not home-schooled on the seas like so many children of cruisers. So, I left him a note," she said. "I put it in our favorite book of love poems."

Her face reddened when I pulled the book out of my pack. She took it from me and glanced through its pages. "This book," she said. "I bought it in Bermuda. For Ferd —"

I put my hand up. "You truly don't need to tell me the circumstances surrounding this book."

She closed it, turned it over and laid it on her lap, and continued. "I had no idea what Samson would do, me showing up on his doorstep like that. I mean, what if he was seeing someone else? He could have thrown me out on my face. He could have moved. He could have been in an entirely different place." She leaned back a bit and looked up as if gathering her thoughts. "But it didn't happen like that. I stood there, bedraggled with just my sea bag. It was cold. I remember that. I remember it was cold."

Her voice became so low I had to strain to hear her story. She didn't even own a warm winter jacket anymore, she told me. She hadn't needed one with Ferd. She was afraid to touch the door, to ring the bell, to raise her hand to knock. She thought about fleeing. She stood there by herself for the longest time.

Suddenly, Samson was there. And she was crying. And he went to her and he held her, and held her, and held her until she stopped crying.

"I kept saying over and over, 'I'm sorry. I'm sorry. I'm so sorry.' He never asked why I came back. He never asked what had happened. He just took me in. Eight months later, I gave birth to our daughter. Our daughter."

Her story over, she sighed deeply. The sun was now gone and the wind had picked up even more.

I knew somehow this was all related. Ferd's new family and the murders of Stan and Simon, the money, possibly even Dr. Papa. It all came around to this.

"Ocean." I looked at her. "Her name?"

"I named her for Ferd. It was the last thing I would do for him. He…" She paused. "We connected about a year after I left. I was there. In Maine. Visiting my parents. My mother was ailing. Ferd found me on their boat. Tried to talk me into coming back to him. Ocean was a little girl. She was napping inside the boat. He…he never knew."

"Why now?" I asked. "Why tell them now? Why, after all this time? Samson has been gone for a while now."

"Four years."

"Then why now?"

"Maybe, uh, maybe it was just a bit of conscience. Finally.

After all the heartache I've caused."

I told her I didn't believe her.

She looked at me. "You're right. That's not the entire reason. I needed someone to help me with Stan."

I raised my eyebrows and she went on, "Ocean was in a very bad marriage..."

I nodded.

"Losing her father..." She took a breath. "Losing Samson was such a blow to her. The two of them were very close. He was so good to her, good to her in ways I could not be. The two of us, Ocean and me, we never much got along. Always fighting, especially during her teen years." She looked up at me. "He even took her to church. I never went. I could never make myself walk through those doors. I was not good enough for church. I had too much of a secret ever to be welcomed into the church." She looked up at the tall steeple of the church and said, "I'm still not. That's why I garden. If I make it beautiful enough, maybe I'll be welcomed in. But church. It was between us always. It was her father she was close to. And then he died, and when he did, my daughter went sort of wild. Well, I guess the apple doesn't fall far from the tree. I think she married the first guy who came along. Stan. I think she married him simply because I had such a visceral reaction to him. I could tell from the outset that he was no good. She married him to spite me. I'm sure of that. I was not a very good mother. I wish to God it had been me who died and not Samson."

"I'm sure you did your best," I said gently.

"I loved her. I love my daughter beyond reason, yet could never reach her. Even when Stan would send her to the emergency with another black eye or broken bone, she refused to see me. I did the only thing I could think of. I contacted Ferd. Even though we had not spoken in twenty-six years, I sent him an email. I told him he had a daughter. I told him everything. I wrote it all down. Maybe if Ocean knew that Ferd was her real father, she would listen to him. And maybe Ferd could talk some sense into Stan. Ferd called me when he got the email. He was so angry —" She bent her head into her hands. "So angry. But I had to do something. I had to try. A mother will do anything to protect her child. Anything."

"Do you blame him for being angry?" I asked. "After all this time to find out not only that he has a daughter, but also a granddaughter?"

"I wanted him to understand. I needed his help."

"Do you know where he is now?" I asked. "Is Ferd with you? Is he at your house now?"

She looked up and regarded me through wet eyes. "No. That is absurd. He would not be here. Why do you even ask?"

"I just thought..."

"I wish he was," she said. "I wish to God he was. I wish I knew where he was. I don't. He hates me. He will have nothing to do with me."

"I'm quite certain he doesn't hate you. I know that because of the gardening books."

"The what?" She looked up at me.

"My uncle collects gardening magazines and books. There is a shelf of them on *Wandering Soul,* plus magazines in plastic."

"Why?" She stopped. "Really?"

I told her about the entire bookshelf being full of them. About the book of poetry being in a prominent spot.

Her thoughts seemed to go back to some far off place. "Really?" She said it again, "Really?"

"Yes."

"Imagine that."

"So," I rose. "You asked my uncle to come and help you with the wife-beater Stan. He does and comes and kills him."

She rose to full height and began visibly shaking, her mouth working. "That was never my plan! I just wanted her to be helped! I never meant for him to be killed."

We heard a noise and both of us looked toward the front of the church at the same time.

Dot was standing there.

CHAPTER 35

The air around Ella sizzled into something you could almost touch—fear maybe, or dread. She seemed to shrink into herself. Twenty-six years after the married woman who'd stolen her friend's boyfriend, and the woman who did not want to even walk on the same planet with her former friend, faced each other. Ella's hands were clenching too tightly to the zinnia and the blue petals began falling to the ground around her feet one by one like confetti, like rain. I said nothing, just took a few steps ever so slightly back, and waited, wondering if I would have to intervene at some point, hands outstretched and say, "Hey now."

Ella looked like a scared and frightened child. Had she suffered enough? Dot's face was entirely passive as she stood there, tall and in command. But then I saw a slight twitching, a blinking of her eyes. How much of Ella's incredible story did Dot know? I guessed quite a bit. Probably all of it. She had kept track of her nemesis all these years, after all. I remembered the Dot of a few days ago, the angry Dot, the cursing Dot, the stomping from room to room Dot. And then the Dot who was on *Wandering Soul* with me, the sad Dot, the pensive one, the one whose shoulders shook as she stood for a long time in front of all those gardening books and magazines.

She moved toward Ella, silent steps on the carpet of grass. In a moment, the two women were in each other's arms. I watched, mesmerized. I saw the heaving shoulders of Dot, the red and wet face of Ella, the tears from both of them, the trembling hands.

Later, we three sat down at a wooden picnic table at the

side of the church. Ella seemed exhausted as if she couldn't sit down fast enough. I moved into the bench beside her while Dot sat down across from us.

They talked, hesitantly at first, and then in more earnest. They began with things from a long time ago. Remember this? Remember that? I felt like an interloper, a weird kind of third wheel. I looked beyond them to the church building, studying its ornateness. It took a while, but eventually, they brought up Ferd. I was surprised they would talk about him at all. As with Ben, some things get moved to the back of our souls, only to come out when ready. And maybe even not then.

Dot said, "I should have been more understanding." She placed both palms on the top of the rough boards of the tabletop. "He never loved me, even before you came along. I should have realized this. It was my own stubbornness. I've held onto it for too long. It's time to let go. I'm sorry, Ella."

"No." Ella folded her hands and placed them on the table. "I'm the one who is sorry. I have lived a lie my whole life. A lie." Ella's voice was barely above a whisper.

"No. You have lived a decent and good life with your husband."

"I have kept a secret for the whole of my life." Her voice was quiet. "My daughter, Ocean. Ferd is her father."

I don't know what I expected. Fireworks from Dot? Sudden screaming? Sudden pulling out of hair? All Dot said was, "I know."

"How..?"

"I think I've always known."

"But…" Ella's voice broke at the end of her sentence. She coughed into her hand.

"As soon as I heard you and Samson had a child, I knew." Dot looked away. "I just knew."

I thought I heard a baby crying, wondered if it was my imagination or simply the power of suggestion. I looked over at the church, and specifically the church basement, the shadow of light beyond the chintz curtains. Dot looked at me. We had both heard it. When I had come here the first time,

Ella had told me her minister brought his cat to church. Really? I said to Ella, "It's not Ferd you are providing sanctuary to, is it? It's your daughter and granddaughter."

For a while, Ella picked at a splinter in the board on the table. The two of us, Dot and I, said nothing. "Come with me." Ella rose. "You may as well. Both of you."

We followed her to the back of the building where she pulled open the heavy door. We followed her through a short narrow dungeon-like hall and then down steep stone steps with a rail along one sides. Our footsteps sounded hollow on the old boards, and I was reminded of haunted places. We said nothing. It was cool down here, and I clasped my arms around me, wishing I had remembered a jacket.

On either side of this hallway were doors. I wondered if they led to Sunday School classrooms but decided no one would put children down here. No, they had to be storage rooms. I imagined them overfilled with boxes of choir robes, sooty hymnals and prayer books, Sunday School papers and dusty Christmas decorations.

Finally, Ella pushed open a door which led to a brightly lit and cheerfully painted room. The dark atmosphere of the hallway had not entered this place. Ocean was there, sitting on a wooden rocker and softly rocking her sleeping baby and humming. Her back was to us and she said, "Mother," and turned. When she saw Dot and me, she held her baby tightly to her chest and stared at us. I couldn't read her expression.

"Ocean?" Ella said tentatively. "I've brought some people."

"I see that," she said still staring at us.

I stood in front of her. "Marie is worried about you. The police are looking for you."

"I'm here."

"So I can see. You've been here the whole time." I moved closer to her. "Why?"

"I needed to get away." She carefully moved strands of hair from the sleeping baby's head. "I had no place else to go." She looked up into her mother's face when she said, "This was the only place I could think of to come. I guess I needed to figure some things out. Get answers, you might say. Answers to everything. My mother was the only person who could give them to me."

"And did you get them?" This came from Dot.

"I know who you are." Ocean regarded her. "You're the other one. The other lover. The original one."

A pained expression crossed her mother's face.

"You told her," Dot said.

"I'm tired of lies and secrets," Ella said. "I invited her here. I told her I wanted to explain everything. I wanted her to know everything before she disowned me. Her father has disowned me."

"My father would never disown you." Ocean's tone was bitter. "Even when he should have." She paused. "And my real father is dead."

"Your biological father," Ella said.

"He's not my real father. I just want you to know that."

"I know that."

"I didn't want his money."

"Of course."

Dot said to Ella, "Ferd disowned you?"

"He wants nothing to do with me anymore I'm afraid, so, I invited Ocean. I wanted to see if there was anything to salvage between the two of us."

"Is there?" Dot asked.

I thought I heard a softening in Ocean's voice when she said, "We're working on it. Ask me tomorrow."

"That's good," I said. There seemed to be a hint of a smile on Ella's face. "It's always good when families can get along." Not that this is anything I knew from experience.

"Well, I wouldn't go that far," Ocean said. "I still have a lot of unanswered questions. Such as, why wait until now to totally disrupt my life and tear it apart from top to bottom?"

"I told you why," I heard Ella say.

"Yeah. My father. She didn't want my father to know."

I was momentarily confused until I realized that by

"father" she meant Samson.

Ella said quietly, "It wouldn't have served any purpose for him to know."

"You don't think the truth serves any purpose?" Ocean's words were biting. Corrie moved ever so slightly in her sleep.

"I couldn't..." Ella looked down.

This girl with the baby was my cousin. I looked at her, and said, "Yet, despite all of this, you came up here. When things went south in Pennsylvania, you came up here."

A green ribbon in the baby's hair was coming loose, and gently, she pulled it out of the soft hair and laid it on the table beside her. "I came because I had nowhere else to go. That's the only reason."

"Why did you set your table with food?" I asked. "That totally creeped Marie and Tim out."

She smiled a bit. "Cute wasn't it? I wanted the police to think I'd been kidnapped, that I was in the middle of a meal and someone just came."

"Ronny Joe."

"They think that?"

"It's a theory," I said. "How did you know to mimic the Bermuda Triangle?"

She looked away. "I have no idea what you're talking about."

"Of course you do."

It was Ella who answered for her. "That was in the papers..."

I stared at the two of them. Something was off here. Something was wrong. Still wrong. Ocean said, "I'm here because I would like not to go back to that town where I've made so many mistakes, marrying Stan being the biggest one. Not running away when he hit me the first time being the second one."

"People there are worried about you," I said. "You need to tell Marie, at least, that you're okay."

Ella moved forward and came between us. "The police will arrest her if she goes back there."

"Arrest her for what?" I asked.

"The murder of my husband," Ocean said matter of factly. "The murder of my cheating, bully of a husband. They think I did it. They were getting ready to arrest me."

I said, "When I was at your house, you were sure that Ferd did this."

She looked down at the baby. "I don't know. He could have. He had the motive."

"What motive?" I asked, confused.

Ella answered for her. "I asked him to take care of Ocean and the baby for me. That was what the card was all about. I was asking him to take care of his daughter. I didn't expect him to take it that far when I asked him to take care of her."

I took a breath. "Ferd didn't do it," I said. "Ronny Joe did."

"What?" The two exchanged looks.

"You haven't heard? Ronny Joe's confessed to the crime."

Mother and daughter said in almost the same breath, "Is that true?"

"Yes," I said. "He wrote it down. He's confessed."

Ella said to Ocean, "You're safe then, Ocean. If what she is saying is true, it's over."

"What about the money?" I asked.

"We may never find the money," Ella answered. "That two hundred thousand may be a treasure that someone in some far distant future will dig up and find."

"It could be in the water," Ocean said. "Like overboard where you found the boat. He might've taken it there."

I looked from one to the other. Just as in the police station, something here felt very off. I looked over at Dot who regarded me with one raised eyebrow.

"I have a friend in the police," I said looking at Ocean. "You know I have to tell him you're here."

"Do what you have to do, cuz."

****

Dot and I met just outside of town in a coffee shop before heading home in our respective cars.

"Well," I said. "What do you make of those two?"

She picked up the salt shaker. "They're hiding something."

"No duh, but what?"

"The money?" Dot added milk to her tea. "Here's what I think. I don't think Ferd did it. I know him. He would never do such a thing. I think Ocean killed her husband, and the mother is protecting her. Or was protecting her. But now that Ronny Joe has confessed —"

"You might be right. I don't think Ronny Joe did it, either."

"But..." Dot continued, "if she did kill him, and he was abusive, it would have been self-defence anyway. I've known too many abusive men in my life, more than I care to count at this point. You said Ronny Joe was in love with Ocean. Maybe he only confessed to take the blame off of her. Who knows? But the money. That seems to be missing, doesn't it?"

"Maybe Ella was the one who killed him," I finally said.

Dot stared at me.

I was remembering Ella's words that a mother will do anything to protect her child.

Did that include murder?

CHAPTER 36

When I got to Portland, I had two hours before tide so I stopped in at the police station. "I went to see her again," I told Ben, "Ella. I'm just getting back. Do you have time? I have an idea about who did kill Stan."

"The word I'm getting from Pennsylvania is that the case is pretty much solved."

"Ronny Joe."

Ben nodded. "He's admitted to everything."

"I still don't think he did it." I paused. "And now more than ever."

"Let's walk. You have time for a walk?"

"Two hours, so I'm good."

There was a hint of coolness in the air as we made our way side by side down toward the waterfront. Ben began, "Ronny Joe has been taken to Mount Joy where he will stand trial for the murder of his brother. He has denied assaulting and killing Simon Towers and doesn't know where his body is. We know this is true because he was promised a shorter sentence if he could produce the body, but he couldn't. Oh, he guessed, but the body was never where he said."

"What about my uncle?"

"Ronny Joe doesn't know where he is. I believe that part. When he came out to the boat when we were on it, I had the idea he was also looking for Ferd."

"And Dr. Papa?"

"Still a suicide. Still unconnected."

"Do you believe that?"

"I don't know what to believe. You said you went to see Ella again?"

"Yes, and it was very interesting. Here's what I think — I think Ella might have killed her daughter's abusive husband to save her daughter."

"Why would Ronny Joe confess if he didn't do it? How would he know the things he knew?"

"Ronny Joe was in love with Ocean and thought that Ocean did it and wanted to take the blame? Maybe Ocean told him things about the crime scene. Or maybe Ella herself did." I took a breath. "Ocean was there with her mother. Ella is afraid that Ocean is going to be arrested."

"Ocean is there? I got the feeling they didn't have much of a relationship."

"I think they're working on that. I think she was there because she was afraid she was going to be arrested."

"No chance now. She may be called at the trial, but that's all."

We were near the water now. It was windy, the kind of crisp early fall wind, which is a harbinger of winter to come. Ahead of us, some smaller boats were out there enjoying it, as well as a few large schooners. I saw a wet-suited windsurfer sail by near the shore.

"Dot was at Ella's, too," I told him. "It was quite informative."

"Your neighbor Dot? She was there? What was she doing there?"

I gave him most of the story about Dot and Ella and Ferd while we walked into a park near the waterfront, which was pretty much deserted at this time of day. We headed over and sat down on two swings next to each other.

"What about the money?" I asked.

"As we speak, forensics is going through their survivalist bunker with a pick and shovel and a fine tooth comb. They think the brothers and their friend buried it somewhere out there. They're practically excavating the place. They're also looking for Simon's body. They're excavating and looking all through Stan's Mount Joy home, digging up the backyard. Maybe it's good Ocean isn't there."

"They have a warrant for that?"

"They certainly do."

"Ocean is scared," I said. "Living with Stan, she's been scared for a long time. Her and her baby. I feel so sorry for her. Her life's been turned upside down."

"You care about her."

"We're family."

Ben stopped his swing for a moment and looked at me.

I told him that Ferd was Ocean's father. "That makes Ocean and me cousins. That's why I feel a bit invested here."

He nodded.

Feeling a sudden chill, I zipped my green fleece to my neck. A part of me wanted to forget the whole thing. If Ronny Joe had confessed to the murder, and if the police were satisfied with this, then who was I to argue? At least then, Ella and Ocean would be in the clear. But yet, in my soul, I knew I couldn't do that. Ronny Joe hadn't done this. I knew this. I don't know how I knew this, but I did.

It mattered because of the other thought that I kept pushing aside. Maybe it was Ferd after all. Maybe he'd gone to Mount Joy to protect the daughter that he had only just learned he had.

A mother will do anything to protect her child. But, so would a father.

CHAPTER 37

Was that why my uncle had taken off without a word? Was that why he'd left his boat out there in the ocean for me to find? He was escaping the best way he knew how, and what better way than to leave your boat abandoned in the middle of the Bermuda Triangle with food prepared and the table set?

The money? A plain and simple coincidence. He came to Mount Joy to see his new daughter and granddaughter at about the same time that the three lowlifes just happened to win a pile of cash at a racetrack. Had he been that cowardly? To leave after killing someone and let them take the blame? *And* steal the money? Unless—

"Maybe Ella wasn't working alone," I offered.

"Ronny Joe insisted he acted alone," Ben said.

"No, not Ella and Ronny Joe. Ella and my uncle."

He stopped still on the swing and looked at me. "Em?"

"I can't think that my uncle would kill someone, but what he would do is defend a daughter and a granddaughter he just found out he had. I can see him doing that. Defending them to the death. He's an honorable man."

"Honorable men don't commit murder."

"Really, Ben? Really? Not even when they're defending someone they love. Not even when they're up against a wall? Not even when there's no other choice? Sometimes people can get pushed too far, and they act out the only way they know how."

Ben looked away from me and out toward the water. I wondered about him. His own story. Is this what had happened to him? Had he been pushed too far in Montana?

He said, "If he is so honorable, then where is he? Why did

he run off?"

"People run away for all sorts of reasons. I'm sure his were good ones. Sometimes people's reasons are good ones."

"Perhaps." He looked down at the ground beneath his feet when he said this.

"I think he has that famous racetrack money with him," I said, "that's the only explanation."

"You could be right."

"So, if he has the money with him, that means he stole it like Ocean maintains."

"Maybe," he said.

"Unless he's dead. Because, the thing is, I can't see my uncle letting someone else take the blame for a murder they didn't do. That's why I'm beginning to resign myself to the fact that he's dead." I toed at the dirt underneath my swing with my sandal. "You can tell I don't know what to think."

"I know the police are pretty sure about Ronny Joe."

I nodded.

"But I, too, have my doubts."

I looked at him. "You do?"

"Sometimes, the police can be too quick to get a conviction."

I nodded.

"Sometimes, they try to find the quickest way out of things…" He regarded me with an expression I couldn't read. Slowly, I swung gently forward and aft.

We were quiet for a while before I said, "I had a thought, Ben. I've got *Wandering Soul* in at the dock. Sometimes when I have a lot on my mind, I go out for a sail. I'm thinking of doing that when I get home. Just wondering, would you like to come along? I know you said you wouldn't mind sailing every so often." What was I doing inviting this married man to go sailing with me? As quickly as I said the words, I wanted to call them all back in.

I made circles in the dirt under the swing with my sandals.

"I'd love to, Em. Unfortunately, I've got a couple meetings this afternoon that I can't get out of."

"Yeah, um, that's okay. It was just a thought. Some other time maybe."

"Here's an idea, how about I bring supper out to your place later, and we can have it on the boat?"

"Supper?" *Really?*

"I'm sure I can rustle something up. And you've been through hell lately. And so, um, have I. There's a whole lot I'd like to talk to you about, Em. Explain." I looked at his face. "I know you saw that envelope from my, ah, wife. Former. Wife."

"It's okay, Ben."

"And I'm sure you've read all the internet has to say about me."

"Ben—"

"I want to explain my side of things."

"It's okay. Really."

"It's not okay. This is something I need to do." His eyes on me were sad. So blue. The way the sun was shining on them, I could see the individual lashes. "I'll get two restaurant meals to go."

"Okay. Um. That would be nice. You don't have to, but, ah, okay."

We settled on a time, which meant that once I got back, I'd only have maybe an hour of good sailing. If I had an hour, I'd take it. Because of the tides, Ben would have to get Geoff to drive him across the channel. I texted him Geoff's number. "Just text me when you leave Portland," I told him. "And I'll pick you up at the old ferry landing."

We coordinated our watches, and I left wondering what the heck I was doing with Ben. Yet again. Former wife. He'd called her his former wife after he'd slipped and just called her his plain, old, ordinary wife. Not ex-wife? Don't you refer to people you've divorced as an "ex"-whatever? Well, maybe, finally, I'd find out. I wondered idly what kind of food Ben would bring. Something left over from Jilly's restaurant? That would take the cake, wouldn't it? *Stop it!* I told myself.

On top of everything to do with my uncle and my

newfound cousin, I also needed to figure out about Ben. Was I ready to leave the memory of Jesse behind? My thoughts went to the star quilt I'd ordered. It was the first major improvement I would be making to the house since my husband died. Before he died we had so many plans for our little cottage—a new dock, clear the trees, a new and more efficient fireplace, new stove, new sink. New bedspread. We wanted finally to get rid of that ratty old blanket and get something new. Since he died I had done nothing. Was this a beginning? Maybe. Just maybe.

When I need to think, when I need time by myself, I exchange the noise of traffic and people for the sound of the wind in the sails and the sea moving under my boat. And today, the wind was so fine. All the way up the coast with Joan and Ben, we hadn't sailed. Because we were intent on just getting there, we did a lot of motoring or motor sailing with just the main up. Today, I wanted to unfurl both sails and see what she would do.

When my husband, Jesse, needed to get away and think, he would kayak. When I need to get away, I hop on my small sailboat, *Wanderer,* and go out for an hour or two by myself, the rougher and windier, the better I like it. But instead of *Wanderer* today, I'd take out *Wandering Soul.* Even the names were similar. That's how much in my blood my uncle was.

The sun was bright, and the day was wild with wind, the kind that *Wandering Soul* loves. I grabbed an extra fleece. It was that kind of day, getting cooler by the minute. I was alone down on the dock. The place next door was all dark and locked up. The summer people with the kids and sandals and shovels and towels on the line must have packed up and driven back to Boston or New Haven or wherever they came from. I didn't see any life at Dot and Isabelle's, either. I wondered how much Dot had told her sister about what had transpired at Ella's. I easily cast off and had both sails up and sailing even before I was out of my bay.

Out on the ocean, I probably should have reefed the main, it was that kind of day, but I decided the more I had to work to keep the boat on an even keel, the less I would have to think — which seems quite counterintuitive to why I came out here. That's what I like about sailing, I can get so involved with a job to do that I don't think about much else. When the job is over, suddenly the solution comes and all becomes clear. I was hoping that would happen today.

We were on a twenty-degree heel, and I leaned my head back and drank in the wind and sun on my face. Soon, I would be having supper with a man I was falling for. And maybe tonight — maybe tonight — he would share with me about his wife and child and whatever happened in Montana, and I would come to understand him and all would be well. All would be well.

I thought of my uncle. "Ferd, I got your boat," I yelled loudly into the wind. "You want it? Come and get it! And bring the money while you're at it. I could use it!" Then I laughed. It felt good to laugh out loud at the wind.

"Yeah. Get him to bring that effing money back!"

I muffled a startled scream and jumped a mile. The voice that said this belonged to a man, a very big man in camo fatigues who stood in the companionway. This was not Ronny Joe. This man was bigger than Ronny Joe, chunkier and thicker about the shoulders and neck. His eyes were bloodshot and what looked like a fresh scar ran from his forehead and down one cheek. As well, his nose was crooked and large and swollen, as if it had been recently broken. His right arm was in a sling, and with his left, he held a gun. I noticed the gun. It wasn't a big assault rifle like the one Ronny Joe had. This was a handgun, a small pistol. But pistols are still guns. And guns can do irreparable harm on boats. Guns can do irreparable damage anywhere.

"Who," I said holding the wheel tightly, swallowing and feeling bile rise in my throat, "are you?"

"Simon Towers. But you already know that."

"What!" *What the hell?* "You're dead. Everybody's looking for your body. The police are digging up the whole of Pennsylvania. What?"

"Don't you know? I'm a zombie. The Bermuda Triangle has followed you here."

He stared at me with such intensity, that his eyes almost seemed red in the light. I lost my balance, let go of the wheel, and the boat veered dangerously in a gust. Had I been transported to some alternate universe? Was I still in the Bermuda Triangle? The momentary discombobulating terror lasted half an instant before he laughed out loud. "Had you there, didn't I? As you can see, I'm not dead. Everyone thought I was dead. That's the way I wanted it."

"The police—"

"The."

"The word is you were left for dead."

"Idiots. Left for dead isn't the same as *dead* dead." He held that gun, but I noticed he wasn't aiming it at me. He seemed to be holding it awkwardly with his left hand, and probably he was right handed.

"What do you want? Wait." I steadied the boat. "Let me guess, you want me to give you the money. The mysterious money that no one can find."

"Ferd left it on this boat. That's what he told us. That's why I'm here." His voice cracked. With his gun hand, he rubbed his nose and ever so slightly, he winced. I also noticed that he limped a bit as he leaned against the companionway.

"You've been on this boat the whole time?"

"No, I just flew in and landed. I told you, I'm a zombie. I was hiding in the bathroom."

"I don't have the money. I don't know where it is. I haven't heard from my uncle in a long time. I've told everyone this. Everyone knows this."

I was suddenly not afraid of him. He was big, yes, and on good days, I'm sure he could overpower me with no problem, but today didn't seem like a good day. I was sure a hit to his face would cause him more than a little pain. We were heeling pretty much on our side, and while I'm used to that and wear the proper footwear, he was clutching the sliding hatch to keep his balance. Like his cohort who'd blasted my car into the tide, his smooth bottomed leather boots were questionable on the boat deck.

He said, "It's supposed to be on this boat. That's what friggin' Ferd told us. That's all I want. You give me the money, I'm outta here."

"Oh, you'll swim to shore?"

"Funny girl." He raised the pistol and aimed it at me and said, "Pow."

"Sorry to have wasted your time, but it's not here. The police have torn this boat apart looking for it. I've torn this boat apart looking for it."

"Ferd took it then. He took it back. He comes in with this grand gift. He gives it to Ocean and then he comes and takes it all back. But he owes me! After what he did to me, he owes me!"

I was quiet for a moment. "What are you talking about?"

"Ronny Joe, he told you all that money was a racetrack win, right? That we were going to divide three ways, right?"

Momentarily, I lost track of the sail and the boat broached dangerously. He fell against the side of the companionway. I could tell he was in pain. I let out the main sail and the boat righted somewhat.

I said, "What do you mean, Ronny Joe told me it was a racetrack win?"

"Ferd brought the money with him. He was all set out to give it to Ocean. Then Stan and I caught wind of it."

"So Ferd was at the racetrack?" I was indeed becoming confused. "He was at the racetrack with Ronny Joe? What?"

"There was no friggin' racetrack. I don't the hell know where this old man gets his money. But he brought it all with him in a gym bag. Cash. It was to help Ocean and her kid escape. Stupid bitch."

"Really?" I was transfixed by this new information. Was he lying? Surely, the police would have checked the racetrack, right? And where did my uncle get close to two hundred thousand dollars if not from some sort of gambling win?

He was still holding the gun with his left hand, but his arm seemed shaky and unsteady. Everything about him seemed shaky and unsteady. "I want that money," he said.

With the boat somewhat steady now, in two steps, he had grabbed me and with one hand, held me in a sort of chokehold. If I doubted his strength before, I didn't doubt it now.

"I want that money, I want that man. You take me to him or you're dead. I've killed others. I'll kill you."

"I told you—"

"Take us to shore. Take me to Ferd now."

"You killed your brother," I said. "You killed Stan."

"Wasn't me. Was not me."

"Then who?"

"Your uncle did, Ferdinand." He pronounced each syllable in the name.

"Ronny Joe admitted to it."

"Ronny Joe's a jerk."

"What about Dr. Papa Hoho? Did you kill him?"

"Who?"

"Norman Tomson. You kill him?"

He laughed. "Guy was an idiot." He aimed his gun up toward the mast and shot. The bullet went clean through the mainsail, one small hole, but the boat kept sailing. "Guy knew too much."

"You shut down his websites, too?"

"Had to. He found me. Knew I was still alive. Get this friggin' boat to shore," he said to me. "And then get your uncle."

"I told you—"

"He deserves to die for what he did to me."

"What'd he do to you? Take his own money back?"

Without letting go of me, he said, "You see all of this?" He indicated his arm, his broken nose, his scar.

"What? Ferd beat you up? Ferd was the one?" I was absolutely incredulous. "My uncle's probably twice your age and half your size." I was almost laughing. He squeezed my neck harder.

"Okay. Okay." I felt like I couldn't breathe. "Let go of me, please. I'll take you back to shore, and I'll get my uncle for you. He's at my house. I've been hiding him at my house. I'll take you there now." Any lie to get him to stop.

"You better not be lying, bitch." He let go of my neck, sat on the seat but kept the gun aimed at me.

I changed the direction of the boat. Instead of beating into the wind, I headed downwind. Running with the wind, the boat flattened a bit. I headed around ten degrees to port. If we kept on this course, maybe my captor would succumb to seasickness. Seasickness is always worse in a following sea. But that might take a while and was not guaranteed. I spread out the full sails wing on wing, dangerous in these high seas, but I decided we were not going to sail easily.

Trying to implant the idea, I said to him. "If you're feeling seasick, the best place to be is standing up right where you are and look straight behind us."

"Wha...?"

"I'm just telling you. Lots of people get seasick in these kinds of winds and in this kind of sea. Do you have a headache yet? That's how it starts with most people, a headache that gets really bad and then moves to your stomach. Oh, and if you're going to throw up, lean over the side there, the left side. That's the most downwind part of the boat now."

"Shut up."

"You called my mother, didn't you?" I asked.

"I was looking for your uncle. And his money."

Something that both Ronny Joe and Simon hadn't counted on was meeting me on my own turf. Rocks and sailing. I know all the trails and paths and rocks in the channels, and I'm also good at sailing in rough weather. Like this.

He sat down on the seat, his back to the bulkhead, gun aimed at me.

I said, "You don't want to be sitting there leaning into the boat like that if you're feeling sick. You want to be up higher. Standing up."

He looked around. I didn't know if he believed me or not.

I opened up a cockpit locker and threw him a life jacket. "Put this on. It's going to get wild in a minute." I was coming up with an idea. I wanted him overboard, but I didn't want him dead. Hence, the lifejacket. I called to him. "But I'm telling you, you feel sick stand up and look to the stern. Look behind us."

I smiled a little at this advice. On the old sailing ships in bad weather, captains routinely forbade their crew to look behind them. The winds look worse there. The waves look higher there. And if you're seasick, looking behind only makes it worse.

He stood up, hesitantly. What I decided to do was a very dangerous move. It's dangerous to jibe quickly in such high winds. It's usually even dangerous to jibe slowly in such winds. But I had a murderer with a gun aimed at me. Things change when you have a murderer on board with a gun aimed at you.

He stood, held onto the coach roof and looked hesitantly behind us. With one motion, I quickly jibed the boat to the other side and the boom swung across the boat, as I knew it would. It knocked him over the side and into the water. As I knew it would. The gun lay in the bottom of the cockpit. I kicked it away from me. The police would probably want this gun, but I did not want it going off accidentally on this boat.

"Can you swim?" I called to him over the wind.

"No." He came up sputtering.

"Well," I called, "good thing you're wearing a life jacket then."

I dropped the sails and started the engine. When I got close enough, I threw him a line and told him how to put it around him. Simon was not going anywhere. I wanted him not only wet but also cold.

After he was secured, I pulled him to the boat and he climbed on board, wet, shivering, and in pain. I quickly tied him up with the line I had thrown to him. Another thing I'm good at is tying knots.

I put the engine in gear and we headed in. Half an hour later, we were back on my dock. My sails were down, and my drenched and whimpering cargo was sitting cold and tied up in my cockpit.

I got on my phone and texted Ben: *Hey, about tonight? Change of plans.*

CHAPTER 38

Bit by bit the story came out. When Ella realized what a brute her daughter had married, she felt helpless. She had never had a good relationship with Ocean, and now with Samson gone, it had deteriorated even further. Yet, despite her faults, Ella loved her daughter, would not give up on her. She finally decided that the truth needed to be told. Maybe if Ferd knew he had a daughter, he could do something about her abusive husband.

Ferd was furious that Ella had kept this fact from him all these years, but finally decided to help his daughter and granddaughter. It was Ferd's money—all two hundred thousand dollars of it—that he had brought with him. And no, the police had not checked with the racetrack. It was a major miscommunication.

When Ben told me all of this, I was simply numb. I had no idea where my uncle had gotten all of this money, and in the end decided that maybe it was simply money he'd saved through the years. It could be from anything—gambling wins, money for odd jobs he'd done. Who knew Ferd had that kind of money squirreled away in a Caribbean bank?

From what we could piece together, Ferd intended to give all of this money to Ocean and the baby. Never one to completely trust bank drafts and even plain old ordinary checks, Ferd brought all the money with him in a gym bag.

The room safe, I thought. That's why my uncle wanted a safe in his motel room in Mount Joy. I told Ben this as we sat together on a park bench on a late fall day. I'd wanted to know everything and so we'd been walking and enjoying the fall colors. And now we were sitting on a park bench above the bright and windy harbor. There was snow in the air.

According to Ella, when Ferd gave Ocean the money, she refused it. This whole idea of her beloved father Samson not being her father was a wrench to her and the money felt like a betrayal. She hated her mother for keeping this from her. By this time Stan, Ronny Joe and their friend Simon had gotten wind of the money. Stan decided the money was his.

The story of Ferd leaving it on the table was a lie. Ocean had finally taken the money and hidden it and told her husband that Ferd had taken it back. To completely keep Ronny Joe off the trail, they told him it was a racetrack win. Ocean told Ferd that Simon had stolen the money. Ferd went after Simon and beat him up.

After Stan died, Ocean took her baby and the money and fled to her mother's home. The web of lies she was entangling herself in, was threatening to come undone. Ella buried the money in the church garden.

I just kept shaking my head as the details of all of this came out. No one yet had been arrested for Stan's murder, although Ben said they were working on building a case. Against who, I didn't ask. I had my own suspicions. I still had not heard from Ferd. The police were still looking for his body, and I was kind of resigning myself to the fact that he was gone.

That changed this morning, which is why I'd immediately called Ben. Which is why we were sitting here. His very short email to me simply read, *Everything's okay. I'll be in touch. Ferd.*

The police tech guys had looked through my computer that morning, trying to find where Ferd's email originated. The nearest they could find was South America somewhere. They were still working on it when Ben and I had decided to go for a walk down by the waterfront.

"I still don't understand why Ferd would carry all that money around with him in a gym bag," Ben said.

I grinned. "That's my uncle. You'd see him on the street you'd never imagine that that gym bag he's carrying around had all that money in it."

"It was his savings," Ben said. "That's what the police have determined."

I nodded. "He's always been a thrifty man."

I brushed my hair behind my ears and wondered how far back it went. The tentacles of the crime were set in motion way back almost thirty years ago when Ella left her husband for a time, and took up with Ferd. She had a baby named Ocean and raised her as another man's child. Reaping what you sow, I thought. Bad Karma. It always comes back in one way or another.

We finished our talk and since I had a tide to catch, we said goodbye and I drove home in my new-to-me car, a three-year-old gray Nissan Sentra. It was a fine car, nothing special, and as long as I kept it off the ocean floor and away from survivalists with assault rifles, I'd be fine. I also have made a new resolution — I will never again chase the tide to get home.

A week later, Ocean, accompanied by her mother Ella, and an expensive lawyer who was well-known for taking on women's cases, especially abusive husband cases, went to the police station in Mount Joy where Ocean confessed to shooting and killing her husband. After years of abuse, and in fear of hers and her daughter's life, she had purchased a gun.

When Stan came into the café demanding the money that Ferd had given her. She refused. He hit her. All of this occurred in the kitchen of the café. Ferd was there and after Ocean left, Stan and Ferd had a heated argument. Marie demanded that Stan leave by the back door, rather than disturbing the customers in the restaurant. He did, followed by Ferd. Little did the two of them know that Ocean was waiting there with a gun. She shot and killed Stan, whose body was discovered the next morning. Ferd begged his daughter to go to the police. Deathly afraid, she would not. Ferd did the only thing he knew to do. He tried to put the blame on himself, by fleeing. When he heard that his favorite niece would be in the Bermuda Triangle for a couple of weeks, he ripped his mainsail, set his boat out there and left his dinghy in an island of mangroves. All to make him look like a crazy, insane killer. It almost worked. And leaving Bear? He knew someone would be along, if not me, then someone else. And he made sure Bear had plenty of food and water.

Ben called and told me all of this the morning Ocean confessed. I had already heard it on the news, though. "Maybe your uncle will come home now," he said.

"Maybe."

"Em…" There was a pause on the line. "Is it too cold to go sailing today?"

"Ben, it's never too cold to go sailing."

"I just wanted to go out sailing before you're off to Florida for the winter."

I gripped my cell phone. "I don't know. I might not go this year. There are repairs I've been wanting to make in my house. And I have a quilt coming."

"A what?"

"An Amish quilt. I may stay here. At least for a little while. I have to see about more work." Suddenly my future loomed long and uncertain in front of me. "But we have today," I said. "Why don't you come today?"

"I could bring supper. Provided you don't have any more murderous stowaways."

I laughed.

"We never had that conversation," he said.

"No," I said. "I guess we never did."

ABOUT THE AUTHOR

Linda Hall spent the early years of her writing career as a journalist and freelance writer. She also worked in the field of adult literacy and wrote curriculum materials for adults reading at basic reading levels. In 1990 Linda decided to do something she'd always dreamed of doing, she began working on her first novel. The book she wrote, *The Josiah Files* was published in 1992.

Since that time she's written twenty-one more mystery and suspense novels and many short stories and essays.

Most of her novels have something to do with the sea. Linda grew up in New Jersey and her love of the ocean was born there. When she was a little girl Linda remembers sitting on the shore and watching the waves and contemplating what was beyond. She could do that for hours.

Linda has roots in two countries. In 1971, she married a Canadian who loves the water just as much as she does. They moved to Canada and have lived there ever since. One of the things they enjoy is sailing. In the summer they basically move aboard their 34' sailboat, aptly named - *Mystery*.

Both Linda's husband Rik and Linda have achieved the rank of Senior Navigator, the highest rank possible in CPS. The U.S. sister organization is the U.S.P.S. Linda's Senior Navigator diploma hangs proudly on her office wall. What this all means is that she knows how to use a sextant and can 'theoretically' find her way home by looking at the stars.

Rik and Linda have two grown children, seven grandchildren and a very spoiled cat.

CONNECT WITH LINDA

Newsletter
http://writerhall.com/newsletter

Website
http://writerhall.com

Facebook
http://www.facebook.com/writerhall

Twitter
@writerhall
#emridgemysteries

OTHER BOOKS BY LINDA HALL

Em Ridge Mystery Series
Night Watch

Short Story Collection
Strange Faces

Whisper Lake Series - Harlequin Love Inspired Suspense
Storm Warning
On Thin Ice
Critical Impact

Shadows Series - Harlequin Love Inspired Suspense
Shadows in the Mirror
Shadows at the Window
Shadows on the River

Fog Point series
Dark Water
Black Ice

Teri Blake-Addison mysteries
Steal Away
Chat Room

Coast of Maine novels
Margaret's Peace
Island of Refuge
Katheryn's Secret
Sadie's Song

The Canadian Mountie Series
August Gamble
November Veil
April Operation

30030824R10169

Made in the USA
Middletown, DE
11 March 2016